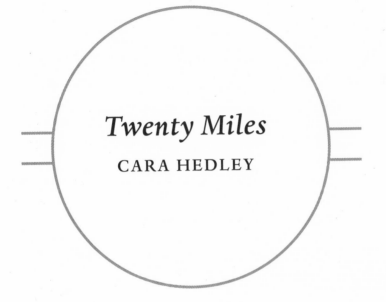

Twenty Miles

CARA HEDLEY

COACH HOUSE BOOKS

first edition

 Canada Council   Conseil des Arts   ONTARIO ARTS COUNCIL   Canadä
for the Arts   du Canada   CONSEIL DES ARTS DE L'ONTARIO

Published with the generous assistance of the Canada Council for the Arts
and the Ontario Arts Council. Coach House also acknowledges the
support of the Government of Ontario through the Ontario Book Publishing Tax Credit Program and the Government of Canada through the Book
Publishing Industry Development Program.

LIBRARY AND ARCHIVES CANADA CATALOGUING IN PUBLICATION

Hedley, Cara, 1979-
Twenty miles / Cara Hedley.
ISBN 978-1-55245-186-1
I. Title.
PS8615.E315T84 2007   C813'.6   C2007-905766-7

To my parents,
for early-morning practices

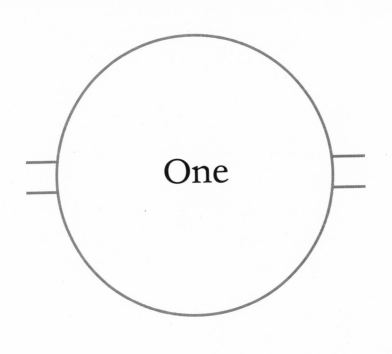

One

Light smacked the ice in Sam Hall Arena and bounced off, blooming bright in the air above. The empty stands looked tired in their worn tiers, the sag of a wilted wedding cake. And the same smell, always, in every rink. Mineral, metallic, but something else too. Something unnameable, old, the smell of a museum. It's in this smell, maybe, where a person can start to get lost.

A player strode across my path from the hallway joining Sam Hall to the Phys. Ed. building. She carried a black hockey bag branded with the Scarlets' red W over one shoulder and a red backpack over the other, handling each as though it were the weight of a purse. I fell in behind. Sandals yawned from her heels, calloused the colour of potatoes – the three-headed-monster heels of hockey players, skate-boot friction over the years wrenching eruptions in the bone. A ragged swath of red at the tip of each toenail. Her hair's dark waves moved stiffly as she walked.

We passed a desk, the gel-headed guy behind the counter dwarfed by the giant wall of shelves behind him, overflowing with every type of ball imaginable, their colourful skins scattered among helmets, skates, racquets, sticks. He looked up from a textbook spread on the counter and smiled.

'What's up, Hal?' he said, saluting with a highlighter. 'Back to work, eh?'

She nodded at him like she was the CEO returning from lunch and he was the secretary. 'You bet.'

Tall, with the bulk of her thighs given away by the jeans – loose waist bunched in by an old leather belt but tight across her quads and butt – and the wide-legged strut dictated by those skating muscles, the hockey legs. I felt the narrowness of my own legs and pictured Hal shovelling me like a pile of snow from the crease as I went in for a rebound.

We entered the long hallway of yellow dressing-room doors and my stomach spasmed – I couldn't picture what I was about to walk into. Hal opened a door near the end and an off smell leaked from the room. The sharpness of onions and something else – chili powder? She groaned under her breath. The door opened onto a short, dim hallway inhabited by a stick rack. It was still early, but a few sticks were propped crooked in there already, sloppy numbers written in black marker on their handles. Hal glanced back at me briefly as she threw her sticks into the rack and then warbled 'Burrito!' like a war cry. She stalked into the room, dropping her hockey bag to the floor with a dull *whump*, and her back burst suddenly into light.

I tucked my sticks into the far corner of the rack and followed her. Stood in the entrance to the room behind the small hill of Hal's bag. She was framed now by the bathroom doorway cut out of the far wall, hand outstretched toward a player decked out in Scarlet hockey gear: baseball cap, T-shirt, sweatpants. The top of her head reached Hal's chin, and Sig – my grandmother – would have called her, with approval, sturdy. They were between the sinks and a tattered brown velour couch, stuffing bursting from an arm, a green toilet stall looming in the background. The short player jockeyed from foot to foot, mirroring Hal's moves, as though she were trying to hide with her back the giant faux-wood microwave that was buzzing with geriatric exertion. On the wall above the bathroom door, a mural: the huge red W, penned in on three sides with *Character, Dedication, Excellence*. These words startled me. They reminded me of the campus holding Sam Hall in its palm, the university unfolding layers all around it, and how this made me lost.

'Just give it to me,' Hal said.

'You're confused.'

'Toad. Do you see this?' Hal pointed to her face. 'This is a nose. Rule number thirty-eight. Now take it out and put it in my fucking hand. I can't believe we're already doing this.'

'Your nostrils are uncommonly large, friend.' Toad turned and fished a burrito swaddled in paper towels from the microwave. She took an exaggerated bite, her back to Hal.

'Delicious!' she mumbled, chewing.

'It's that extra-spicy, extra-heinous kind too, isn't it? You bastard.'

I felt the mounting vertigo of a tourist. They might have been speaking Spanish. Only a few spots were taken around the room, a handful of players taping sticks, pawing through their bags, so I looked for the biggest gap. The benches lining each wall were broken up into stalls, black wooden partitions separating them and a shelf traversing the top of each. Small, empty porches. Silver-tusked hooks everywhere and clear Tupperware bins under the benches. All the stall walls were bare except for one with a poster of David Hasselhoff in a green Speedo and a Santa hat.

'Hugo, how's it smell in here?' Hal poked her head around the corner of the doorway and Hugo looked up from her stall wearily, shoulders dropping a bit, like a seasoned little sister who didn't want to be enlisted. She was pale and small, but with a veined bulge in her forearms as she leaned over her bag, elbows on her thighs.

'Like ass,' she said dully.

'And rule thirty-eight. Say it.'

Hugo pulled a pair of long underwear from the bag and mumbled, 'Thou shalt not eat burrito.'

'*Thank* you.'

I dropped my bag in front of a stall in a deserted corner, across from David Hasselhoff and a few down from the next closest player, and then someone grabbed the back of my shirt and pulled, steering me away. I turned; her face was inches from mine, nose wrinkled, tongue crooked, unsnagging a lip from braces. Her mouth shifted into an apologetic smile.

'Diss one,' she said, gesturing to a stall four down, now smoothing my shirt where she'd grabbed it. 'That's the one you want.' French accent throwing a kink into some of her words. She nodded encouragement and I moved away from her hand on my back.

'Oh? Okay.' I picked up my bag. 'Thanks.'

She nodded again and hung her backpack in the stall next to the one she'd assigned me. We both looked to the bathroom. Toad now held the burrito above her head.

'If you cut it, does it not bleed?' she said, gesturing at it.

'Don't do this. You can still do the right thing.' Hal shook her head, hands on her hips.

My neighbour clucked her tongue, rolled her eyes at the display. She turned to me. 'I'm Pelly,' she said.

'Hi. I'm Iz.' We smiled at each other and then she smiled a bit too long and I unzipped my bag.

'You're discriminating against my favourite food just because it has body-odour issues – which is a fucking tragedy, Hally. Listen, I'm an elite athlete. I'm a leader of this team. I'm giving my body the sustenance it needs to give a hundred and ten today and you're trying to sabotage this? Let's look at the underlying issues here, let's talk about this, let's have a chat. Are you worried that someone's going to be a little, um, more of a champ than someone else today? 'Cause you know – '

At this, Hal turned on her heel and strode over to her hockey bag. She yanked it up and then threw it down in front of the stall I'd first chosen. Toad devoured the burrito, a victorious grin. 'Kisses!' she called, mouth full.

Pelly shook her head, turned to me. 'It's always like this,' she said, apologetic.

Three stalls down, Hal pulled off her T-shirt and bent over her bag in a black lace bra, a ridge of muscle moving over the small etches of rib in her side. The intricate stitches and eyelets of the bra. With brisk, businesslike motions, she sat up, unhooked it and I looked away and knew they must be older, these players.

Pelly went to the toilet stall and Toad shoved her a bit as she passed, Pelly squeaking protest. Toad had taken off the hat; her eyebrows surprised me. Thin, high arcs. They seemed to set the rest of her face off balance, working against the sweats, mocking them, and I wondered if she plucked the eyebrows to make them go like that, to go so high and ironic, or if they were some freak genetic occurrence she tried to hide with a baseball cap.

I pulled off my shirt and jeans and got into my old under-equipment clothes – the lull that always comes at the beginning of the equipment dance, my limbs falling into the familiar rhythms, the pattern looped and repeated a million times. Shirt. Left leg of the tights. Right leg. Right shin pad: hold and tape. The creaking trumpet of tape as I yanked it off the roll, drawing quick circles around my calves.

A cluster of voices echoed hollow down the hallway and then four more players burst in and greetings ricocheted rapidly around the room. Then two more and another and another in quick succession, like someone had rung a bell and they'd all come running, and the windowless room swelled suddenly with sound, their voices getting all tangled up in each other, a laugh track layered in. Angles of conversation grew more complex as the empty stalls filled, voices now in competition, cross-room shouts, players craning their necks to talk over neighbours' heads. Someone turned on the CD player in the corner where I sat and the Tragically Hip screamed, pinning everyone's voices back. But they just adjusted, cranked up their own volume, veins bulging in the side of Toad's neck as she talked to Heezer, who sat in the Hasselhoff stall wearing a bowling jersey with 'Juan' stitched on the pocket. Heezer smiling and nodding, leaning forward to lip-read. Turning down the music wasn't an option. They carried on around it, some mild affliction they just had to live with.

Hockey pants, cinched in. Left skate, the lace burn on my summer-thin skin. Right skate.

The stalls began to run out. A stack of orange plastic chairs that looked like imports from a Grade Six classroom scattered into available spaces around the room. I guessed at the other rookies – the ones who went straight to the plastic chairs, kept their heads down, weren't pelted with insults or nicknames when they walked in. Darting quick glances at them, I tried to decide whether or not they looked like they'd be good. A broad-faced player ambled in then with a stubby but tall hockey bag bulging like an overstuffed cushion. Goalie. She let the bag drop in the entrance to the room and spread her arms wide.

'What's up, savages?' she bellowed. Two players on the plastic chairs looked over with the eyes of startled horses and then I knew for a fact they were rookies and I felt comfort for a moment in their disoriented stare.

Shoulder pads, left elbow pad, right elbow pad. I pulled my practice jersey over my head. I usually left my helmet off until I was walking out of the room, but I put it on now and leaned back into the shadowed nether regions of the stall, letting the little walls on either side close me in.

Hal slipped on a pair of hockey gloves, scuffed, with beaten-looking edges. I wondered how long she'd been playing. She dropped her chin to her chest and began to slowly hit the gloves together; the sound was like a thick book being slammed shut over and over again. She kept doing it and others joined in and the sound got into my chest and found the adrenalin that began its snake-charmed dance through my limbs, murmuring to my legs, my hands, my heart. Humming them awake.

Sig ashed a cigarette out the open window, smoke and leaf-bloated air layering September into the cab of the sagging grey pick-up. The ashtray overflowed with mottled butts, Styrofoam cups from the Laketime coffee shop and Coke cans littering the passenger side floor. She flicked a butt out the window. Iz always got after her for doing that – the reason behind the ashtray affront. She'd spot Sig winding up with a butt and say, 'Sig.' That's all she'd say, just her name, and Sig would wink and stuff the butt into the ashtray.

She'd left Iz standing in her miniature room in the residence. The room held a cot the university supplied, Iz's childhood dresser, a couple of old suitcases bursting with winter clothes, and her hockey equipment, the black bag pocked with dust from its trip on the truck bed. She'd have to lug the equipment across campus to the arena later that afternoon by herself. Sig wanted to stay and help her unpack, find her a good meal, drive her and the hockey bag over to the arena later. But a quiet insistence in Iz's posture, the way she stood in the centre of the small room, told Sig that if this move was going to work at all, it would have to start right then, right there. No use dragging it out.

She closed the door against the tears threatening to spill from Iz's eyes, the embarrassed tilt of her head. Her steps down the worn hallway carpet, her opening of the door, her turning of the key in the truck's ignition, each felt like a failing.

Stacy Moon, the Winnipeg University Head Coach, had found Sig in the stands at the Rec Centre during one of Iz's games last year – Iz still playing in the Midget boys' league, although she was older than most of them by then, her old teammates all moved on to the Junior league, if they were good, or the Friday-night beer league. Sig saw the Scarlet Hockey crest on the woman's jacket, and then Moon explained how they'd come to see Iz and how excited they were with what they'd seen so far. She said this with the necessary confidence of a small woman wearing big shoes, cut with a strangely girlish enthusiasm. Sig had heard about this already – 1997 and they'd finally started a women's hockey program in Canadian universities, the next logical step for the sport that seemed to be gathering force with a why-didn't-we-think-of-this-before energy. The hockey parents had already begun to ask Sig about it, about getting Iz in there.

Moon explained the team was still in the building phase and didn't have a lot of money, but the program was growing, and then she lost Sig a bit in the spiel about costs and retroactive scholarships, and Sig looked out and found Iz on the ice, striding through centre, looking for a pass from the boards and getting it. The way Moon told this part of the story sounded more like they were getting off welfare to take a job at McDonald's, but Sig didn't care about this. Then they stood and watched the girl stick-handle around a cement-footed defenceman, big oafish boy, in for a shot. The puck left her stick and stopped the breath in the crowd's throat, one huge gulp, and Sig saw science textbooks. She saw a bed-in-a-bag and bulk sweat socks and five-pack Jockey bikini briefs from Zellers. She saw the numbers in the bank account they'd opened for Kristjan's university fund and that they'd continued for Iz instead. Kristjan – Iz's father – gone two months before the girl was born, but some parts of him, like this, overlapped into her. The density of the fund's sediment and the way it bloomed thick stalks of intention. She saw notebooks and ballpoint pens and highlighters. She saw a woman, an older woman with Iz's face, wearing a white coat, a child's knee in her hands, bending and straightening the leg like a wing. A physiotherapist, Iz had said once, shyly. What she wanted to be. This woman holding the leg made sense to Sig and she'd often gone there in her mind, placed her own aching joints in those hands, let them bend her back into health. The goalie covered the puck. Breath out with the whistle and Sig knew she'd pass Iz to Moon. To those faceless girls. As though the whistle sliced open the inevitability.

'We'll see,' she'd said to Moon.

Truth be told, she'd waited after dropping Iz off at the residence. She'd sat out the afternoon in the parking lot of Sam Hall Arena, the truck hidden among the students' shit-heaps, the accidents-waiting-to-happen all decked out in skateboarding stickers and rust. The players began to arrive, small in the distance with the growth-like bump of hockey bag across their backs, and Sig squinted until she had a headache, watching the gaggles of girls disappear into the blank face of Sam Hall.

She held her breath as she watched Iz walk slowly up the arena sidewalk, leaning slightly against the weight of her shouldered hockey bag. She'd changed into a different pair of jeans, different T-shirt. 'What're you going to wear?' Sig had asked her on the way out. 'Dunno,' Iz grunted as though she didn't care.

Chin up, Sig thought angrily as she squinted at Iz's hunched back. *Get your goddamn head up.* She couldn't walk into a murder of girls with her eyes glued to the bloody floor. She'd be eaten alive.

Her ponytail was crooked.

She walked through the door.

We fell into a swarm around the gate to the ice, watching the Zamboni amble a lazy line down the far boards, erasing the remains of the practice before ours.

The players' chatter sawed through the Zamboni's stretched movements. I stood in their middle and felt the waiting in my legs. The transformation always begins here, in the drum roll off the ice, waiting for a Zamboni, or for the rest of the team or the coaches, summer leaking from your body, muscles rearranging themselves under the weight of equipment into memories of this theatre of winter contained by the boards. How to act.

After the final lick of the Zamboni's slow tongue, its last lazy circle, the ice lay smooth, a thin-skinned sheen. Dizzying mirror. The Zamboni inched toward its door and our swarm shifted, tightened, everyone moving toward the gate, lifting their sticks off the floor. Muscles flooding with memory.

Tykes league – me and all the boys. Chad Trenholm, a notorious parent-clinger, crying his eyes out beside the other team's net, stick on the ice, wailing, 'I want my mommy.' Even the motherless among us could feel his loss there on the ice, small but urgent. It spread among us, contagious as head lice.

Our coach, Uncle Larry as we all called him, stood on the bench behind us, unmoved, the sloppy game going on around Chad's inert body.

His leather mitts formed a fat bracket around his mouth. 'Keep it off the ice, Chad!' he called, a voice scrubbed porous by cigarettes and rink air. 'Off the ice!'

Our ice grew walls this way, conjured gradually through Uncle Larry's mantra. *Keep it off the ice, boys. Off the ice, Isabel. Am I speaking Chinese here, or what? I said, Keep it off the ice.*

Even if we did miss our moms, dads, grandparents – if their faces flickered lonely in the stands, an impossible distance away, if our toes were so cold we were convinced they'd fallen off and were rattling around in our skates, none of it was to touch our ice. This was our first training as men.

I wasn't a girl then. Not a tomboy either – that word, like some ragged misfit cat, tripping on the tails of others. I was a girl, of course, but not a *girl*. We were the same size, had the same voices, the same disguised faces behind our too-big helmet cages. And we all pretended we were someone else when we were out there. Someone bigger, faster. Someone with hands, as Uncle Larry said, as though the ones we owned were imposters, all the real hands leading disembodied lives out there, magic bleeding from their elusive fingers like the coins Sig used to conjure out of nowhere, silver blooming from the crack between her ring finger and pinky before her arthritis got too bad.

We played together, so we were the same. That was a long time ago.

But it can't all be kept off the ice. Even after the Zamboni has licked away the violence of our skate blades, there is always more. There's more and more.

I glided up the ice, right wing, playground squawk of voices behind me, eyes on Pelly's strides like a speedskater through the middle, but she'd lose the puck, I saw this in her flimsy grip. Voices around me calling for the puck, calling Pelly's name, along the boards, behind me, voices circling like seagulls, and I should call, I should call, but why didn't Pelly see me open? Head down, Pelly wouldn't look up, and she'd lose the puck, she was about to lose the puck. Open. And Pelly, head up, finally, cage tilting toward me and the puck coming fast, *tock* of the puck on my tape. Breathless, ready. And legs springing long, eyes breathing the bobbing helmets, and the jerseys all different colours – shit, different colours – and holding on to the puck, keeping it – who was on my team, I didn't know – their voices shouting my own name hot in my ears, coming from behind and beside, the heated jazz of the Z, sawing me open. Chest growing in breath, red bloom of lungs, ribs' tectonic shift. Open.

Breath moving in smooth currents, in and out of my lungs, puck clinging tight to the stick, and bodies everywhere, colours everywhere. But now I saw only the spaces between, precise. Incisions in the frozen air. The smooth slice of blades, alignment of joints and muscle, angles measured and tight. Mathematical wonder.

And then Hal was bearing down on me, and I could feel the swing, tumbling back into myself, but not quite, logic still strung down the electrical wires of my legs, Hal bearing down, script unravelling in my limbs, legs coiling and then boneless, not thinking, feeling Hal's hard bones against my shoulder, all of Hal's bones at once against the boards, and then I was looking down, spine still buzzing.

Hal sprawled, her gloves and stick littering the ice in a circumference appropriate to impact, like a plane wreck.

'Yard sale!' someone shouted across the ice.

Hal lay on her stomach, hands clutching at her helmet, ragged gasps. She rolled on to her back.

'I'm – I'm sorry – I forgot – I played hockey with guys, and – ' I couldn't breathe, Hal's face red and crumpled. Moon sprinted over.

'Jesus Christ! What's wrong with – ?' She saw my face. 'Oh – well, there's no hitting – Hal, are you okay?'

'I'm fine,' Hal said and hoisted herself up off the ice with a sharp breath.

'I'm really sorry. I – '

Hal turned her back and skated away. I looked to Moon, throat tight.

'Hey, no,' Moon said, as though reprimanding a puppy. 'No. You injure one of our players and that's – Hal's our captain – if she got bumped off pre-season, I don't – ' Tears elbowed the backs of my eyes. Moon touched my arm with her glove and tilted her head slightly. 'Hey, I know – listen. It's like this. Just don't do it again.'

I glided back to the line at the boards.

'You okay, buddy?' Toad asked Hal. I slouched behind them, making myself small. I could see the muscle in Hal's jaw clenching through the side of her cage.

'I was just laid out by a fucking Barbie doll. Other than that, I'm great,' she said.

I cleared my throat and looked over into Pelly's stall where she hid, face red and wet, her braces exposed in a pained grimace, silver gleaming from the vague shadow cast by the shelves above. Her shoulder pads spun slowly on their hook, like a mobile, shrouding half her face.

'Are you okay?' I asked. Pelly shook her head, hopeless. Toad came over and sat on the other side of her, nudging her to make room.

'I won't steal your tape any more, champ. You don't have to cry about it.' She smiled into the stall.

'I sucked.' An echo.

'If you sucked, Pelter, then we all did. It was a fucking gong show. Mooner got a heinous haircut, and she's taking it out on us.'

'I'm going to get cut.'

'Nope.'

'I am, Toad. You don't know.'

'I do know. And, anyways, it's just the first day. You can get better, but Mooner's mullet won't improve for a long time, unless she shaves her head. And that's a good thing, you know?'

Silence.

'It is a mullet,' Pelly said.

Toad hit her on the knee. 'It really is. Boz says no, but it is. Heinous Hall of Fame material. Just don't worry about stuff right now, Pelter, okay? Seriously.'

Toad went back to her stall. Pelly's head emerged after a bit and she leaned over again, attacking her laces.

'I'm okay,' she said to me, wiping her nose with the back of her hand.

I nodded. 'That's good.' We undressed in silence. I looked over at Hal, speaking gravely to Boz, eyebrows raised. Boz nodded her head over and over, the tiny tips of braids dancing on her shoulders. Her glasses filled with the yellow light of the room, burning bright ovals against her dark skin.

'Are you okay?' Pelly asked.

'What? Oh, yeah, I'm fine.'

'You worried about Hal?'

'No, no.' I wiped my skate blades with an old T-shirt, kept my head down. 'A little bit, I guess.'

'Just stay away from her for a while. She'll forget about it. Pretty sweet hit though, eh?'

'I just – I didn't mean to, that's all.'

'It was like, *Pow!* And we were all like, *Holy shit, did that happen?* And we were laughing a bit?'

I walked along the curve of boards toward the rink door that would spit me onto the road leading back to Rez. The ice lay empty and gleaming. Fluorescent lights hung a steady hum in the rafters, their blurred reflections crowding the surface of the ice. I passed an open door cut into the stands like a mountain cave, seats rearing up high above it. A man's voice called out the door. 'Is that Isabel?'

I thought it was Stan, the assistant coach. I turned around and a stranger stepped from the doorway, craning his neck nervously.

'Look at you, then,' he said quietly, as though we'd been reunited after years apart. 'There's the face.'

He looked kind of lost standing there in the small doorway, no one else around. He wore navy blue sweatpants that rode up a bit around the ankles, a white polo shirt tucked in. The shirt was old and thinned so you could see the orangey hue of skin and roughly sketched chest hairs beneath. A black leather fanny pack hung crooked around his thin hips.

I smiled awkwardly, my feet still pointing toward the door to the parking lot.

'Oh – pardon me. Sorry.' A high-pitched little laugh. 'My – I'm Ed.' He took a couple of hesitant steps over and then shook my hand. Strong shake, then, as though he'd just remembered something, he dropped my hand and combed his fingers through his hair with the quick motions of habit, adjusted the strands into a consistency meant to keep up the illusion his scalp wasn't peeking through. But he had this look while he made the adjustment – he crouched his head down like he was about to be hit and rolled his eyes upward, hand performing the furtive adjustment, so it looked like he was pleading for me not to notice and, although I was confused, I instantly wanted to tell him he was handsome. I wanted to pat him on the back like a dog.

'You don't know me, I guess,' he said. 'You don't. I knew your, uh, dad. I played with Kristjan back in the day.' An apologetic tone.

Of course.

'You're from Kenora?' I said.

'No, we played Junior that one year here in Winnipeg. Billeted together. Geez, you look like him, eh?' Amazed eyes.

'That's what I'm told.'

'Okay, well.' His eyes slid to the ground, then over to his door.

'You work for the team?' I asked.

He smiled quickly, then ran a hand over his mouth. Long fingers with knotted knuckles. 'You could say that, I guess.' He pointed past my head. 'I drive the beast.'

The black nose of the Zamboni poked out from its stall beyond the boards, the headlights glowing dully in the shadows.

'Oh, okay,' I said and made a movement toward the door. 'I see.'

'You going out? Just hang on one second, I'll come with you. Need a smoke.'

Ed patted the fanny pack. He went through the door, then came out pulling on a beaten-up windbreaker, fluorescent green stripes on the sleeves. He shut the door behind him and the room disappeared into the stands.

He held the door open for me. The late summer air felt curdled after the rink's ice-thinned atmosphere; walking into the dark parking lot felt like an escape.

I'd stay away from the paths on the way back, take the lit road that wound around the perimeter of campus and smacked straight into the residence. Sig and I had mapped this route earlier in the day. A million years ago. Ed picked up a dusty pylon and used it to prop open the door, then pulled his cigarettes from the fanny pack. The lighter's tiny flare and then the orange tip of the cigarette brightened against the shadows of his face. I hovered for a moment.

He squinted against the smoke blowing into his eyes and tilted his head at me. 'You walking?' he said.

'Yeah, it's not far. The residence. McMurtry.'

He clicked his tongue and looked down the road. 'Murch, eh?' The curving line of amber street lights. A rusty station wagon sped past, a thud of bass coming out the window with a tortured twist of song. It went around the bend and the low hum of distant traffic took over again.

'Decent amount of people, I guess,' Ed said. 'You best keep under those lights, though. And stay off the street else one of those morons will mow you down.'

'Yeah, I will,' I said. 'Okay, well, see you.' I raised my hand and started to walk.

'Buddy a mine told me about you,' Ed called at my back. 'His nephew plays in Dryden and he seen you play against him at some tournament. Said he couldn't believe it – Norse has a girl and she has his hands. So Stan and me are having beers last winter, I tell him about it. We drove down – Moon too – that weekend to watch you play. I told them, "She has his hands, you know, you'll want to see this."'

I knew the game he was talking about. Moon had approached me afterward and we'd talked about the team. Then Sig and I took the ice road, plowed across the lake, home from the rink like we always did because it was quicker, but it felt like Sig was speeding, and I was scared the tires would spin out and the ice would twirl the car around and around like a toy.

'I never really knew how they found out about me,' I said.

Ed gave an embarrassed laugh. He waved his cigarette through the air like a ref saying *No Goal* and stepped away from the long triangle of light cast over the pylon onto the cement.

'Just wanted to say hi is all,' he said. 'You best get going before you get cold.'

I took a couple of steps backwards. A crescent moon rubbed against the dark bulk of Sam Hall. 'Bye, Ed.'

''Night, Isabel.'

Sig relinquished Kristjan in chunks. Every night, a dose of him, as though it might cure what ailed me. She'd start with something tangible, something I could see there in the pictures – his teeth, say. Scraping at his grin in one of the old albums. She'd start with a tooth, the hard fact of enamel, and it would be hard to tell when she crept away from these small truths of his body into something bigger. That unknowable lake of myth that grew and grew.

'Ah, but his teeth were such beauts,' she'd start. 'Teeth like your grandpa's, big and strong. Kid drank milk like it was going out of style – jugs and jugs. We had our milk delivered then – none of this Safeway garbage. Charlie – that's it. He was the milkman, and lugged all those jugs to the back porch for years thinking we must have twenty kids or thereabouts, me and your grandpa. But he only ever seen Kristjan slamming in and out of the house. So one day, finally, when he's collecting money from me, he says, "Where you hiding all those other youngsters?" I laugh and say, "It's just the one for us. The boy." And you should've seen his eyes, they went real wide, and he says, "I don't believe it." And I just nod – what do you say to that? And he says, "Well, ma'am," – called me *ma'am*, if you can believe it, only time I was a ma'am in my life – "Well, ma'am," he says, "we'll have to look into getting that boy a cow all his own."'

I shifted in my bed, and Sig shimmied in so she could swing her other leg up onto the mattress. She sat on top of the comforter, pinning me into a tight cocoon. The dim bedside light rippled shadows over the bed like water, so it seemed as though we were tucked into the cabin of a boat.

'Well, I forgot ol' Charlie and what he'd said, busy with Kristjan and his baseball – spring at the time. But not a couple of weeks later, if I don't arrive home from bowling to find a big fat cow on our front lawn, chewing on the grass like the old doll owned the place!'

'Liar!' My eyes sparked open.

'How can you call your poor old grandma names like that, child? A cow in *that front yard.*' Sig feigned indignation, a hand thrown across her chest, and pointed in the direction of the lake.

'Could it swim?'

'Oh, she swam like a fish, Isabel. Can't you just see it? She was too slow to take out for walks, real lazylike. So Kristjan would swim her way over to Eagle's Nest Island and back. You'd just see their two heads bobbing along, way in the distance, Kristjan circling back once in a while to help her along. Hot summer, and Kristjan was a prune the whole time.

'And that milkman, Charlie, never came again. We didn't need him with Bobby Orr – that's what we called her – right there in our front yard. Kristjan had as much milk as he could drink, eh? Kid needed his own cow.'

I inherited a lot of his stuff. People die and their hockey equipment lives on. Sig joked that she'd cross-dressed me as a kid, decking me out in his old clothes all worn at the knees and elbows, but why the hell not, the clothes were there in the attic, ripe for the picking. But that wasn't it – I knew Sig found some sort of satisfaction in the reincarnation of the clothes, seeing them walk again, seeing them run and climb trees.

So I got the clothes and the equipment and the following parts as well: his eyes, his laugh, his cowlick and his hockey hands, among others. Apparently this is the most unbelievable part, these hands of mine: I handle the puck the same way, have the same moves, have his *hands*. As though I'd grown from these hands somehow. Hands growing arms like branches, skin, crawling into bloom, growing a heart, eyes, a mouth. But first, the hands. The rest: an afterthought, a revision.

As I walked down the hall cutting the third floor of Rez in two, my neighbour slipped through his door and then slammed it behind him, as though he were being chased. I'd met the neighbour, Gavin, as I lugged my hockey bag out of my room before practice. The extreme straightness of his part looked like a wound, a pinkish line carved in his head, and I had to dodge his bad breath as he stepped in centimetres from me and said, 'Greetings,' eyebrows pulled down gravely. His dad had walked up behind him then, wrangling a huge stereo speaker that looked seventies, and gestured a sort of apology at me with his reddened face, moving his grey handlebar moustache in weary acknowledgement of this son of his, as he angled his elbows through the door.

All day, throughout the building, parents had been depositing kids. Handing us off. The hallways crackled with the static of separation, the hot worry of mothers. When the brown hallway door closed behind Sig, cleanly, quietly, I disappeared.

The smell of Windex and musty carpet spilled out as I opened the door. I yanked up the window and propped it open with the amputated arm of a hockey stick. Then I stood in the middle of the room and rotated a full circle, assessing my options. I sat on the plastic chair in front of the narrow desk that had only two legs, the front ones, and was bolted to the wall at the back, as though they'd sawed it in two and Gavin or someone else had the other half. I unpacked the box of school supplies Sig had put together and then arranged the binders and notebooks in the scarred wooden shelf above the desk and resisted the sadness offered to me in the pages of the little blue Daytimer – Sig pulling it proudly from the Zellers bag: 'Thought you'd need one of these.'

I lay on the bed and closed my eyes and tried to paint the space behind my eyelids the exact blue shade of the living-room walls at home.

Music boomed suddenly into my room from next door. Prince began to croon. I groaned. That huge speaker. I thought of the blue emptiness of the living room. Sig sitting in its bruise. She hated quiet. She would choose Prince over quiet. I picked up the phone.

'Hello,' she snapped, because a phone call was an insult to whatever she was doing.

'It's garbage day tomorrow,' I said. She chuckled, slow, and then harder, gaining momentum until she severed it with a cough.

'So?' she said.

'Did you put it out?'

She snorted. 'Yes, Mother. Mother dearest. Four bags, all your junk, thanks a lot. Anything else?'

'Nope,' I said.

'Well, the sky hasn't goddamn fallen since the departure of Your Excellency, but you'll be the first to know when it does. I even remembered to feed the dog. We may just survive this, kiddo.' Sig snorted again. 'How was it?'

I paused, weighed the possible answers. I could tell her about Ed.

'I hit a girl,' I said.

About how, when he watched me play, Ed saw Kristjan's hands and in a poof of diesel and snow the Zamboni man became my fairy godmother.

'She big?'

And I ended up there, lying in the narrowest bed I'd ever seen, in the smallest room, listening to the complaints of my muscles and Prince.

'Pretty big.'

'You hurt?'

And Sig had ended up alone.

'Nah.'

'She hurt?'

'Well, didn't seem like it. She was spread all over the ice, though.'

'Ah,' Sig said.

'Yeah.'

'She got up, though?'

'Eventually.'

'Ah. Well, no harm done, kiddo. Shake it off. All your equipment in there?'

'Yeah.'

'What'd you eat for supper?'

'Bought a tuna sandwich from the food court.'

'The food court – look at you, eh?'

'It was pretty crappy.'

'Ah. Not bad for practice anyways. What are you doing now?'

I looked around the room. 'Lying on my bed. My neighbour's a nerd and he's listening to Prince.'

'Oh, hey now, you watch it, kid. You jocks. Nerds grow up to rule the world, you know, so you be nice to him. He could be prime minister one day and you'll be in the beer leagues, Miss Big Time. Just watch it.'

I laughed. 'I'll be driving the Zamboni,' I said, and Sig snorted.

'You know you are not in the beer gardens if you can hear me right now.' The bullhorn voice echoed into the room from the hallway, sending a ripple of surprised laughter around the lecture hall. 'You are not in the beer gardens. You are in class. I know this because I am walking down the hall, past your classroom – ' A woman in a long skirt and Doc Marten boots walked up the stairs and closed the door with a grudging smile. This door opened into the upper atmosphere of the lecture hall, the rest of the room dropping down from where she stood like a swim-down cave, old brown seats forming walls. It had rained the night before and the smell of wet grass and mud had been carried in on the soles of sneakers and sandals. I'd chosen a seat next to the stairs, midway down, and now I sat and waited, clutching my backpack on my lap. The woman descended the stairs. Was this the professor, Dr. Hurlitzer? Based on the name, I'd pictured old and tall and square and moustached. She picked up a stack of papers from the desk in the pit of the room and looked up with a small twitch of her ponytail. She couldn't have been more than thirty. I looked around the half-full room, wondering if I had the wrong one.

That summer, I'd swum blindly through numbers in the course catalogue – section numbers, lab numbers, course numbers. Awkwardly trying on the descriptions. I'd talked to a career counsellor at the university. Physiotherapist, I threw out to her. This was the one Sig liked. Teacher, I also said. Biologist. Hockey coach. Each answer felt like confessing an exotic, hidden desire, but none of it seemed to surprise her. General first year, she told me, with conviction, and these words had calmed me instantly. And so: Psychology, English, Biology, History. A huge island to roam around until. That was as far as I'd gotten: *until.*

'Okay, everyone,' the woman said. 'I have the syllabuses here. Dr. Hurlitzer is in Germany still, so just grab one and then you can go. She'll be back next week. I'm the TA – my name is Morag. Any questions, I can answer them for you. Otherwise, see you next week.'

That was it. The beginning and end of my first class and the room stirred suddenly with swooping students, flying down to the TA and her papers, then fleeing the room, syllabus in hand, back out into the sun. These moments in the classroom a minor setback to the anarchy of a beer-drenched first day.

Student traffic swelled into a thick orbit around University Centre, a gravitational pull toward the beer gardens set up behind the building. Moon was out of town, so no tryouts that afternoon. Without the ice time to move toward, the afternoon loomed. Going back to Rez wasn't an option. In the past couple of days leading to the start of classes, the halls had become crammed. The soundtrack of endlessly colliding schedules: relentless door slamming, muffled beating of shoes on the carpet, voices glancing off each other. A hotel of teenagers freed, completely, from the leashes of their parents' eyes for the first time. Musk of hormones and hangovers. Students staggering down the halls in pyjamas and bedhead well into the afternoon.

27

That morning, at breakfast, I'd watched Gavin as he whirled around carrying a plate of waffles like he was trying to find his bearings. Then, his spine straightening in epiphany, he made a beeline for the ice-cream dispenser and buried the waffles in a messy white heap of vanilla. That plate had filled me with dread. Oozing from the ice-cream machine's udder: a graphic confirmation of the lawlessness I'd sensed since I arrived.

I let myself be drawn into the pull around the periphery of University Centre and heard the beer gardens before I saw them: a denser raft of voice mingled with the jangling undertow of music and laughter. A plastic fence was strung around the area, the drinking students corralled. The fence fell into a small maze formation around the entrance like an airport security gate and students were lined up, fumbling in their bags for ID, tilting their faces toward the sun while they waited.

I walked slowly around the edge of the fence, heading in the direction of Sam Hall because that was the only other place I could think of to go and I wanted to look like I was on my way somewhere. Maybe Pelly would be there, maybe one of the other rookies.

I heard a long, loud laugh I recognized from the dressing room. The unmistakable, throaty laughter of Boz. I looked in its direction and saw them in the far corner of the beer gardens: Heezer, Hal, Pelly, Toad, Boz, mixed in with a circle of football players, all of them, beer in hand. Toad – knees bent, elbows jutting a competitive angle – chugged a beer against a colossal guy wearing a skull cap, head angled casually back with the plastic cup tilted perpendicular to his face. His other hand fisted on his hip, a cocky gesture toward boredom. Boz and Heezer's mouths moved with encouragement I couldn't hear, Hal looking on, arms crossed, a bemused smile. Pelly glanced up nervously at the blond football player next to her. She looked like a toy he could pick up and carry under his arm. When Toad spiked her cup to the ground, Heezer howled with victory and the blond guy picked her up by the waist and flung her over his shoulder, Heezer shrieking and pummelling him on the back with her palms. Toad's competitor flung his cup on the ground with an exaggerated twitch of his wrist and then turned his back on the circle and began to walk away, a slow, loping stride like he was in a rap video limping to the beat.

I recognized the football player from the gym. We'd done a team workout the day before – circuits in the Gritty Grotto, the gym in the bowels of the Phys. Ed. building. A sprawling, low-ceilinged space you descended into, the sweat-bloated air pulling you down. The gym was arranged in a series of concentric circles, weight machines surrounding the free weights, all lassoed by a rubber track, the track surrounded by a halo of gravel. I'd left the Grotto with a taste in my mouth like I'd been eating chalk.

Here, the Gritty Grotto, was where the teams all roamed, different herds mingling in their Scarlet athletic gear. A marked division of species. The giraffe pack of the women's volleyball team, high ponytails and black spandex shorts. The men's hockey team: a lean, shaggy-haired, baseball-capped pack of wolves, their smooth strides. The bearish football players, vibrating size, confident in their tattooed bulk. I lay on my back next to Pelly on a mat that smelled of socks, resting between sets of crunches, and watched a group of football players collide with Boz, Heezer and Toad, who were on their way to squats. Heezer and Toad had a Tweedledee and Tweedledum thing going in their workout gear, both wearing knee-high sweat socks with stripes around the top – Heezer's blue, Toad's red – and matching black shorts with the Scarlet symbol on the thigh and the word *Hockey* sprawled in bold across the butt. Toad had snorted at Heezer in the shorts as she followed her out of the dressing room, swigging from a water bottle.

'I love how the shorts announce our junk in the trunk. Like everyone can't tell what we play, come on. Yeah, we're fucking gymnasts. Look at us. You know what they should have? One of those alarms built in like garbage trucks have, you know? Like every time we back up the shorts go BEEP ... BEEP ... BEEP. Warning. Junk in reverse.'

The two groups, football and hockey, collided in high-fives, the beer-chugging football player greeting them all as Tough Bruce, holding his palm down low for them to slap in succession.

To Heezer: 'Tough Bruce, what's up.' Slap. To Toad: 'Tough Bruce, pleasure as always.' Slap. 'DariUS!' Toad barked. To Boz: 'Looking fine, Tough Bruce. Touch it out, sister.'

The armholes of the football players' T-shirts had frayed edges where they'd ripped off the sleeves. The teams separated, football to bench press, hockey to squats, and Pelly and I started the crunches again.

Of course they wouldn't be at the rink on their day off. Of course they'd be there, drinking beer in the sun. But it was strange seeing them outside the dressing room, away from the ice, the gym, away from Sam Hall. Seeing Hal there in sunglasses, her smirk behind the plastic glass of beer as she talked to Heezer, felt like seeing a teacher on a weekend at Zellers.

I floated in the current of students, heading toward the rink. The crowd thinned out as the path emptied into the long, sheared lawn bordering the Sam Hall parking lot. Green humidity hung in the air. A bike bell behind me and then the rushing winged sound of tires grew, a quick touch of wind on my legs as Clare Segal whizzed past – 'Heya, Iz!' – her teeth a quick flash at her shoulder, a Metallica sticker stuck crooked on the back of her helmet. She shot into the maze of trees and buildings beside the arena. Clare was my other stall neighbour, the southerly one. She wore the daily uniform of jeans and plain T-shirts that most of the other players did, but once in a while she wore a T-shirt that said *Birtle Quilting Bee, 1982* or *I'd Rather be Sailing* or *St. Rose Pie-Eating Champion, 1994* and I'd wonder about the rest of her life outside Sam Hall.

Quick footsteps behind me and I stepped to the side as a guy brushed up against my elbow. But then he slowed down, loosened his stride to match my own and grinned down into my face.

'Hi,' he said.

'Hello.' I made my face a question mark and took another step sideways. He stepped diagonally toward me again, that amused smile, like we were two-stepping.

'You played hockey in Kenora – Beachview,' he said, his dark eyes skating zigzags across my face.

'Yeah?'

'Isabel.' As though he'd been searching for a punchline and it was my name.

'Uh. Yeah.' I combed his face for a thread of memory. Dark hair, eyes. The scar on his upper lip. Nothing.

'I played Peewee with you a couple of years. Jacob. Copenace.'

'Oh, um, did you go to Beachview? Elementary?'

'I came in from Redbear. The reserve.' His smile curling the scar up into a crescent.

A round kid, swollen cheeks, wisps of hair glued damp on his forehead. Crying as his feet thawed after outdoor practice, that burn that follows numbness, the cruel trick. No sound, but steady streams of tears down his cheeks. His parents whispered to him, their voices like Buck's brother-in-law, Uncle Noah, the S that continued after the word was done. His dad removed his shoulder pads, pulled his arms through a winter jacket; his mom rubbed his curled feet. They arrived in a long van filled with relatives. Colourful jackets, long leather mitts with beads that winked under the fluorescent lights in the stands.

'You look different,' I said.

'I was fat.' A fact, unapologetic. 'You're playing hockey here now? I saw you in the rink the other day.'

'Yeah. Well, trying out. You know. They invited me to.'

'That's wicked, Isabel. Wicked. Congratulations.' He put his hand on my shoulder, the padded plush of fingertips through my T-shirt, sincerity etched in the crow's feet beside his eyes, and my shoulder steadied itself under his grasp for a moment, then dropped like the wing of a plane. 'Second year for me now. It's a good place to be. You in Rez?'

'McMurtry.'

'Ah, I was there last year. I'm in St. Mark's now. How do you like it?' He caught a leaf in the air, a fluid swipe of his palm, and twirled it between a thumb and forefinger.

'It's not bad.' A siren wailed behind us, the sound sifting through distance until it was small.

'There's a lot more of that,' I added.

'Of what?'

'Noise.'

'Yeah. In Redbear I can hear my grandmother sneezing down the street every morning.'

I laughed.

'Seriously, I can. Every morning, three sneezes. Good projection.' Jacob smiled, laid the leaf in his palm.

'Hey.' He turned to me like he'd just remembered something. 'We should go for a skate sometime. You know, like the old days.'

I teetered on the edge of this suggestion. Sudden fear licking the back of my neck.

'Well, I guess we both live at the same rink now, so.' I laughed like a girl.

'What are you doing tomorrow?' he said, leaning down. I felt wedged in by his teeth.

'Skating.' That fake laugh again. I'd just invented it and now wanted to send it into extinction.

'With me?'

'With the team.'

'And me?'

'Are you trying out for the women's team too?' I tried to throw my eyebrows at him.

'I wish.'

I shrugged, struggling to keep my feet under me. The conversation was too fast.

'We should have a coffee,' he said. 'You know, we K-towners gotta keep the spirit alive here. Yeah?'

'I don't drink coffee.' True.

Jacob stopped in his tracks and tilted back his head, his laughter low and smooth. I looked at him over my shoulder, kept walking.

'You're giving me a workout, eh?' he said, catching up to me. 'Going for coffee – it's like a metaphor, you know?'

'A metaphor for what?'

'Well, for lots of stuff.' A stretch of silence. I didn't know where I was going.

'Anyways, if you don't drink coffee now, you will soon,' Jacob said. 'Believe me. Morning practice. Vats of it in the dining hall. You'll get hooked.'

'No, I won't.'

'You will.'

'*Nope.*'

We both paused. I hadn't meant to say it like that.

'Okay, maybe you won't,' Jacob said finally. 'Okay. I can tell – you're a woman with willpower. Balls of steel.'

He called me a woman.

'So, tomorrow, then?' he said.

'Tomorrow what?'

'Coffee.'

I looked at his face, the slant of kid's eyes I'd caught. 'How did you recognize me?' I asked.

He tilted his head to the side, slightly.

'You look the same,' he said. 'I remember, that second year, you started to have your own change room. You were so small. I thought you might be lonely.'

While the liver hissed in the frying pan, filling the house with the smell of cooked blood, two people won brand-new cars. First, the blond trollop whose laughter sounded like a baby bird plummeting from a nest to its death on the ground. Then the college boy with the crewcut and gold chains and abuse of the thumbs-up sign, who, when Bob Barker asked his name, bent so he was practically eating the microphone and screamed, 'Eagles rule!,' triggering a small uprising in the back row of the studio audience, visibly drunk hooligans in matching college sweatshirts, each with a huge red hole in his face where a civilized mouth should have been. When the boy opened the door to that brand-new car and stepped in, screaming non-language into Bob Barker's extended microphone, a dark cloud gathered above Sig's dinner plate, throwing a shadow over the gelatinous patch of liver, over the pea rubble, and when she chewed the food and swallowed, this darkness slid down into her stomach.

She threw a chunk of liver to Jack, resident golden retriever, then pushed her plate to the edge of the TV table and tallied a list of all the people she knew who deserved brand-new cars above these idiots. She saw Iz popping the trunk, throwing in her hockey gear, picking up a couple of teammates on the way to a game, music pouring golden from the CD player onto their laps, the car's shining red curves articulating the shape of their laughter. The college boy brayed, voice cracking. Sig slammed her thumb into the remote and threw it to the ground and the TV inhaled all the bright flares of voices and laughter and applause and held them there in its dark, obstinate stomach, and the house caved in on her once again.

Dwarfed in Buck's armchair, the sky still dribbling dirty light through the window, Sig fell asleep because, she thought angrily as she let herself drift away – up toward the ceiling spangled with brand-new cars and Iz and all the negative space surrounding a slab of lonely liver – this is what old people do.

Hot chocolate with whipped cream, not coffee. From the Tim Hortons in the food court. Jacob drank his coffee black and tall, and when he ordered it, speaking this language of coffee, he became instantly older.

He needed a textbook. I followed him to the Used Book Store, in one of the tunnels that spread like roots beneath the campus, where he said everyone fled in the winter.

'Rocks for jocks,' he said, holding up a textbook in the geology section, the two of us small among the shelves of books, yellow *Used* stickers crooked vaccinations on dulled spines. 'And it's kinda sad, but it really is that. It's obscene. Back row's all football and about five of us hockey guys wanted to take it together, so we're all there. A couple of the basketball guys. You know, no one'll ever show anyway, so.' He snorted, flipped through the book, put it back. Picked up another.

'Looking for something?' I said.

Jacob looked down at the book in his hand. 'I'm looking for the one I like best,' he said.

I paused. 'Aren't they all the same?'

'No. Here.' Jacob picked up another book, flipped through it quickly, handed it to me, and reached for another.

'This one,' he said and waved the book he held. 'See? This one's it.'

He handed the book to me, and I turned it over in my hand.

'It looks like someone ran over it with a car,' I said.

'Open it.'

The name Cam Hennig sprawled across the inside of the cover in jagged lettering, three phone numbers, tagged with names, layered crooked beneath; an alligator drawn on the neighbouring page locked its jaws around the words of the title. Pages flipped lethargic, sodden with orange and yellow highlighter and the oil of fingertips.

'Do you know this Cam person?' I asked, pointing.

Jacob tilted his head at me. 'No.'

'Does he have the answers to the exam in here or something?' I laughed.

'I don't think so.'

'Oh.' Silence, and we both looked down at the book, its punched-up face.

'I guess it's just more interesting this way. It's not just you in there.' He tapped the cover. 'All alone.'

We hovered for a bit, the text between us, and the books ganged up on me. All the eyes that had swam through them. This wasn't how I'd imagined a typical, knee-weakening first date. Then again, when I imagined a knee-weakening first date, the girl I saw was never me. But then Jacob touched my elbow and my arm hairs sighed and we walked toward the cashier, a slow amble. I had no idea if this was a date.

'You having some fun with the girls?' *Girls*. Like he was my uncle.

'The team?'

'Yeah. They seem like a laugh. I hung out with some of them last year a couple times. Hal. And what do you call her – Toad?'

'Toad, yeah. And Hal.' I shrugged. 'Yeah, they're. Well.' I took a deep breath, tried to sum up the essence. 'Scary.'

Jacob stopped walking and laughed.

'They are,' I said.

'Fair enough, fair enough.' Jacob swatted my arm lightly with the book.

I shrugged.

'You should never be scared to *live the dream*,' he said in a fake grave tone, laughing again. He didn't discriminate much, laughter-wise. It made me suspicious. Too girly.

'Well.' I considered this. 'They asked me to play with them. So.'

'So you're saying you're not living the dream?'

'Are you?'

'What?'

Annoying. 'What's *the dream*?' I said.

'What?' he said again, winked this time. I glared at him and he laughed.

'Okay.' He cleared his throat. 'The season after that last year I played with you?'

I nodded.

'My old man's car busted down. Just gave up one day in the summer and we didn't get another one for months and so I couldn't play in town any more. I cried.' He laughed. 'I'm sorry, but I did. Big time. For days. I mean, of all things, right? And so my dad – he's a good guy, Merv – he set up some nets in our back lane, right, so we could play street hockey whenever we wanted. My cousins and me. We were out there every day, into the night. Merv set up some lights for us, so it was a pretty good set-up, I guess. Anyway, my Uncle Grant comes one night while we're all asleep and crashes through it all in his truck. We'd put it off to the side in one place to get it out of the way and he steamrolled it all anyway – the nets, the lights, all our sticks. Gets out of his truck laughing his head off, like it's this great joke. He used to play when he was younger. I guess he was pretty decent but then he found booze young and that was it. How it goes. So now he's just busting everything up in the middle of the night and we wake up the next morning and all our shit's completely totalled and hockey's done.' He shrugged. 'It got me away from there for a bit. Hockey. The only way I was.' Shrugged again and slid the text-book across the counter, looked at me. 'No idea if that's a dream.'

I wanted to fix that car. As Jacob counted money into the cashier's palm, I had this off-kilter, impossible desire to go back and fix his parents' car, to put him on the ice with me that lost season. It didn't make any sense.

'We can always take this back, if you want,' Buck had said and handed Sig the gift, a shy grin. Sig placed it on her lap.

'Geez. I don't want to ruin it by opening it,' she said, her voice still hoarse with sleep. Her eyes were swollen, her hair tangled; it was the second Christmas of their marriage, and she'd barely slept, prodding Buck out of bed at five-thirty, their room still filled with the metallic taste of night.

The present was exquisite, a thick, red velvet ribbon intersecting the middle of its green face, paper folded and taped under in precise angles. A fountain of curled ribbon spilled over the edges, trapping in sharp slivers the Christmas tree lights that slowly burnt away the early-morning darkness.

Buck exposed a startling chord from time to time, an unexpected flash. Sig didn't know what to do with the jarring intimacy, distant from anything she'd expected of this silent husband. He wrapped birthday gifts for his parents, scrutinized the boxes with an intense eye. Pink ribbons and pastel tissue paper clutched in his giant hand. He occasionally added flourishes to the dinner table when he set it: folded the serviettes into pyramids, picked some wildflowers that grew among the crevices of rock bracing the lake and placed them right there on the table, next to their knives and forks, or plucked a few petals from a daisy and sprinkled them onto Sig's plate. He didn't say anything when Sig sat down for dinner, his head bowed to the fingers bearing the mill's rough calligraphy, scratches and stains, and neither did she, the petals slid off the plate and put aside without a word, hidden in the folds of her yellow serviette.

There were some things Sig expected of this marriage. She hadn't expected the silly romantic junk mewled by the mouths of daisies, and she didn't believe in it either.

'Don't mind the wrapping,' Buck said. His head dipped and he twisted his wedding ring. 'It's yours to open, anyways.'

'Here I go,' Sig said. She tore into the gift, putting the ribbon to the side, yelped as she lifted a skate out of the box.

'If they're not the right size, or they're –' Buck watched Sig's face.

Leather seeped pungent into the living room, overthrowing the scent of pine. Sig, a low chuckle, examined the liquid curves of the black boot, the slow touch of lights, red and green, on the long blade.

'They're the same kind as mine,' Buck said. 'Figured mine have done the trick, so – But if you want something different, something –'

'No,' Sig said and laughed. 'No. No.'

The lake snapped and creaked beneath them. Sig moved in staccato strides, her arms swooping beside her. Her ankles caved in toward each other, echo of her blades against the ice.

'Goddammit,' she slurred through her balaclava as she snagged a blade and keeled forward.

Buck caught her elbow, pulled her upright.

Docks frozen in summer amnesia dotted the shoreline behind them. White rolled out in front of them, until it hit and shattered the horizon. The sky didn't move, wind locked away. The shovel Buck used to clear the ice lay half-buried nearby. Delicate tendrils of cold snaked up Sig's toes, toward her ankles. She moved the toes with satisfaction. They were nearly numb – the way it should be, skating on the deserted lake Christmas day.

'How the hell do you do this?' Sig said and wrenched her elbow free from Buck's grasp. She plunged forward, mouth a straight line, and glided for a moment before her feet gave way and she tumbled to the ice.

'Bloody hell sonofabitch skates!' she spat and put her cheek against the ice for a moment before rolling onto her back. Buck loomed above her, his face red, breath steaming around his head. The woollen flaps on his hat lolled forward like dogs ears.

'Help up?' he said and extended his hand. Sig found the dull seep of the cold to her winter skin, lethargic through the layers of clothing – wool undershirt, Icelandic wool sweater, parka – preferable to the stuttering vertigo carved out by the skates.

'No, I'm just looking at the sky,' she said. The ice creaked in her ear. She flung her arms and legs out, made a snow angel in the sheet that covered the ice. Buck sat down next to her, arms around his knees.

'You're a natural,' he said. Sig blew rings of frozen breath, her eyes narrowed against the raw blue of the sky.

'Nope,' she said and heaved herself up. Buck held her elbow as she got to her feet.

'Here,' he said and faced her, held both her forearms. His grip was strong, almost bruising. When he skated backwards slowly, Sig inching forward in his wake, she imagined music.

'Making up for the Legion, eh?' Sig laughed, stared down at her shuffling feet.

Friday nights, Buck sat in a darkened corner of the Legion with Chuck and Harold and sipped beer. He watched the dance floor while Sig swooped by, feet and hands blurred under the dimmed lights. She laughed into the faces of neighbours, effortlessly balanced a gin in her hand through the dips and twirls. Bert Mulcahey, a notorious pervert but incomparable dancer, liked to inch his hand down Sig's back, pushing his luck. It was all an act, and he set Sig off every time, her head tilted back, laughing and slapping his arm. Buck's eyes caught sharply on these exchanges; those sitting next to him could practically hear the rip. He blinked hard, cleared his throat, tore off a strip of skin next to a stunted thumbnail. Sig never mentioned these reactions to him; he would be embarrassed, she knew, probably didn't even realize he was doing it. He smiled, told her to go have fun when she came over to sit, with her damp band of hair, forehead glistening under the weak light cast into the hall's outskirts.

When Sig looked up, she saw his eyes circling her face. Her blond hair poked out around the perimeter of the balaclava, trapped her breath in stiff, white tufts. Buck's own breath travelled in small clouds toward her face, faintly sour, the smell of morning twisted into flannel sheets. Icicles clung, heavy, to her eyelashes, and their shadows teased the rounded edges of her vision. The lake boomed under their feet.

As the egg began its obese somersaults, a dull gonging against the sides of the pot, Sig leaned against the window frame and scanned the mess in the yard. Then she surprised herself. She leaned over and grabbed her pack of smokes from the table and lit up, right there in the middle of the kitchen. She inhaled deeply, lungs wincing with guilt. Since the girl had gone, a kind of anarchy had overtaken the house, the rooms stretching into obtuse outlines, hours billowing in and out of them like slackened sails. She snorted and smoke jerked from her nostrils – she felt like a teenager whose parents had left her alone for a weekend.

The egg timer chimed and she threw the cigarette into the sink and turned on the tap, ushering smoke toward the open window with her hands as she crossed the kitchen floor. Near the stove, she stumbled, toe catching on the linoleum.

'Goddamn!' she gasped and grabbed on to the edge of the stove, looking behind her on the floor. Nothing. Jesus, she might as well be literally drunk if her legs were going to act like it. She glanced at the liquor cabinet, a Pavlovian tickle at the back of her tongue, and then looked at the clock. Not yet, she told the ready mouth.

She poured the water from the pot over the cigarette in the sink and then took the egg into her hands, passing it back and forth between her palms, letting its heat leak into her skin. She rapped the egg against the edge of the counter and began to pick away at the gash of shell rubble, sharp shards falling over the garbage can. Some still clung stubbornly to the flesh of the egg, resisting the clumsy intentions of her fingers. It should not be so hard to peel a goddamn egg. She breathed around a knot of frustration and leaned against the counter, took a break.

It was that she had too much time for the egg, this act she'd done on automatic pilot throughout her life – always while doing something else: while feeding a toddler, or reading the paper, or talking to Buck over her shoulder. Now, though, she had the leisure to plumb every motion with all her concentration, eyes weighting each fragment of shell. She was forced to throw herself headlong into the stretched, yawning minutes of peeling because she didn't have anything better to do. And now the egg was not co-operating. Her finger tripped while trying to lever up a larger chunk of shell and instead shattered the piece into smaller shards. Her fingers were always forced to go at peeling with a kind of athletic gusto, the nubbed tips getting right down into the meat of the egg to wedge off the shell, since she had no fingernails to speak of, every one bitten to the quick, unable to perform any graceful, manicured shearing of shell. She had to rely on contortion instead, on the joint pliability of egg and skin. But now, with every piece shattering into smaller ones under these missteps, the fingers said no, no, and the egg fell into an unconquerable labyrinth of shell.

A few years ago, Grace had dragged her to an art show. Grace knew the artist and Sig had laughed when she first told her about it. The woman had saved the garbage from each of her breakfasts over the course of a year. She dried out orange and grapefruit rinds, apple cores, banana peels and then painted them with varnish. She kept milk and orange juice cartons and oatmeal packages and coffee filters and grinds and arranged them all in glass boxes. She saved every piece of eggshell. Sig was ribbing Grace – Grace quietly trying to shut her up – when they rounded a corner of the exhibit and came upon these shells. They were glued onto a vast red canvas, arranged in no particular pattern or form, just their own small broken shapes jostling sharp against one another, and Sig stopped suddenly, halted by this landscape, the unexpected violence. She didn't say a word.

Sig finally gave up on the egg. Spiked it into the garbage can with a frustrated grunt. Then, turning toward the sunlight coming in from the window, she held the hand up to her face as she might a misbehaving child, peering angrily into its stubborn flesh. And there. Proof. The fluttering thumb, its movement like a butterfly wing. A rhythm-less beating, fumbled attempt at flight. She felt a strange thrust of relief: it wasn't her after all. It was this thumb, this separate thing. Wriggling like some insect caught by her hand. Held captive by skin.

We all got letters one day, those of us who remained. The cool white envelopes neatly containing three weeks' worth of anxiety. Over the course of tryouts the orange plastic chairs in the dressing room had begun to disappear one by one. A couple of players didn't make it through the first week. Tall, quiet Sandra with the wobbling slapshot, the sad eyes when the puck didn't get off the ice, watching it dribble to the net. Christy, whose mascara ran macabre rivers down her face beneath her cage when she sweated. Her glacial stride. These two cut in the first week. Then, with what seemed like random whim, a pack of ducklings picked off by a muskie, others disappeared. There were covert meetings involved, I knew, hushed requests to visit Moon in her office. But I didn't witness any of this, kept my head down in the halls, avoiding the crosshairs of the coaches' eyes. Small mumbles before practice announcing the room's latest losses: 'Christy got cut. Sara got cut.'

The stack of orange chairs grew higher and the team tightened, drills quicker with fewer skaters, the weaker links gone and a different friction now during scrimmages, the taut motions of teammates used to each other's play, each other's hands. I tried to attach names to strides, to playing posture, to ponytails. I began to get it right more often. I stayed away from Hal on the ice. The dressing room distilling slowly to its core of stalls.

The hockey itself was the easy part: hands remembering the story, legs revising, improvising, that self-renewing drama unfolding in the white space between thought, the hard-breath moments when your brain forgets itself and the hands take over. Those seconds around the net during scrimmage when we looped a tentative sinew across the ice, the pulsing geometry of the puck as we attached ourselves briefly to our linemates, willing ourselves to connect into different bodies, into moving, breathing shapes. These moments were muscle.

There was a weight outside these seconds, though. Sabrina was cut. Theresa was cut. The suggestion of a blade hidden somewhere – behind the coaches' eyes, buried in the bones of our own hands – and how deep this blade might go, where it would hit, how much blood. And whose blood – my own, Kristjan's, Sig's? I tried to keep it off the ice.

Another possibility, a simple solution: I'd get cut, I'd go home. Freed suddenly from Sam Hall, from the thin stall walls dividing me from the Scarlets, from Rez, from books. They'd invited me but they didn't have to keep me. Cut: rebounding off the grey edges of the city, down the highway. Home. Jamey was cut. Jana was cut. They took their bags and didn't come back.

Stan, the assistant coach, stood outside the dressing-room door and handed the letters to everyone as they left. He held the envelope toward me, stone-faced, but then he winked and I took the envelope and had to force myself not to run, pulse knocking around in my ears. I marched stiffly out to the ice, vaguely registering the weak-ankled circles skated by a Peewee team in orange and red practice pinnies, and sank down against the wall. Tore open the envelope. 'We're looking forward to having you onboard.' Undoubtedly, a contribution of Stan's; he had a penchant for metaphors involving cars and trains. *You need to fuel up, ladies, get those wheels moving, shift gears, park it in the garage, ten minutes ten miles, running on empty, eh, running out of steam?* An impersonal letter, my name written into a blank following 'Congratulations,' but there it was. Another season.

Boz came through the door holding her own identical envelope. I was still slouched against the wall and she stood in front of me, watching the shaky trajectory of the Peewees. She shook her head and smiled.

'So cute.' She wore capri jeans and runners and her dark ankles shone a smooth gleam. They looked like they'd be cool to the touch, like stone. She looked down at me and then crouched and grabbed both of my wrists and pulled me to my feet. She smiled and then wrapped her arms tight around my shoulders. I could feel the muscles in her arms as she moved her palm in a slow circle on my back. I understood instantly the currency of Boz's hugs, the way some of the players fell so easily against her body, in the dressing room, in the hallways of Sam Hall. I felt a blush plunge from my cheeks down my neck.

'Welcome,' she said. The warmth of her face, one hand still on my shoulder. 'We're celebrating tomorrow. Someone will call you.' And then she walked off toward the parking lot door.

I was a Scarlet.

I stood, flattered and shipwrecked, and watched the coach lob pucks into the corner, a surge of kids following it in, their comic hunger for that skittish black dot. I walked around the boards toward the door.

'Made the team, eh Isabel?' Ed called as I walked past his office.

The door was cracked open wide and Ed sat in the middle of the tiny room on a narrow wooden chair, red paint peeling off it like a bad sunburn. He leaned back, hands folded behind his head, feet up on an orange plastic chair like the ones in the dressing room, those sweatpants riding up around his ankles. A small TV flickered silently on another plastic chair next to a mini fridge. He grinned widely, as though he'd just given me the news himself.

'I did,' I said and held the envelope up.

'Already knew,' he said, still grinning. 'Friends in high places, you know. Congratulations to you.'

'Thanks,' I said. I put my hand to my mouth, tried to cover a smile.

'Naw, you should be proud, Isabel. This is a big deal, you know? Norse'd be proud as shizz, I'll tell ya that. Yep.' He bobbed his head and took his feet off the chair. Eyes darting nervously around the room, he made a jokey Vanna White gesture at the chair. 'Take a load off for a sec, eh? We should celebrate or something.' He cleared his throat, embarrassed.

I hesitated. The prospect of returning to my Rez room at night after practice, after team workouts, had begun to cause small pebbles of dread to roll around in my stomach. Gavin had been play-ing Rammstein the night before, their German shouts jerking guttural anger through the wall. The night before that had been the Goo Goo Dolls. It was less the music itself, more the unpredictabil-ity of Gavin's taste, that unsettled me, a musical identity crisis enveloping me every night. And there was a Pizza Hut just down the street from our building, so there was always someone eating pizza. There was never no one eating pizza. The ghosts of pizzas past, present and future roamed the hallways. They got in under my door. The unshakable cologne of melted cheese in the fibres of my clothes.

I walked into Ed's office, sat in the chair across from him. He examined my face with the same surprised look he had when we first met.

'You want a pop?' he said, going over to the fridge. He leaned over it, a fist on the fanny pack belt on his hip. 'I got Coke here. I got Sprite. Grape Crush. Beer.' He turned, eyebrows raised, and put a finger to his lip. 'Not that I drink and drive the beast ever.' A nervous laugh.

'I'll have a Grape Crush,' I said.

'Excellent choice.' Ed opened the can for me and handed it over. Then he picked up an empty Coke can sitting beside the fridge and poured a Molson Canadian into it.

'To celebrate,' he said and we touched cans. The Grape Crush on my tongue tasted of swimming lessons at Clementine Beach when I was a kid, of Buck counting out quarters at the canteen. Ed settled down into his chair like he was getting ready for a class to start. He took a sip, cleared his throat.

'So, Norse and me billeted together at the Ferrys,' he began. 'Old couple, real nice. Didn't know what they were getting themselves into, I guess. Didn't know Junior hockey players were all shizz disturbers as a rule, you know. Just a nice little couple wanting to do their part for the team. First night there, Norse and me didn't get home till five in the morning. Old Mrs. Ferry waiting up for us in this heartbreaking nightgown all worried. Norse didn't even make it inside. We get to the door, it's like his knees just buckle. Had a little nap on the front step. That's what he called it – having a little nap. I sent her a card a few years ago, feeling all bad thinking about the way we acted, the two of us, and them just trying to be nice. But it came back to me. Guess they're probably gone by now too.

'Anyway, you live with a guy, you share the same room, you play hockey together, you get to know him pretty well. We were like Siamese frickin' twins,' Ed snorted.

As though I was interviewing him. He didn't stop until he'd covered the first month of his relationship with Kristjan. The two of them dating sisters. Rookie Night and Kristjan so drunk he passed out in his underwear and a scuba mask in a bathtub at somebody's friend's brother's party.

As far as I can tell, a hockey player dies young in a small town and his death grants him a different sort of fame. Even people who had never spoken a word to Kristjan seemed to feel they knew him intimately. To know him was to know the grief that had covered the town like a rough, wool blanket. They felt compelled to tell me about him, as though I were some walking, talking memorial wearing a sandwich board that said, *Please deposit testimony here.*

Ed's nostalgia was a less polished brand. He talked about Kristjan like Kristjan was in the room and Ed was bringing up these stories with me to razz him. Like we were all shooting the shit over beers, recalling the glory days, the three of us. There was a kind of recklessness around the edges of his stories that I hadn't heard before, that made me wary. But I listened. I nodded my head and asked small questions and let Kristjan spill, drunk and disorderly, into the room.

Ed stopped talking suddenly and cocked his head to the side. He put a finger to his ear. 'You hear that?'

Just the mosquito song of the fluorescent light. I shook my head.

'Quiet, right?' he said. We listened again and now I heard that the Peewees' high-pitched shouts, the puck tocks and blade rasps, were gone. Ed's office flooded with the absence.

'That means I'm on.' He grinned quickly, feeling the pocket of his old dress shirt, and then grabbed his jacket from the back of his chair.

I watched him pull the Zamboni out of its bay, his palm drawing the steering wheel in a slow circle, popping the gears, the Zamboni's black bulk jumping slightly and then falling into a sluggish pace, trailing a tail of gleaming ice behind it. Ed looked over and steered toward me. He shouted down from the high black chair, over the boards, 'Talk to you again soon, Norse.' Then he winked and drove off. The Zamboni ambled slow across the empty rink. In its wake, strips of licked-raw ice, perfectly aligned.

'Shove over, then,' Sig said and perched awkwardly on the bed's edge. I wormed over to the other side and Sig paused, my expectant breath at her elbow. I reached beside my bed and hauled up a photo album, the blue one all cracked at the corners like dry lips.

'I've got one,' Sig said and shuffled around in the album until she found the newspaper clipping the colour of a nicotine stain.

Norse Giant Crushes Pykes. Kristjan, a teenager, winced, crunching a wan-faced opponent along the boards.

'I've heard this one,' I said gently. 'I think.'

'No, no,' Sig was impatient; I could hear the words building up gritty in her throat. 'You haven't heard this one. Just listen.'

She cleared her throat, a loose rattle. This sound made goosebumps wave up along my arms, underneath the flannel pyjamas. Sig's Ready-Go whistle. Her voice would change now; it would get bigger. She'd be a different person.

'Well, then. You see, Kristjan, he wasn't always this big.' Sig tapped the photo with her wedding band. 'In fact, when he was your age, he was smaller than most kids. A real runt, you know? Much smaller than you. And he was probably about your age when he met the bear.' Sig paused for dramatic effect, and I didn't move, breaths long and sleep-heavy, eyes measuring Sig's mouth in dreamy sweeps.

'Well, so Kristjan was taking Elskin for a run, out back of the Keewatin baseball diamonds – that old path where we saw the beaver with its babies and the snapping turtle last summer? You know the one. I warned Kristjan not to go back there. "You'll be eaten by a bear," I told him, but when he started running, that boy, it's like his legs kidnapped the rest of his body, mind of their own, you know. So he finds himself on this path, sun going down. "You be back before sunset," I told him, but his legs wouldn't listen. And it's real quiet on the path, just old Elskin panting and Kristjan's heart going *ba-boom, ba-boom, ba-boom*. And the path runs beside the lake, so he can see it the whole time, and you know how when you see the lake, it's as though it's watching you and Kristjan feels safe.

'It starts with a rustling in the bush, like it always does, in all the scary movies. But it's real this time. Kristjan looks up to the treetops, and I'd always told him, "If you see one tree shaking when there isn't any wind, that's a bear scratching its back on the bark." And sure enough, there's one tree shaking in its boots. Right there. The fur on the back of Elskin's neck stands right up and she starts growling – a pistol, that dog. She was. Kristjan starts running faster, yanking Elskin along – she stopped right there on the path and started growling and snapping at the air. And that's when it happens. This bear comes slinking out of the bush. And isn't it always a Jesus surprise when you see a bear – do you remember that bear that walked into the backyard when we were having your birthday party, just like he'd been invited, the saucy old thing?

'So sure enough, a bear walks out onto the path, right in front of Kristjan and Elskin, a giant bear, bigger than any we've seen, kiddo. Likely about ten times the size of Grandpa. Maybe more. Just huge, with paws the size of your head, and teeth the length of your hand. And Kristjan stands there with Elskin still growling beside him. Remember, he's just small. And the bear staring them both down. Kristjan – he's thinking of everything everyone has told him to do at this moment. You know, play dead, cover your neck, clap your hands, make yourself big. And he doesn't have much time, he can see the bear's eyes turning red and his neck tensing up like a spring, and so, in that second, he just does it. He's small, but he makes himself big. He raises his arms out like this and thinks himself big, and something happens. He grows tall, up and up until he's looking down on the bear. And he sees the bear's scared, trembling. Bear's the one thinking now, How do I get out of this alive? He's met his match. So he takes a swipe at Kristjan, real quick, and hits him on the shoulder before he disappears back into the bushes, whimpering like a little pup. Kristjan had a scar after that, looked like a sliver moon hung there on his little shoulder. And he was different in other ways too, I'm telling you.

'Next time he plays hockey, couple days later, he's still small, smaller than you, but he's playing big, he's playing gigantic. He's the star of the team now, no one can believe it. They start calling him the Norse Giant. And then that's all they call him. On the ice – "Norse! Norse!" And he really is giant. He's huge out there. Something of the bear in him after that day, I'd guess.'

Tipsy Cups: one table, longish. Ten plastic beer cups in total, the cheap kind but not too flimsy, five lined up on each side of the table.

Three inches of beer in each. The first people on each team do a cheers, then chug the beer. Empty cup is placed face down on the edge of the table, a fraction of the cup's rim hanging over the side. Using your pointer finger, lightly flick the cup upward. When the cup lands upright, the next person chugs. Flicks the cup. Lands it. And on down the line. First team to finish wins, obviously. Winning was the point – it was the point for most things when it came to the team. Eating, drinking, pranks. And hockey.

I mounted these details in my mind with the urgency of a physics student about to take a pop quiz. I watched Boz's technique carefully. The placement of the cup on the table. How much rim hanging over. How light the flick.

Boz's basement apartment was an amber-filled cave. The kitchen walls surrounding the Tipsy Cups table were painted dark orange, round lanterns of yellow paper hung in the corners, dribbling out muted light. On the wall above the crooked pyramid of beer boxes across the room: a framed painting of an African woman in a colourful dress, grinning and barefoot. On the adjoining wall, a huge poster of Mario Lemieux. A trophy towered in the centre of the table, complicated scaffolding of flaking gold leading to a bowling man. A piece of masking tape with the title *Rookie of the Year* taped over the nameplate on the trophy's base. Boz assured our group of dubious, slouching rookies that this title didn't rest on the outcome of Tipsy Cups. The trophy was present instead, I assumed, to remind us of our continuing obligation to compete.

Hal placed me second in line on Boz's team. Up first versus Toad's team. Hal took her position as ref at the head of the table, raising her whistle. This triggered a rash of shouts and cheers, team members strung along both sides, encouragement shouted down to number one. Subs swarming around the table, the friction of bodies in Boz's cramped kitchen, not enough elbow room. The competitive lean of my teammates' faces down the line was as heavy as if they were sitting on me. I was going to choke, I could feel it. How far over the edge? How light the flick? My hands didn't know this game.

'And the losers each have to say something real nice about Toad's daddy,' Heezer said, performing some deep knee bends, a pre-competition stretch. 'Eh, buddy?' She grinned across the table at Toad, who stirred the air with her hand and then cupped her ear like Hulk Hogan.

'Oh, sorry! I didn't catch that, sport. I don't speak Asshole.'

'All right, on your marks, ladies,' Hal boomed. The chatter rose to a din. Adrenalin burned the back of my throat. Pelly, first in line on the opposite team, cracked her knuckles. Boz, our number one, cleared her throat, looked at me.

'All set, babe?' she said.

'What if I can't do the flick thing right?'

Boz laughed. 'You'll get it. No prob.'

Hal put the whistle in her mouth. I bent my knees a bit.

Whistle.

Boz and Pelly crashed their cups together, then threw the beer back. Pelly spluttered a bit and belched, but got the cup down quicker than Boz and fumbled her first attempt at the flick, the cup over-rotating and landing on its side with a hollow clatter.

'Shit!' she shrieked.

'Light as a feather, Pell!' Toad yelled next to her. 'Light as a feather!'

Boz fumbled her first try too – the landing was almost there, but not quite, the cup catching too much of an edge, and my pulse picked up on the cusp of my turn. Boz reset the cup, calm in her speed, while Pelly's bounced on its side again.

'Mother of, mother of – '

You could tell Boz's second try was going to be it, the smooth, arcing flow, and it landed firm, my hands in motion on its landing, to the laughing chants of my teammates. Choked the beer back in two gulps, the raw tickle of it in the back of my nostrils, holding back a cough while I swooped the cup down to the edge of the table. That's when the hands kicked in. I could feel the cup's centre of gravity in my palm as I moved it swift into place over the edge. The weight of it, how it would fly. I flicked the rim like turning on a light switch and knew the way it would go even as I made contact, like hitting a baseball in the sweet spot of the bat, and it soared up smooth and landed solid. First try. Boz and Pelly yelped congratulations, Boz grabbing my shoulder, and relief flooded the tension in my arms, cheers swelling over the table, over me. Thank God.

Another rookie, Roxy, flubbed six times at the end of our line and I felt a bump of sympathy and validation every time she screwed up. We lost, but not because of me, so I didn't care.

But then, immediately, the next obstacle: saying something about Toad's dad, a heavy red-headed man with a sarcastic smile who picked her up after practice in a rusted K-Car and called her Toots.

'Mo is a silver fox,' Boz said. Toad gave an uninterested shrug.

'Iz?' Heezer said, pointing like a director. I didn't have enough time.

'Well,' I stammered. Toad faux-glared at me. I looked at Pelly. She flexed a bicep and tapped it furtively. 'Mo has nice muscles?'

'Clearly, she's drunk and confused,' Toad said, and that was it. Another pass. Heezer pointed to Tillsy, the goalie.

'Uh, okay, Mo. Well.' Tillsy looked at the floor, deep in thought, then grinned up at Toad. 'Mo wears extra large bikini briefs.' Mild groans and Toad gave an exaggerated *so what?* shrug. Tillsy followed it up: 'And I know this because we do it every weekend.'

Heezer grabbed the whistle hanging around Hal's neck and gave a couple of supportive bursts. Light applause around the table.

'You know what, Tillsy?' Toad shouted, her face reddening. 'You can say whatever you want and it will roll off my fucking back. It's extremely unconvincing, frankly. Not to mention disturbing that you would sacrifice your gay fucking pride for a childish game. Honestly.' Toad shook her head in disgust and Tillsy shrieked with delight, hands clasped, like Toad had just surprised her with a present.

'So if any more lesbians,' Toad continued, 'would like to jump in and testify on behalf of my dad's sexiness? Then step right the fuck up. I will open the door for you.'

Heezer blew the whistle again and Hal wrenched it out of her hand. I examined Tillsy uncertainly. I couldn't tell whether Toad was countering Tillsy's burn with a false accusation, or if Tillsy really was gay. In the dressing room, lines between burns and reality were perpetually blurred. Tillsy seemed thrilled with the exchange, red-cheeked and laughing.

'Toady, drop the F-bomb a little more, champ,' Hal said. 'We're not convinced you're rattled yet.'

'Oh, Toad,' Tillsy giggled. 'I'd sacrifice my gay pride any day to rattle you.'

'You have no pride,' Toad shot back. 'This has become alarmingly evident in the last few minutes, friend. I don't like what I'm seeing here.'

'Heez, you're up,' Hal boomed, raising her voice over the room, a seasoned team orator.

'Excellent,' Heezer said, rubbing her hands together. 'Okay, well, the other night, when Mo and I were taking turns fondling each other's C cups, he said – '

'Fuck you guys, fuck this game,' Toad exploded, fighting a smile. 'I'm leaving now. I'm going to get you assholes some chips because none of you thoughtless pricks brought any and I'm a benevolent entity and you're all a bunch of heinous, bush-league peasants.' She stalked to the door as the room breathed *ohhhhh* and, as an afterthought, she turned back and grabbed my arm. 'And I'm taking a rookie.'

Boz's 7-Eleven was mine too – the one just off campus. This was essential in Winnipeg – that everyone have a Sev they could claim as their own. This one teeming with Rez-bians, as Toad called them, a vigil of the drunk and hungover circling the Slurpee machine around the clock.

We entered the Sev's searing light and made a beeline to the chip section. The radio blared through speakers, every aisle inhabited with students, friends shouting to each other from opposite sides of the store.

'I like All-Dressed,' Toad said, clutching two giant bags to her chest. 'I'm devoted to All-Dressed. I can't believe those sows didn't bring any chips. What's your fancy?'

I felt a tap on my back then and turned to find Jacob, clasping, like a bouquet, three long pieces of red licorice that bowed flaccidly over his hands. He thrust them toward me.

'Pour vous,' he said and Toad squeaked beside me. My cheek skin itched.

'Oh wow,' I said. Bad acting. I darted a glance at Toad.

'What's this, kiddies?' she said. 'Sweets for your sweet, Copes, or what?'

Jacob grinned at me, eyebrows raised. I took the licorice reluctantly.

'Jacob and I played hockey together back home,' I explained to Toad.

'Well, everyone wants a piece of our Barbie, don't they?' Toad said. 'She's good shit.'

'Barbie?' Jacob said. 'Like the doll?'

'No.' Toad paused. 'Her real name's Barbarella.'

I grabbed a bag of chips from Toad's arms and wagged it at Jacob and then moved toward the cashier. 'We better get going, eh Toad?'

'See you tomorrow, Isabel,' Jacob called at our backs.

I turned and held the licorice toward him like something dead. 'Did you pay for these already?'

He laughed and shook his head. I could hear him laughing again as we walked out the door.

'Wow. Boy can giggle,' Toad said.

It had rained at some point during Tipsy Cups. The asphalt gleamed darkly, air thick with the smell of wet gravel.

'Isabel, eh?' Toad kicked a rock like it was a soccer ball. Followed through. 'You guys are all Victorian with each other or something, eh? Can't imagine that translates well in the bedroom.' She stopped suddenly and swung the plastic bag, hitting me on the hip. I stopped and waited while she opened the All-Dressed chips, the bag wafting a smell of vinegar and socks. She stuffed a handful in her mouth, sighing dreamily, shoulders sinking like a heroin addict finally getting a hit. 'You sitting on it yet?' she said thickly, mouth full.

I felt like I'd been spinning around and around and was now trying to walk a straight line.

'Sitting on what?' I said.

'That's what I thought.' Toad nodded sagely and we kept walking. 'Watch out for those dudes, though. Seriously. The guys' team.

Know what they started calling us last year? The Scarlet-ettes. First of all, what? Second of all, they have their panties all tied up in knots 'cause they think our team's going to end up taking away their money from the program. Um, have you seen their dressing room compared to ours? Have you seen their equipment compared to ours? I say lick my bone, princesses. They're the Scarlet-ettes.'

She chewed the chips angrily for a bit.

'That sucks,' I said. 'But Jacob and I – '

'Keepin' it in the Scarlet family though, eh Barb? Classic tale of incest. Not that our team's never dabbled in theirs if you know what I mean. I won't tell on you, though. Secret's safe with me.'

'Well, it's not a secret,' I said. 'It's nothing.'

'Fuck, it's cold out. Chips?'

'Yeah.'

We could hear them laughing from down the street.

About three minutes after we walked through Boz's door, Toad announced, 'Well, you know what they say. You learn something new every trip to Sev. I'd like to announce that Barbie's a slut – in the best sense of the term, of course. But I can't reveal who the lucky guy is at this juncture – yeah, sorry, it's a guy, Tillsy. I'm not at liberty to say. Although it's fascinating.'

At the Rec Centre back home I had dressing room number three every game. Buck used to carry my bag for me when I was young. On his big shoulder, it looked like an oversized purse and echoed a thick clatter when he dropped it on the floor from up there. When he and Sig left the room for the social mixer around the canteen, the door sucked closed behind them and sealed me into the staleness of the room. As though the dark breath from the inside of every hockey bag opened in there had escaped and been trapped between the walls. As I dressed, I listened to the sound next door, tried to pull words from the dulled jumble of boys' voices. This was my team, this mess of laughter and words thickened by the wall, the timbre of their voices taking on weight, as though they were speaking through water.

I could remember a period as a kid when I absorbed all the intimacies of my private dressing rooms – crushed beer cans from rec league the night before, tape balls, empty shampoo bottles, small graffiti scattered over the benches and walls – with archaeological pleasure. My teammates' voices inflating my anticipation. I'd perfected the seven-minute change over the years, though, so by the end of Midget, I arrived before each game with just enough time. Then the coach would poke his head in before he went to talk to the boys and I'd walk over to their room and sit in for the two-minute speech and then we'd play.

Once we were all dressed for the Home Opener, Hal began to pound her thighs with her gloves. I felt this beat in my stomach. On one side of me, Clare Segal had a sneeze attack. On the other side, Pelly tilted her grin toward me, nervous, expectant. Hal leaned over.

'Twenty minutes, twenty miles,' she said loudly. She looked at me.

The path from the dressing room to the ice went like this: down the hall, a right turn, and there was the door that opened onto the rink itself. Tillsy pushed through, a wide-legged stride in her goalie pads, and we walked into a corridor like a mountain tunnel, the stands high above.

As soon as Tillsy reached the gate to the ice she stopped, all of us held in the thrumming tension of our line. The lights dimmed like it was our birthday and they were bringing in the cake and then the music began. 'Thunderstruck,' by AC/DC. The crazed moaning sound at the beginning that got louder and louder, like the band was creeping up behind you and then the first hit of *THUN-DER!*, a crack felt in the knees.

Hal's gloves still beating inside my chest. Pelly, in front of me, bounced her shoulders up and down, she shook her head from side to side like a horse.

THUN-DER!

Alberta circled their end of the ice, green and yellow, picking up pucks from a spilled pile of them in front of their box, where a suited coach paced the bench, pissed-off face, studying a clipboard.

Players began to sprint arcs up around the red line, coming around the boards and slowing down. Hard slow hard slow.

''S go, White!' Heezer shouted near the front. 'Showtime, White!'

'C'mon, Scarlets!' someone yelled behind. ''S do this!'

Hal, ahead of Pelly, horked out the side of her cage onto the floor. When she turned her head to the side, her face was tight.

The announcer cleared his throat into the microphone and then he yelled in a talk-show-host baritone above the AC/DC: 'Here. Come. Your Winnipeg University Scarrrr-lettttts!' And the beat jumped into my throat and cracked open.

One of the Events guys, dressed like a Puck Bunny in a Scarlet Hockey T-shirt, flung open the gate for us like it was a rodeo and we were the bulls, and my team began to waddle-sprint down the hallway, and soon I was leaping through the gate into light and the thick applause of a crowd in mitts and the manic screech of AC/DC and I skated the fastest warm-up circle I ever had because if I stopped skating I would throw up.

Sig sat in an empty row near the back of the stands and searched for Iz on the ice. She found her in the other team's end, pinning a girl against the boards, the two trapped in the tangle of their bodies, writhing for the puck hidden between their feet. Sig was surprised: Iz, her back leg dug in strong, had the girl caught like a fly by the wings.

She was used to seeing Iz knocked around. The games played out fast when Iz was a teenager, and the boys sometimes didn't realize they were hitting a girl until she was crumpled on the ice, head curled into her body, trying to disguise the pain. The boys' bodies slumped when they realized what they'd done, and they'd crouch next to her on the ice, suddenly gentle, offering a hand up. Iz refused. The regret of those boys was what she hated most about hockey. She'd rather have her ribs cracked than hear their sheepish apologies.

The whistle went and Iz skated to the bench. Sig watched her move to the middle, lean an arm over the boards, the other bracing her upside-down stick. The player next to her poked her with an elbow and gestured at the ref, her helmet moving up and down as she spoke. Iz nodded.

They didn't look so different from the boys, Sig thought. A bit shorter, but they still had that bulky, square-shouldered look about them, the same loping stride. Ponytails whipping around in their wake.

A gust of perfume, and a woman sat down on the seat next to Sig. Sig looked over briefly, caught the bones in the woman's face, purple scarf wound like a turban around her sharp head, the red lipstick that arrowed from her lips into the outskirts of her mouth. A man in the row ahead of them twisted stiffly. He'd smelled the perfume, no doubt, the exotic scent moving uneasily among the worn rink seats.

'How are ya, Terry?' the man smiled through a moustache, eyes slits in his wide face.

'Just fine, Mo. Hi, Eileen.'

'Oh hi, Terry! Oh shoot, did you just get here? You missed Hal's goal.' Eileen, dwarfed next to the huge man, had the tendoned neck of a bodybuilder, a restless mouth.

'A beauty, Terry. Top right-hand corner. Deked the goalie. Fucking goalie's a mess, anyways, but Hal schooled her.' Mo chuckled.

'I'll catch the next one,' Terry said, and the couple turned back to the game, Eileen gripping Mo's jacket sleeve as the team threw the puck around the net.

'Oh. Oh! Oh!' Eileen breathed.

'Shoot! Shoot! Corinne, you bloody scag – girl's got the puck glued to her stick,' Mo spat as the whistle went. Sig chuckled. Terry looked over at her as she pulled a fleece blanket from a handbag patterned with parrots. She wrapped it slowly around her legs.

'Hi there,' she said, smiled.

'Hello.'

'Who are you cheering for?'

Sig craned her neck, looked for Iz on the ice.

'Number Five. Isabel, my kid – my grandkid,' she said, pointed to the faceoff circle where Iz was locked, arm in arm, with a short girl on the other team, her jersey practically a dress.

'Oh yes, of course. She's a rookie.'

'That's her.'

The women followed the play to the opposite end of the ice. 'Poor thing,' Terry said. 'How is she holding up? They're not being too mean, I hope. Those girls can be so silly.'

'Iz's tough. Played with boys all her life.'

'Oh,' Terry nodded knowingly. 'What did you call her?'

'Iz.'

'Right, right.' Terry nodded. 'I'm Terry, by the way. Chris's mom – Number Seventeen. Right there.'

'Sig.' She reached her hand over and Terry took it, her fingers collapsing in Sig's grip. 'Good to meet you.' They were silent for a while, cheers climbing up to them from the rows ahead, contagious spurts of clapping. Clouds of heated air, coils glowing orange on the rafters above.

'Funny, I was just thinking – you said you call your grand-daughter Iz?'

'Yes.' Sig looked over, tilted her head.

'My daughter goes by Hal – that's what the girls call her. Our last name is Hallendorf – ' Terry coughed suddenly, her head whipping forward, hand flying to her mouth. She cleared her throat and smiled, one front tooth tilted in toward the other. A cheer swelled above the benches as the team scored.

Eileen, hands blurred in a feverish clap, turned. 'That's her third point, Ter,' she said. 'She's on a roll.'

'Oh, good. She'll be in a good mood tonight.' Terry clapped quietly, watched Hal skate past the bench. She drummed her team-mates' extended gloves, stick dragging next to her on the ice.

'That her?' Sig asked, pointing to the pin on the lapel of Terry's purple coat. Behind a circle of scratched plastic, a girl posed in a jersey, tangled hair, her teeth too big for her head. Terry looked down, rubbed at a smudge on the plastic.

'That's her. She's about ten there, I guess.' She leaned toward Sig. 'She hates that I wear it. It's so embarrassing. I like to razz her, Sig. Is that bad?' She laughed. 'Well, and look how darling she is too.'

'Nothing wrong with a bit of razzing,' Sig said. 'So that's Hal, eh? I think Iz's mentioned her name before.'

'Oh, lord. I take no responsibility.'

'What's her real name, her girl's name?'

'Her girl's name,' Terry laughed. 'Oh God, she would kill me if I called her by her girl's name.' Terry looked, distracted, toward the bench. 'Don't you dare, Mum,' she mimicked in a high-pitched voice. Skin pulled tight across her cheekbones, patches of blush like burns. 'I'm bigger than you, you know, I can kick your ass.' She chuckled and turned toward Sig, leaned in. 'Her name's Crystalline,' she whispered. 'This is a big secret, apparently.'

'Crystalline?'

'Yes.'

'Unusual, eh?'

Terry leaned back, pulled the blanket tighter across her knees. She took a deep breath, raising her hands, palms up, as she inhaled. 'I was so tired when they brought her in after she was born. You need a name, they kept saying. And this was about the time I got into makeup with my friends – I was sixteen, you know – and my favourite – ' Terry began to laugh. She leaned toward Sig and grasped her knee. 'My favourite eyeshadow was called Crystalline! The seventies, right? So it was kind of whitish with these sparkles. "Mom!" Chris says, "You named me after a bloody eyeshadow!" I don't know how to defend myself.' Terry picked a tear from her eye with a raspberry nail.

'Don't know if you can defend yourself on that one,' Sig chuckled.

She looked back to the ice and searched for Iz.

Number Three on Alberta had her priorities mixed, as Stan suggested gently between the first and second periods.

'Mixed!' Toad said, furious and dripping sweat, gulping for words. 'Mixed! She'll get fucking mixed!'

Moon shrugged in a not-discouraging way. Voices sprung up along the benches, adrenalin shared around the room in an electric surge. *Come on, guys. We can do this. Come on. We're doing awesome, come on. We can beat them, you know we can.* Then Hal began to beat her gloves together, head down, over and over, a tribal drum, until a knock on our door told us the ice was ready.

I raced back to our net alongside Three, dropping back for Heezer, who was scraping herself geriatrically from the boards after a collision at the other end. The Pandas' power play schooling us all over our end, like a game of Keep Away.

And there was Three all over Tillsy, and me trying to get Three out of there, shovelling at her concrete shins, Tillsy still getting thrown off balance, Three all over our goddamn goalie, and I kept hearing this word in my ears, pushed like blood with every breath, on the knife edge of hyperventilation. *Priorities, priorities*, the word over and over again like my brain had shrunk for lack of oxygen and lassoed this word, just this word, and Three's stick still between Tillsy's pads, and they'd score if she kept doing that, and I couldn't breathe, I couldn't breathe.

'Bitch!' Three screamed shrilly as she fell. She sprawled face down on the ice, kicking my shin with her skate until I backed away, blood in my ears.

Whistle.

'Number Five, White, two minutes for cross-checking!' The ref skated at us as though someone might pull out a gun at any second and shoot, Three still kicking and spitting, and I glided into the ref's overeager wake, a handful of road-tripping Panda parents applauding my capture.

Toad opened the door to the penalty box from inside, grinning. She was in for tripping ('Could she have taken a bigger dive? Look – I can dive too. I'm an actress! I'm an actress! Look at me!' Tripping along as she was hauled off to the box).

'Duh, duh, duh – The Sin Bin!' she sang doomfully as I stepped in. 'Yeah, don't do us any favours, Ass Eyes!' This, shouted in the direction of the ref's zebra back as she slammed the door. The box vibrated like the inside of an old piano and I edged around Toad to sit on the bench. I felt a gathering in my throat, adrenalin turning to venom, turning on me – the slow, snake-eyed blink. So embarrassing to be caught like that, acting out a private violence, frozen into a red split-second in your mind, like dreaming of peeing and then wetting the bed. The announcer drawled my penalty over the loud-speaker.

'Hey, Five, you watch your back, eh? Shauna will paralyze you! She has a black belt in karate! You won't feel your goddamn legs! Wheelchair!'

I turned, and a miniature woman five rows up snarled, straining against her husband's forearm grasp. The husband grimaced with embarrassment, eyes sliding side to side.

'Wheelchair!' she shrieked again, her voice cracking. Toad cranked my helmet back to the ice.

'Don't look. Never look,' she said, laughing. She watched the play, darting glances at the clock, and snorted. 'That's awesome – *wheelchair, wheelchair*! Worst fucking heckle in the history of hockey. I love it.' The ref whistled Hugo offside and Toad hit the side of her helmet with her glove, dumbfounded. 'Eleanor!' This was the ref's name and Toad used it throughout the game like they were chummy.

She watched the clock shuck off the last seconds of her penalty and lifted the door handle.

'Keep the Sin Bin warm for me – and don't forget to say your Hail Marys – ' And she leapt out of the box as though skydiving, plummeting toward a snarl of players biting at the puck along the boards.

I half-turned and looked for the heckler out of the corner of my eye. She'd forgotten her promises of my imminent handicapping and was now engrossed in the play, little claws buried into the husband's bicep. I tried to think of the last time I was heckled, but couldn't. Parents of the boys floated threats over the rink, but never at me.

Sleeping Beauty Syndrome, Sig called it. No matter what I did on the ice, no one would touch me. Not the boys, not their parents. 'Princess force field,' Sig would say, drawing an invisible line around my body with her finger. I hated it. To hear those words directed at me – this seemed an impossible decadence.

'Black belt!' the heckler barked behind me, freed from her trance by a whistle.

I sighed and watched the penalty's epileptic countdown on the clock, my gaze seeming to slow it. The box hyperventilated around me, and I imagined the ancient breath of my sinning teammates growing inside me like mould.

'Iz!' Moon bellowed from the bench, on her toes, chin up. I nodded.

'Go right on!' she yelled, pointing to the net where Hal was wrestling the puck around a defenceman.

Seventeen. Sixteen. Fifteen. Fourteen. Thirteen. Hal shot the puck at the goalie's pads, a wicked wrist shot, and the Alberta D scrambled for it.

I threw open the gate and jumped out, the air flooding my mouth like water, ice drenching the bloodied inside of my cheeks – I chewed them while I played, iron tasted later with the vague amazement of a sleepwalker.

'Get her, Shauna! You get her, now!' the heckler shrieked as I sprinted to their net.

We lost. To the *Pandas*.

'Mmm, sewage,' Jacob said. We were walking along the river path – the Red River, thrown around one side of campus like a protective arm. The water looked hard and glossed when we'd first eyed it from the fifth-floor dining hall, trying to decide what to do. A colour that might be gathered like paint in your hands, but up close it swirled and churned, thick tongues of mud lashed in with green and orange.

He was watching me. My muscles shifted in resistance. I knew that if I looked over, he wouldn't flinch. His eyes would still be on me. He'd been watching me like this since the bookstore. In the dining hall at breakfast. At the rink. Like he was trying to figure me out.

A huge squirrel, grizzled black, ran across our path carrying a ragged flag of lifejacket material in its mouth. The wildlife I'd seen around campus all appeared pumped-up, larger than life: the deer lounging aloof around the greenhouse behind Rez, all muscled ribs and supermodel legs, the squirrels like bear cubs. This wasn't what I'd expected from the city.

'Those squirrels,' Jacob said.

I wondered if he was thinking about home.

'My grandfather – Shoomis – when he was really old and had gone a little … squirrelly, so to speak – sorry, that was bad – he was convinced that all squirrels were communists.' Straight-faced, Jacob squinted out at the river. 'He'd get all worked up whenever he saw one. "You commies,"' Jacob mimicked in a husky voice, face crumpled up, '"you stay away from my tomatoes!" – he had this garden he was always protecting from communist takeover. Didn't worry about us, but made sure his cucumbers were safe. He died in his sleep one night, midsummer. Just went, you know. Kookum swore she knew exactly when it happened, even though he didn't make a sound. Said it was like how the end of a thunderstorm can wake you – not the noise, but the quiet, she said. This sudden stillness. So she went out to the kitchen to call my dad, and – middle of the night, remember – a squirrel was sitting on the window ledge, looking into the kitchen. Tiny, this squirrel was, and kind of bird-like, kind of downy, like it just hatched out of an egg. And it just stared at Kookum, not moving. Watched Kookum make all her phone calls. And no one could understand what she was talking about because she was telling everyone she called, not that Shoomis had died, but that he'd come back as a communist. Proud. He'd come back as a communist.'

Jacob kept staring out at that melted edge where the colour turned solid again. I watched his face, the unmoving creases around his mouth, laugh lines even when he was serious. He snapped his head toward me suddenly and caught me staring, his eyes a trap. He winked. I shook my head, laughed a little as another squirrel pranced by with a swatch of lifejacket, mud crusted around its mouth.

'They're digging a lifejacket graveyard,' Jacob said. 'How's that for a goodbye to summer?'

The way he said summer, the stinging S held for a moment on his tongue. I missed summer when it was gone the same way I missed Buck, and I wanted to tell Jacob this, with his S still buzzing between us, his own grandfather offered toward me like an outstretched hand – I could talk about Buck if I wanted to. I wondered at how calmly he was able to skate the edge of sentimentality. I didn't know how to even start.

Jacob's arm brushed mine. I moved away from him. The sun spun and then lost its pivot, clattering instant shadows, as though the campus buildings were falling down over top of us. A woman with dreadlocks walked a fat Rottweiler along the path toward us. The dog wore a tie-dyed collar and stopped every few trees to lift its leg, standing stork-footed for a few fruitless moments, its bladder run dry.

'Poor guy got no game,' Jacob said quietly. The owner looked vaguely sheepish as she sung a low greeting, and the dog ignored us.

It was as though he'd set a goal for himself. Once the dog had passed. The huge white pine with boughs hanging weary over the path. As soon as we reached that tree he'd try it. Like trying out a head fake on a D – which wasn't fair because I had no warning, just his eyes that forecasted the movement of his lips right before his head swung like a wrecking ball toward my face.

'Oh Jesus,' I breathed and turned my back on him, quick, hands over my mouth like I was about to sneeze. But I hadn't expected this at all. I should have expected this. My hands were still on my mouth so I faked a cough.

'I have to go work out,' I mumbled and scurried down the path, Jacob's laughter at my back.

'Isabel, you're hilarious,' he said.

I saw him next in the rink as we practised. He sprinted down the stairs, hair damp after his own ice time, three others on his heels. Their cheeks all moved, steam coming off their heads. Moon explained the next drill and I looked over at Jacob. On his way up. He wore the blue underwear shirt they all wore under their equipment, with the navy rim around the neck and cuffs. A darker blue square clung to his back, long hoops of sweat under his arms. I imagined the salty smell passed between them. Hair pasted across his forehead as though he hadn't touched it after he removed his helmet. His calves flexed in rhythm with the passing stairs, hamstrings glinting above, a fin of muscle, his mouth open. He had a nice mouth, I decided.

Hal leaned over, helmet lightly knocking mine. Her breath a scratch over my cheek.

'Don't do it,' she said. 'Those guys are all pigs.'

Centre ice, a Pronghorn winger threw a pass a couple of feet in front of me at a high-pitched screamer somewhere just beyond my left shoulder – 'Yeah, yeah, yeah!,' a backup singer gone horribly wrong – and I threw myself at it, feet hungry with a win so close, tied 2-all, and we were winning the third period, coming back from the throbbing red zero below HOME of the first two periods. But you could feel it rising during the second intermission, communicable anger, Hal expelling low, fervent words around the dressing room, a desperation stirred in my legs, a need to show her I'd listened, I'd heard her, all of us turning to each other on the benches when she was done, repeating her words, mouth-to-mouth resuscitation, and then thrown back to the ice and gasping into life.

Moon was juggling lines, searching for the formula that would create the boom, and so I'd been sent on one of her blind dates with Hal, right wing to her centre and I knew her shadow there along the boards as I lunged for the lazy Pronghorn pass – if I could just steal this pass, I'd give her the puck, her shape along the boards I could see in my hands' eye, she could have it. And I sucked the puck off its track, inhaled it with my stick, spinning back toward their net and forgetting Hal in the dazzle of all that empty ice, the Pronghorns having pulled up their defencemen already, too presumptuous, and so I was speeding into the emptiness of their end, the rush and pulse of wind and breath and the rising chords of my teammates and the crowd and the laboured beating sound of a D killing herself to get back in position, the one like an oversized doll draped in a Pronghorn jersey, and their goalie puffing herself bigger like a spooked cat, spreading her arms, bending and widening and shrugging herself into place, my hands reading the net's blank spaces, the holes around her body, the heated grunts of the D just behind me, and Hal shouting, 'Go, Iz, yeah, you got time!,' Scarlet voices carving into my back, my hands and feet flashing a hundred different lives, weighing their choices against the shifting crouch of the goalie, then my eyes saying *there*, pinning the upper left corner of the net, hands sending the puck into flight, up, but something catching, hands tripping, the puck wobbling in the air and then plummeting like a doomed plane, dull thunk into the goalie's pads. The goalie dropped on it.

Whistle.

I stood there on the cusp of the goal crease. Gloves pounded my back, echoes through my chest. *Nice try, Iz. Almost had it. Next time, buddy.* I didn't move. Hal sprayed to a stop in front of me, took off her glove, the wormed push of her fingertips through my cage, yanking my helmet in close to hers, breath hard and hot all over my face, a smell faintly curdled.

'The right was wide open,' she huffed. 'What the fuck happened?' Eyes wide.

Breath delivered breech from my lungs. I gulped and gulped.

'Eh?' Hal demanded, but then she let go. Shook her head.

'I shit the bed,' I breathed. 'I totally shit the bed.'

She backed up a bit, eyebrows raised but I moved toward her.

'I'm sorry,' I said. 'Hal, I – '

She turned her back and skated away, her strides like snapping rope.

Ed ambled toward his office holding a Styrofoam coffee cup from the machine in the lobby. He smiled absently at me and looked away and then his eyes crashed back to my face.

'Hey, nice game there, Norse,' he said. My brain still revving replays of the fanned shot, all the different ways I might have not shit the bed.

'Well,' I said, 'a tie's not a win, right?'

He tilted his head at me, sipped at the coffee with distraction. Leaned in.

'Hey, she would've gotten it either way,' he said quietly, as though telling me a secret. 'She was all over it. It's math, you know. Kristjan always – '

'Okay,' I grunted, Ed's sad nostalgia cuffing me with weariness. 'Gotta go eat. See ya, Ed.'

I didn't care about The Game or math or Kristjan. What made me feel sick was the birth defect in that shot and how this made me weak and the red push of Hal's fingertips through my cage. I stalked off to the door and flung myself into the parking lot, the night, the headlights of Pelly's car pinning me against Sam Hall. Waiting to transport me to the shinier, carb-bloated horizons of Theresa's Pizza and More, where we were to replace the lost potential in our muscles with spaghetti and meatballs.

Ed left to erase the mistakes of our blades.

'I really want to make this happen,' Toad said, peeking under the tail of her lobster. 'I do.'

'You put the ass in class, sport,' Heezer said, leaning over from the next table.

Toad snorted and nodded her head in amazement, jiggling one of the huge mottled claws. 'Totally.'

Pelly reached over without a word and dismantled Toad's lobster in seconds flat, then gargled her wine and worked at a piece of food snared in her braces with her tongue.

'You're a star, child,' Toad said, bowing her head over the opened lobster. Pelly shrugged and tugged on the tip of a napkin folded into a shell shape. The napkin collapsed, and Pelly smoothed it over her lap in one quick motion, simultaneously pulling down the hem of her dress. She crossed her ankles beneath her chair. I tugged on my own napkin and eyed the lobster in front of me. Sig usually cooked a few crayfish in the summer, and I'd learned to leave the house when she put them in the boiling water, still alive. The first time, I watched the crayfish perform a sluggish dance at the bottom of the pot as their shells turned Christmas light red, and I knew they were being lit up on the inside because they screamed, quietly, almost privately. Sig took a hammer to them at the dinner table. She kept it beside her plate and, without warning, swung like she was trying to kill them for the second time. Buck smiled while he watched her, baffled and amused.

Everyone was eating theirs. I glanced around Pelly's parents' restaurant at the spangled constellation of tables the shape of kidney beans, of deformed hearts. Four or five to each table, and my teammates' faces flickered eerily in candlelight as they laughed at each other and ventured with knives and glinting shell-crackers, classical music tinkling faintly in the background. They were strangers in makeup and dresses. Like real girls, I thought.

At the table next to us, Woo was making her lobster perform an energetic dance to a song she only knew some of the words to, hummed loudly and off-tune. She'd drunk more beer than any of the other rookies at the warm-up party Boz had hosted in her apartment, shotgunning beers over the bathtub while Hal and Toad teased and hair-sprayed her black bob into a frizzy, off-kilter pompadour. She'd fallen on the ground laughing when they brought out the dress she was to wear, a pink and purple eighties prom gown with a silk-screened profile of Madonna on the back. She'd expressed jealousy at the two-foot-high inflatable beer-mug hat that was given to Roxy as part of her rookie uniform, while I'd thanked God that I'd managed to escape it. I'd tried to look at the situation like Woo did, tried to come at the humiliation in a different way. I'd attempted a few forced laughs when Toad unveiled my dress, a massive, hot-pink number with shoulder pads and a yellow bow drooping from the waist. Pink Sorel boots to match. I'd managed an additional weak laugh when Toad had turned the dress around to reveal *Hockey Barbie* written in huge black letters across the back. But Woo was drunk, and I could barely swallow sips of my own beer (slapped into my palm by Toad as soon as I walked through the door – 'You'll be needing this, Rooks,') as Hal and Toad improvised the rest of the costume, any small ability to laugh dissolving there in Boz's room while I sat on her bed, listening helplessly. They riffed off each other, grew my horror in sentences.

'You know what we should do? Rip off one of the sleeves so it looks like she was in a fight or something. You know, Hockey Barbie duking it out with that totsi, Skipper, in the corners. You dirty bitch – drop your gloves like a man, or I'll drop them for you – ' Toad said.

Hal jumped in. 'Ooh – we could give her a black eye. Where's that purple eyeshadow I saw over – '

'Holy shit – you know what I just thought of? I think I might still have some of that tooth black-out from that Halloween, like, the football-player Halloween. Oh my God, that would be per – '

'Yeah, and then rainbow eyeshadow on the other eye, and – stitches on her chin.'

They'd followed through.

I looked back down at the lobster. Pelly was disengaging the shell for me, deftly and delicately, as though diffusing a bomb.

'Thanks,' I said.

'No prob.' Her eyes dropped to the Jill strap resting on my lap, worn as a belt, the through-the-legs strap they'd severed swinging taillike between my knees. On it, Toad had scrawled, *DON'T EVEN THINK ABOUT IT, PERV.*

'Hockey Barbie's very own two-in-one Jill strap and chastity belt!' she'd said brightly. 'Watch her fend off hockey crotch shots by day and horn dogs by night! Hockey Barbie, defending her reproductive organs and her virginity all at once!'

'Why do they call it Jill strap?' Pelly asked the table.

'Oh, Pelter-Skelter,' Toad sighed, head down to the lobster, elbows pointing right angles over her plate. The candle splashed kaleidoscope spots across her face.

'You know the nursery rhyme "Jack and Jill"?' Boz said. Pelly shook her head. 'You know, Jack and Jill went up the hill – '

'Oh yeah. Yeah.' Pelly nodded rapidly. 'Oh, okay. Yeah.'

Toad abandoned the lobster, clattering her knife onto her plate, and filled her wineglass as she leaned back in her chair. She threw her hand up like a cheerleader as she chugged the wine, then dabbed daintily at the corners of her mouth with her napkin. I examined the cartoon on the Jill strap. I wondered if I could turn it backwards without them noticing. A bit later, I decided. I could already feel the wine in my legs, a slow tingle working its way up.

'Whatever happened to Jill?' Boz asked. She wore a purple scarf woven with gold flecks that trilled across her chest in the candlelight.

'Jill who?' Pelly said.

'As in Jack and Jill. Jack fell down and broke his crown and Jill came tumbling after. Then what, you know?'

'If women weren't so bad with directions, she could've gone first and they might both be alive today,' Toad said, raising her glass as though offering a toast. Pelly made a clicking sound.

'Oh, Toady, why do you do that? You're such a chauvinist,' Boz said.

'Boz, I've told you. Why must you make me relive the trauma?' Toad pretended to cry. 'I remember when my mom brought home the skates. But there was something wrong with them. I told her there was something wrong with them, and she laughed. What the hell was wrong with them? I thought they were freaks, these albino freaks, you know? My mom, she just laughed. Oh, the horror, when she forced them onto my feet. The horror. And there you have it, ladies. The truth: I was once a … I can't speak the words. I was a fingerpainter. I was a hockey player trapped in a figure skater's body. There you have it. I swear on Mooner's track suits.'

Toad pretended to blow her nose into the napkin. Pelly rolled her eyes and turned to me. She held the wineglass with her pinky finger raised.

'You like?' she nodded at the lobster. I hadn't touched it yet. I nodded, and took another sip of wine. I watched Boz wipe pretend tears from Toad's face. The other tables buzzed like hives around us. Perfume everywhere.

'Shit,' Pelly said under her breath and then Mrs. Pelletier glided up to our table behind Toad and Boz. She wore her hair in a bun and had the same stretched-forehead look Pelly did when her hair was in a ponytail, the corners of her eyes pulled back. Pearls, French manicure. I smiled idiotically at her, my hand travelling instinctively to my hair, pushing it down. Hal and Toad had ultimately decided to compromise on the hair: a crimped pigtail on one side of my head, and one huge back-combed snarl on the other. When Mrs. Pelletier looked at me, I felt the black eye makeup as pointedly as though it were a real bruise, roots plunging into my eye socket.

'What a lovely gown that is,' Mrs. Pelletier said to me, without a trace of irony.

'Ma!' Pelly chided, mortified. 'She's one of the rookie – it's a joke!'

'Well.' Mrs. Pelletier turned to Pelly, nonplussed. Toad bowed her head and closed her eyes in concentration, trying not to laugh. 'It is time now. Before the dessert.'

Pelly wiggled around in her seat a bit in protest, then Mrs. Pelletier dragged her off toward the black piano, angled open and gleaming at the far end of the room, the domino floor pouring shrinking diamonds toward its small stage.

Hal and Toad waited for Mrs. Pelletier to disappear into the kitchen, and then retrieved the garbage bag they'd left between the front doors when we came in. Hal cradled the plastic bulk as she and Toad walked over to our table.

'We're going alphabetically through the rookies, so you're up,' Hal said to me.

'B is for Barbie,' Toad chanted.

'I'll go first!' Woo yelled from the next table, swivelling around in her chair, pompadour wobbling. Her mascara had already streaked below her eyes.

'Ooh, not looking good,' Toad said. 'You're up against the alphabet there, Woo, and looks like you're losing.'

Pelly's first notes boomed out, slamming shut the noise in the room. The kidney-shaped circles of heads rotated toward the piano. Its top opened out toward the room, so that it resembled, from my distance, the hood of a broken-down car, Pelly tinkering angrily in its belly. The notes vibrated during pauses in the song, like the after-shock of a hit, lingering violence.

'Let's go, Barbie,' Hal said, the music shrinking her voice.

I hesitated, eyeing the bag cradled like a baby in Hal's arms. I knew the bag contained King Kong Beer Bong. Toad had sat the rookies on Boz's living-room floor like a group of nursery school-ers and revealed the long contraption, its impressive machinery that she and Bitty, an Engineering student, had built with their own hands using parts from a hot tub. Its name was written in black marker on the large funnel, a thick snout of tube trailing down, these two parts hinged together with a complicated system of levers and valves. Toad had performed a ceremonial bong. When Hal flicked the switch on King Kong, Toad's face had grown alarmingly red and a vein pulsed in her forehead, as though she were being strangled.

As they arranged me around the toilet in the handicapped stall, Toad brushed the front of her dress.

'Do mind the frock, dear,' she said, holding out her hands like a surgeon for King Kong as Hal wrestled it out of the bag. I gazed into the toilet bowl, the bathroom's dim chandelier washing everything with moving, honeyed light. The wine had crawled up from my legs to behind my eyes and the dominoes in the floor moved like a game. Air freshener leaked peaches into the stall.

'Nice,' Toad said as Pelly began to play a new song, a sad song, its notes creeping muffled into the stall. 'Beautiful. A slow dance between Barbie and King Kong. This is incredibly romantic.'

Hal retrieved the hose from Toad's hands and hovered it by my mouth as Toad poured a beer into the funnel. Her heels tapped an absentminded rhythm on the echoing floor, light swimming slowly across her face, red lipstick worn near the inside of her mouth.

'Ooh, too much head. Shit. Hang on a sec, Hal.' Toad peered into the funnel for a few long moments. ''Kay, ready.'

'If you have to puke or spit or anything, do it in there,' Hal pointed to the toilet. She smiled a bit. 'Open up.'

I opened my mouth with a dreamy, detached feeling. Like I'd just been shot to the gills with Novocaine, making my mouth invincible. I briefly recalled Toad's advice about confidence as Hal shoved the hose into my mouth.

I didn't open my throat. They didn't warn us that opening your throat wasn't the same as opening your mouth. In that split-second after Toad flicked the switch, I assumed it was the same. And then the choking began. My head became a water balloon, flooded, swelling. My nostrils smouldered and I lunged toward the toilet as my face exploded, beer spurting out my nose, travelling down and up my throat at the same time. When I sputtered, 'Fuck,' the word felt separate from me, an underwater bomb.

'Wow,' Hal said behind me. Their shoes braced my knees.

'I knew it,' Toad said. 'Hockey Barbie wears her sailor's mouth on the inside. What else are you hiding from us?' A run snaked up Toad's tights from her shoe. It stopped at a mole-like glob of purple nail polish.

I hacked wetly, grasping a chunk of teased hair back with my glove, Hal's hand on my back as Pelly played what sounded like a eulogy.

The bar moved in a dark glow that bruised the arms slanting bottles to mouths, the faces that opened on to our group as we walked in, Toad pushing us rookies ahead as though herding cattle. I stumbled through first, cutting a hall through the crowd, the crush of chests against my shoulders, beery laughter on my face and the flash of teeth. Bare arms humid against mine, the sway of ribs on the room's muscled backbeat, damp skin of hands gripping my shoulders, strangers laughing at the gown, the makeup, their voices insistent and smeared. Roxy's hand curled around my arm from behind as I tugged and pulled her through.

The evening tripping together into a dot-to-dot: blurs and gaps, flares of heady clarity, square moments drenched with light and noise. On the dance floor, my limbs flowing boneless, indigo faces around me exotic among their musky spread of feathers, hips tilting subliminal. I never danced. Why didn't I dance, I never did, but it was this, it was dancing, and why didn't I do it every day? Heezer, on the ground doing the worm to a song that had an accent, and the dancers jumped in circles around her – everyone jumping as soon as the song came on – arms raised, shirts bouncing up with flashes of perfect bruised stomach, and Heezer on the ground, body kinking forward, while Toad mimed a spanking. I never realized this – that Heezer was so hilarious, and I had to crouch to the ground, my laughter was so crippling.

The dim shrill of a whistle across the dance floor, and I gathered the booze-drenched hem of my gown in both hands, heading again toward the bar.

'Ladies. Shooters.' Toad announced when we were all there, all the half-eyed rookies. She had offered the same declaration the past four or five or six times she summoned us with the whistle, extending her palms toward us, a benevolent dip of her chin. 'Ladies. Shooters.' As though bestowing a blessing on our weak-necked heads.

I stumbled fast into the bathroom, catching the toe of a Sorel behind me, and waited. Wait. The bathroom lurched under my feet, as though I stood in a boat. And the tequila. Wait. I could still taste the tequila's burn in the back of my throat as I looked in the mirror and pulled my eyes open with my fingers. I'd forgotten about the hair. God, the hair. I was so incredibly ugly, I had never been uglier.

I pulled myself out of the bathroom, hands on the walls, the room slanted, then lurched through the door, my entrance unintentionally grand. A hand grabbed my arm as I veered back out into the darkness of the bar, and I swept around.

'Those your dancing boots?' Jacob said, his hand still on my arm. I stepped toward him, hovered for a moment, words gathering thick on my tongue, then I punched his shoulder.

'Have I talked to you already?' I said.

Jacob's face twisted into a smile. 'Just got here. The girls got you on some booze, eh? Are you okay?'

I rested my heavy head against the wall, closed my heavy eyes.

'I'm hot,' I said. 'I'm too hot. I'm hot and I'm ugly.' I traced a lazy circle around my face with a finger.

'Hey,' Jacob said. I could feel his breath close to my face. 'Even dressed like that, you're not ugly.'

I opened my eyes, and Jacob peered at me. 'Are you okay?'

The music pushed from inside of my head, trapped. I winced, put my hands over my ears. Jacob's ears peaked up into triangular points. I wanted to touch one of those strange tips. So I did. He smiled and took my hand, brought it down to my side, held it for a moment, and then let go.

'I'm too hot,' I said.

'You wanna go?'

'Yes. Yes.'

Quiet. Away from the bar, sound played a strange inversion, noise only in my head, on the inside, silence lounging foreign all around the dressing room, the brown velour couch behind me so strangely empty, misplaced in its tattered skin.

I dressed fast – I could never go that fast, usually. Someone should have been timing me, I thought, as I waddled out to the ice. Jacob, skating around the far end of the rink, bent over and laughed. He kept laughing as he skated, hair venting out, and sprayed me in the shins with ice as he stopped next to me.

'What?' I said.

'I was wondering what took you so long – what happened to just gloves and skates?'

'No. Full equipment,' I said. Jacob laughed incredulously.

'Why?'

'Safety first.'

'When did you turn into such a comedian, Isabel?'

I stole the puck from Jacob's stick, jockeyed it around, and looked across the rink. Quiet. The ice lay empty, one-dimensional except in the corners where it dropped into skies filled with the looming boards, the belled lights above.

I gave Jacob a sloppy pass and he began to skate, cutting a trail along the boards, his long strides, and I followed, sluggish. My legs filled with tequila.

Momentum. A flood in my legs then, the flash of my reflection on the glass as I stumbled into speed. Chasing Jacob around the periphery. The scrape of my blades tight against my ears, the hum fading slowly down. And Jacob's back shifting under his jacket, shoulders rolling, white of teeth over his shoulder as he looked back at me, catching up. And then he was skating harder, I could see it in the way he crouched closer to the ice, in the lengthening of his strides. My breath magnified in my ears. The tinny scrape of my blades, muscles in my thighs coiling tighter. And my own head caught in the corner of my eye, gliding along the pane of glass, black of the helmet and the cage, and my face unreachable beneath.

Jacob breaking out into the middle of the ice, pivoting backwards to face me, and that smile as though he were cheating and getting away with it, and then the puck on my stick blade, and the instinctive give of the stick. Everything fast now. I didn't see the puck until it was back on Jacob's stick, and then my legs moving for the net, and the pass right before the blue line that made the sting come through my gloves, and my stick lifting, and then the awkward twist in my knee, so fast, the blade edge burying in the ice like an axe, my feet too careless, too slow, and I was falling, limbs tumbling away from each other, away from the slick suck of the ice, the ordered memory of my body. The air thickened. And I hit the ice – knee, elbow, chest, elbow, knee, groin, head. I laughed, face down.

'Good thing you wore your equipment.'

I turned my head, laughter gushing from my belly like a tap I couldn't turn off, and saw Jacob's knee, skate folded underneath, stick nestled against the bottom of his thigh. I gathered myself up into a ball on my side, undid my helmet cage and let it dangle open sideways, the bright lights scratching against my dry eyes. The laughter ran out.

'I'm going to tell you something strange,' I said.

'Okay.' Jacob shifted his legs.

'My dad died, right? Didn't know him and all that. But, I don't know, it's like when you swim.' I took my glove off, made my hand into a wave. 'And you're swimming because there's the lake all around you and you'd drown if you didn't and maybe that's the same with skating. You skate because you're thrown on to the ice because your dad played hockey. So you swim because you have to.' I didn't see the words coming before I said them. They just appeared, magnetic against the ice, logic reversing and colliding and settling. Then silence. Or the absence of the hum in my ears, jarred out when I hit the ice, like getting the wind knocked out of me.

'I can see that,' Jacob said carefully.

I nodded, helmet cage clanging.

He paused. 'Well, look at us here. We haven't drowned yet.'

I was cold. The ice, at eye level, was blinding, fluorescent lights trapped on its surface. Blazing white. I rolled over onto my back, and then sat up, cage swinging. I took off my helmet, tossed it at my feet.

'Ah well,' I said. 'I was just wondering how I got so drunk tonight and then how I got here and so I was just thinking about … '

His eyes on my forehead. He reached over and I felt his fingertips pushing hair back from my face, felt the skin on the pads of his fingers growing damp with my sweat. My eyes heavy on the teeth biting his lower lip, their precise and crooked edges, and then he leaned in, his breath on my nose. And then I was kissing him before his lips were even there. I couldn't see my movements before, couldn't recognize them while they were happening – they were just there, the falling motions of my body, suddenly, and I was wondering if I should stop, his hands in my hair, the strangled snare of tangles against his fingers, dull pain of the tug in my scalp, and then his fingers breaking through. And my back against the ice, not thinking about stopping any more, the chill through my shoulder pads, through my jersey, through my neck guard, and then the back of my neck wet and cold, melting the ice beneath it, while the skin under my chin burned, neck guard gone, although I couldn't remember him taking it off. His hands on my shoulders and back, fingers prying underneath the pads, over top of my jersey, and I moved my hand to his shoulder, down the length of his arm, and there, his muscle unravelling under my hand as his palm moved down my side, the jersey coming up. I arched my back to get it off, and then he stopped, and I didn't care because there under my finger was the birthmark beneath his chin, and it felt like Braille, and tasted like salt, the grained remains of sweat on the nerves of my tongue. My jersey caught under my armpits and Jacob's hands firm on both my shoulders, pushed.

'You're drunk – we shouldn't – '

I pulled the jersey over my head, the grating rip of Velcro, and then the shoulder pads gone, the elbow pads twisted up on my forearms, but I didn't care, kissing him again, pushing his back toward the ice. Hovering over him, his lips moving from side to side, shaking his head, even as he slipped his hand under my T-shirt, fingers flitting past the hockey pants, down to the small of my back. Jacob shaking his head, and me thinking, *I am kissing*, and then not thinking, the crush of my chest on top of his as his head turned. His hands moved out of my shirt, and I wanted them back under, but he was pushing again, gently, and then hard enough to get me off his chest.

'Iz, no. No. Come on, you're drunk.'

Wait. Wait.

Getting up off the ice, and thinking as I skated. Thinking about the word *no*, thinking about bed. Jacob calling my name behind me. Finally, thinking. And then the couch in the bathroom, sitting there so I could sort it out in my mind, all of it draining into place now, my lips swollen and dry, eyes heavy, and Jacob gone.

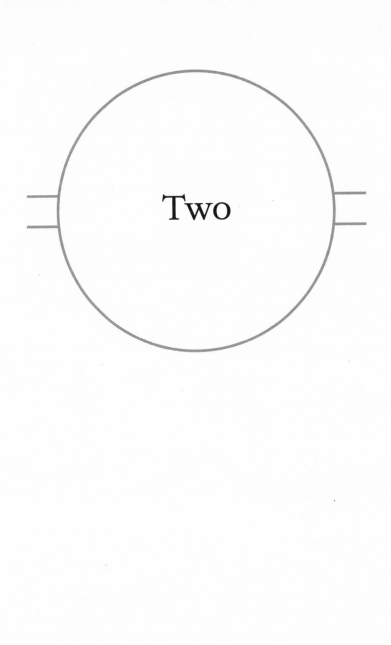

Two

Sig named me. She made it seem as though this task were bestowed upon her, a giant honour – *yes, madame, oh yes*. I recognized the overacting even when I was young. She was trying too hard, but I didn't tie this behaviour to any particular variables, as I didn't link her zealous swearing after Friday-night Bingo, her maudlin embraces of the dog, to the sharp smell on her breath when she bent over my bed to rub noses, Eskimo kisses goodnight. *Goodnight, champ. Sayonara. Bon soir. Ciao.* That incalculable behaviour of grown-ups.

Sig revealed my namesake one summer, around the time when childhood edges began unravelling, icons blown out: first the Tooth Fairy, then Santa Claus and on and on, magic dissolving like a baby tooth in the depths of a Coke bottle.

The girls in my class were named after goddesses: Athena, Helen. They had modern names that seemed directly linked to their popularity: Tiffany, Brittany, Jaime, Brooke. The gorgeous names. They wore them like boas, like diamonds. And in the midst of the attendance sheet's movie-credit names was mine, Isabel. My namesake, apparently, was Isobel Stanley, daughter of Lord Stanley, as in the Stanley Cup. There it was: I was named after a non-mythical hockey goddess, who was probably an ankle-burner.

Sig produced an ancient newspaper clipping. The photograph was black and white and blurry in a vaguely creepy way, like photos of the Loch Ness Monster, so each of the six players – five in black, one white – was faceless. As though someone had gone over the picture and blurred the lines of their bodies, smeared their noses and mouths, their eyes, with an eraser. They looked nearly identical, all around the same height, shadows cast over the blurred faces by extravagant hats, hats tall and angled like wedding cakes. Skirts draped in reverent folds to their ankles, hiding the moving angles of their legs. Those skirts seemed so deliberately elusive, I wondered what they were hiding. Did they wear pants under there? Their legs would have frozen – they were playing on a nameless pond somewhere in Ontario. I knew January in Ontario. Later, I realized that what they were hiding was the fact of these legs, a secret in itself. The hot friction of skin while skating, muscle blooming under the spell of this heat, swelling voluptuous. Quadriceps, hamstrings, gluteus maximus. They were denying these names, pretending none of that heat existed, under the decadent folds. Proper ladies.

Isobel Stanley wore white, the only one, at the heart of the dark pack all lunging toward a puck just outside the photo's frame, sticks thrown out – most of them held their sticks with only one hand ('Two hands, two frigging hands,' Uncle Larry screamed in my mind) – with what I read as unskilled desperation. Equating ankle-bending with the skirts and hats, I thought, was justified.

Fair enough, Sig didn't have much material to work with, and neither, then, did I. Giving Isobel Stanley the title of hockey player was, it seemed to me, grossly out of proportion to the evidence of this picture.

When I was three, legend has it I pounded out a rough version of 'Chopsticks' during Sig and Buck's Christmas get-together for the neighbours. Who taught me or guided me was never revealed, the event shrinking over the years to the circumference of that singular spotlight, the pinprick illuminating tiny me on the piano bench, blond-headed and determined. It was decided by the neighbours that night that I wouldn't be a hockey player after all, I'd be a virtuoso, a black sheep glowing golden among the jocks.

I never touched the lonely piano again. The Sawyers from next door continued to call me The Pianist well into my teens, until Sig, drunk, said, 'For Jesus' sake, the way you say it, you'd think a male member with legs had walked into the room whenever you see the poor girl.'

A three-year-old does not a pianist make. So Isobel Stanley played a couple of shinny games, skirts and all. So what? Would she have wanted to be labelled a hockey player, pinned like a strange butterfly onto that gilt-edged corkboard? Would she have wanted this responsibility? And if she had, wouldn't she have taken it a little more seriously, wouldn't she have traded in the hat and the skirt, wouldn't she have made herself less girly?

There were some things I could never take back. My name was one.

I spent an awkward few moments clasped between Marge Pernsky's breasts – I'd played hockey with her son since we were five – in the freezer aisle at Safeway a couple months before the Scarlets.

'I'm just so thrilled for you!' she sang. 'Finally, a team full of girls for you!'

I'd gotten this a lot. As though I'd been held hostage by that long line of boys' teams, as though I finally got to choose. But choice had never been part of it. I don't remember when I first started to play. I don't remember not knowing how to play. I must have been an ankle-burner at some point; my muscles must have made a series of corrections, found their way into the story, but I don't know how. Playing became one of those unexamined functions, a muscle memory that came before any real memories. And so, skating like walking. Skating like breathing. This isn't one of those destiny manifestos – *the sport chose me! We were meant to be together!* No. But choice was never part of it. Following Hal through the yellow door my first day with the Scarlets was the next correction.

The bottom half of the red B trailed a wavy cowlick behind it, the top half hinging a jaw around the first part of my name – Isa – making it look like a question. I sat very still in my seat in the lecture hall, holding the essay, as though the mark might begin to seep some sort of significance into my hands, dripping past the skin, my veins absorbing it like a phosphorescent dye, travelling up, up, illuminating parts of my brain like rooms in a house. Nothing. I scanned the chicken-scratch comments at the back. I did a few things decently and needed to work on some others. No mutations or deformities to speak of. I skimmed my conclusion and it didn't sound like me.

All around me, students were swooping from the recesses of the lecture hall, flooding up the stairs, papers flapping in their hands. A girl in round glasses, a red smattering of eczema on her hands, sat a few seats away from me, essay flipped to the last page, reading intently. She moved her mouth slightly as she read and looked like she was about to cry. As I watched the quiver in the girl's bottom lip, devastation welling around her eyes, my own essay developed a kind of weightlessness; it lost its sense of gravity. It could have winged up, flown from my hand, out of the room, and my world would have looked exactly the same. I pictured Dr. Spencer glancing up, finding me there in the balcony, extracting the marrow from my reaction as he did with other students' mean-well, stammered answers.

'So, what I'm … getting from you,' he'd say, head bent, fingers tapping the bridge of his glasses, 'is that you don't give a shit. Essentially. This is what you're saying.'

Looking at the B in my hands, pig-Latin alphabet. 'Yes, yes. That's it.'

This carelessness surprised me. I'd expected some change to come with my first mark – a knowing. This lack trickled into a form of bravery that buoyed me up from my seat, down the stairs, toward Dr. Spencer of the big words, that distant character on the room's small stage. From my perch in the nosebleeds, he spewed a Tom Hanks–ish charm. Lisping, boyish energy cut with a kind of mediating care. He had a way of joking with the entire room as though we were one person, having a tête-à-tête at a dinner party. He was hospitable, a host; students laughed when he meant them to and then he smiled modestly and slipped into lush, segued trails that lost me again. I couldn't help it: I kept slipping off the surface of his words, I drifted. I thought about hockey instead. Sig. Jacob. Those words on the ice returning to me as I flipped through *The Great Gatsby* to the pages Dr. Spencer shouted out like an aerobics instructor: *No. We shouldn't.* How that bony place behind his ear felt on the tip of my nose. Dr. Spencer wore plaid, button-up shirts and corduroys except for once when he wore a Toronto Maple Leafs jersey. He was far away.

As I slunk up, he was levering an unruly stack of paper into a brown leather satchel, his furrowed brow cordoning his face into a VIP lounge. Standing next to him, I initiated conversation the only way I could think of: I said, 'Uh,' and then I cleared my throat. His eyes drifted over and then latched weakly onto my face, distracted.

'Hellooo,' he said, the O's dropping into ironical depths into which I didn't possess the skills to rapel.

'Hi. Dr. Spencer, um – ' A blush burnt two distinct territories on my cheeks. There he was, *bam*, like happening upon a movie star at Arby's. But it was as though, now that the show was over, his makeup had dissolved, his orangey aura had turned off like a neon sign. He was far older than I thought, the creases around his eyes that, from my seat, made his face crackle into a smile, up close, anchored the eyes into a kind of wariness.

'I just wanted to tell you – ' I winced a bit at this, the intimacy around its edges inappropriate for a person who clearly had no idea who I was. 'I'm missing class on Friday? I play on the hockey team, so we're out of town. I just thought.'

Moon had told us we should do this, tell our professors when we'd be missing class. A courtesy. But Dr. Spencer seemed to get a kick out of it. A smile tugged on one side of his mouth, slowly, uncurling amusement. 'The hockey team, eh? Well. Good for you. Well.' He chuckled once, scratched his brow. 'Just borrow some-one's notes when you get back.' He gave an *I dunno* kind of shrug. 'And win, of course.' He looked back down at the papers now sprouting a bouquet from his bag, brow tenting again, slicing off the conversation. Done with me. I could miss every class and he'd never know, the mysteries of my schedule inconsequential to him. The strange hygiene of these huge classes. I could tweeze myself so cleanly from their middle.

Students flowed through the beige hallways, streams of coloured chatter, the smell of soup weaving salty currents among us from the café by the entrance. Everyone with the burdened pos-tures of backpack wearers, or leaning like wind-blown trees to balance messenger bags anchored with books. The girl ahead of me wove a highlighter through the air like a baton, conducting her conversation with a guy in a trenchcoat, laughter peeling off and falling behind them, over me. I looked around for Jacob. I'd seen him between classes in this hallway before, rolling to Sport Psych in his Scarlet Hockey jacket. I watched for him at the rink, in the dining hall, on the paths leading to Sam Hall, mentally mapping escape routes. The humiliation of Rookie Night could be isolated in this way, made into some far-off island. If necessary, I was prepared to deliver a deke, a head fake, to go wheeling around him. Head on a swivel, quick feet, as Moon would say.

Outside, I crouched beside the sidewalk and opened my backpack. Stuffed the essay inside the black cover of my Scarlets Play Book, a hefty binder crammed with hockey's arithmetic – permutations and combinations, algebra and angles, as though a goal might start here, on a page, spilling its story onto the ice with us, its bulky heroines. Pages and pages of happily-ever-after pitches.

The campus was built on paper, everything boiled down into books – parts of the human heart, the fall of civilizations, hockey. I'd never seen so many books in my life. But we were moving forward. We were making something happen. Weren't we? Moon had us working on the 2-3 Press last practice and it was a good system, a smart system if we used it against the right team – the Pronghorns, maybe – and if we got it down, if we perfected it there during practice – all of us treading ice, free from the pressure of opponents – I could see it working, I could almost picture it, that shining, future game.

As I zipped my backpack, I saw Jacob, late for class, jogging toward the Meade building doors, the collar of his hockey track jacket twisted under at the back, the front half-zipped and billowing. I crouched down farther and let another swell of students coming out through the doors crush my view. When they'd passed, Jacob had disappeared into Meade.

Dr. Chester had a tiny smudge of peanut butter on the corner of his mouth, and Sig was supposed to listen to him say all this garbage with peanut butter on his mouth like a five-year-old? He repeated himself, slower this time. His elegiac voice and the perfectly-straight part through his black hair. As though she were hard of hearing.

She thought of old Arnie Talbot at Bingo, his bobbing head. Sitting, yet never still. Feet battering the floor beneath the table. He, and his wife and daughter and son-in-law all arriving one Friday night at the Hall, all of them but him with ice cream cones from the Dairy Queen, his hands and tongue not stopping long enough for such meditative licking. How bereft he'd looked without an ice cream cone.

'Yes, uh huh, I heard it all the first time, thank you.' Sig plucked a Kleenex from Dr. Chester's immaculate desk and thrust it toward him, tapped the side of her mouth. He made a surprised sound and swabbed idiotically across his lips as though she'd told him he was wearing lipstick. 'Now, how's your mother?'

She began to mourn ice cream cones.

Hal put on cowboy music while we got dressed. Limp Bizkit whining about breaking shit, then silence for a moment, Toad freezing mid head-thrash. Johnny Cash began to croon, and Toad looked accusingly at Hal, clucking her tongue.

'Please, not this crap again,' she said. Hal ignored her, head down, tying her skates.

'Delia, oh Delia … If I hadn't have shot poor Delia, I'd have had her for my wife,' sang Johnny Cash.

Boz put a hand on her chest. 'Oh, that's awful,' she said.

No one changed it. Toad bellyached, but it was just for show. She'd never change it if Hal didn't say she could. When Heezer put on Sarah McLachlan or Tori Amos, though, Toad sprinted over there, pulled the cord from the wall as though yanking a poisonous barb from a teammate's heart. Heezer started to put on that music as a joke, tried to trip Toad mid-sprint.

The music seemed like strange taste for Hal. I would have guessed she'd like something a little more intense, music that throbbed like a headache, not the banjo-drunk hiccups of the cowboy ballads. Above the CD player, on a bulletin board dripping pictures, their edges curled like leaves from the shower steam, hung a picture of Hal, Toad and Heezer last Halloween. Toad and Heezer, dressed as football players, winced grins as they butted heads in oversized helmets, and Hal glared grimly at the camera from behind a black mask. The Lone Ranger.

I'd heard Toad call this expression of Hal's the FOAD look, which stood for *fuck off and die*. But it was more complicated than this.

Hal's glances held a dictionary of violence, an A to Z of ways to make a person want to die. I wanted to get inside these looks, to speak their tongues. Or to find a way into that locked space surrounding her, like Boz had, the way she leaned against Hal's knee and nodded over and over while Hal spoke gravely, quietly, eyes cast off somewhere just beyond Boz's face, trailing back for confirmation. But my flight instinct was stronger.

Hal shouldn't have been the Lone Ranger. I'm not sure what costume I would have placed her in instead. You learn not to guess at these things. You take cowboy music and Lone Ranger costumes and file them away in that chameleon jumble of other stuff that you never would have guessed. You learn this after a while: you can't guess, because you'd be wrong most of the time.

After practice I visited with Ed. Tuesdays had become Date Night with him. When I walked toward the rink door by his office, he'd be watching TV while some team circled the ice outside his door. He was waiting for me, I could tell, but he pretended he was surprised, making a big fuss about getting a chair, grabbing me a Grape Crush from the fridge.

We talked hockey and Kristjan and he grew younger and tougher and happier and more perverted, falling into a kind of Glory Day swoon when he really got into the stories, staring at some invisible rink beyond my head, he and Kristjan, Siamese frickin' twins, first-line wingers, ruling the ice and keg parties and the lust of underaged girls and the streets of their borrowed suburban neighbourhood. Ed shedding skin and regret and all the layers of ice he'd made since then, since the Zamboni found him.

He liked to get the stories straight, struggled to find the exact words Kristjan used when he woke Ed on the top bunk in their room at the Ferrys, their billets. Kristjan had punched Ed in the chest and when Ed looked up, through the darkness, Kristjan had the window open, one foot on the sill.

'He said, 'You're snoring, buddy. I'm ready to jump.' No, it was, 'That snoring, brother. I'm gonna put myself out of my bloody misery.' *Bloody misery*, that was it. And he kind of makes a move like he's really going to do it and I'm half asleep, right, and I jump from the bunk and grab his arm because I actually thought. He starts laughing his head off but I really thought. Went to save his life.'

There are people who let their ghosts swear at them with one foot on the windowsill in the middle of the night. I nodded and nodded. The patient student. I think he told himself he was doing me a favour. Like he was giving me Kristjan, which he kind of was, except the sound of Kristjan's voice in my head was still Ed.

When the ice time ended and all the voices and blade gasps and echoed shots drained from the office, his eyes cannonballed back to the room, to Sam Hall, to the Zamboni. I hated this moment. When he remembered that the ice had turned on him. He put on his jacket slowly, then pulled a photo from the pocket. Handed it to me.

'Found this the other night, going through some pictures. Thought you might want it.'

The photo was full of Kristjan's head, his face tilted up, smiling peevishly at the camera, one eye half-shut. His mouth was open a bit, saying something that looked like it was probably an insult to whoever was behind the camera.

'That was one of the last ones I had of him. Some Halloween party.' Ed smiled a bit, went to the door. 'And yeah, he's drunk as hell, I'm willing to bet.' Proud.

I tacked the picture on my wall in Rez, in the middle. It was the only thing up there, and when I lay in my bed, it looked like he was sneering right at me. I wanted to tell the kid to shut up.

Legend has it that a boyfriend Boz had the season before punched her, gave her a black eye. Drunk on rye, Hal and Toad climbed into a tree outside this boyfriend's apartment and waited for him. When he walked up the driveway, they pelted him with stones they'd gathered. I pictured Hal selecting the ammunition, turning each stone over in her hands, testing it with a fingertip as she glared through the darkness. She would have chosen the sharpest rocks, the heaviest, the ones like arrowheads. I saw her launching them from the tree, knees bunched up to her chest, and the look she had when winding up for a slapshot – you could tell that whoever got hit with that shot would hurt like hell, like she'd planned – and the muscled arc of her arm, the violent flick of her wrist.

The boyfriend tried to see into the tree at first, shouting, but then he got a stone in the eye and ran into the house, blood on his face. When he came back out, waving a knife, Hal and Toad were halfway down the street, laughing because the knife was so small they could barely see it from that distance, it could have been a butter knife, and because the boyfriend was crying – the sobs echoing off the black pavement.

I watched Boz on the red couch in the lodge where Team Day was being held, the fireplace throwing strands of liquid shadow over her face, and tried to picture her as a punched-up girlfriend, a bruise cloaking her eye. Responding to Question Four on the Team Bonding Questionnaire, she explained to me, right hand threading a pen through the air, how she planned to become a child psychologist: the programs she'd have to take, the schools that offered them, the exams. And why. The blunt-edged kindness cutting these reasons jolted me. I thought she was joking at first, parodying someone, and I almost laughed. But she didn't stumble over any of these words. She didn't flinch.

She touched her fingers to her lips and tilted her head. 'And that's my story.' She smiled. 'What do you think? Have we bonded yet?'

'Pretty close,' I said, and she winked at me and flipped the sheet in her lap. Stan ambled past and gave us a questioning thumbs-up.

'We're good,' Boz said to him, and Stan looked pleased.

'I knew you two would be a good pair,' he said, nodding happily, then wandered off toward Woo and Toad. Stan seemed perpetually on the hunt for some elusive team adhesive: *stick together, tight, like glue, good, we're gelling, girls, we're really coming together now.* He'd walked through twice already and called out 'Team bonding!' like a photographer reciting 'Cheese!' and hoping for that shot with everyone smiling in perfect order, no one caught in a blink.

'Getting to know you, getting to know all about you … ' Boz sang, her singing voice a shade deeper than when she talked. A framed black-and-white next to her head showed two men in buck-skin parkas standing over a deer, its blood casting a Rorschach pattern onto a bed of snow. I wanted to know: did she fight the boyfriend after he punched her?

She cleared her throat.

'Okay, Number Five. Here we go. Number Five – why do you play hockey? Do you want to go first again, babe?'

I shook my head. 'No, you go ahead.'

'Okay … wow. Hmmm.' She cupped her chin with a hand and stared at the floor. 'I guess it's supposed to be a simple answer, huh? You know, "Because I love it," or something along those lines. And I do love it, of course, but I don't want to just … '

She stared at the floor again, head tilted.

'Okay, I'll tell you a story. When I was at home this summer, my brother was watching this show on TV. This gangster movie. And I usually can't stand those movies, with the shooting and all that, but I was hanging out with my brother, so I just sucked it up. Anyways, so there was one scene where they had this guy tied in a chair, and they were trying to get information out of him, but he was resisting – the usual. They say, Tell us or we cut off one of your fingers. But he still doesn't tell them, he's squirming and crying – it was awful. So, of course, they cut it off – I didn't watch that part. But that whole night I was thinking about it, because it was so brutal – but also, I was thinking, what would I do that for? You know, sit there in a chair and let someone cut off my finger. I was up all night. Anyway, you don't need to know all that. My point is, I suppose, hockey. It passed the test. I asked myself, cut off your finger or never play hockey again in your life? I know this probably sounds stupid, but I pictured never playing again and the way that I would just suffer, you know? The way I see it, it comes down to this equation, a sort of math. The physical pain of having a finger cut off goes away, heals in a relatively short period of time, versus losing hockey forever, which, I think, would be like walking around with a broken heart for the rest of your life. Like a never-ending breakup. With your *man*. You know? So do it, then. Chop it off. Done.'

Boz pushed her glasses up the bridge of her nose. 'Whew. I talk too much.'

'What else?' I said.

'Sorry?'

'What else passed the test?'

'Oh. Well.' Boz smiled and counted off on her fingers. 'God. Family. Friends – you guys.'

'Oh.'

Boz settled back on the couch and laced her hands together. 'How about you? Do you think you'd do it?'

'Chop off a finger?' I looked at my hands doubtfully, spread my fingers wide.

'Yeah – goodness, that sounds awful coming from someone else's mouth. You must think I'm morbid.'

'No, no, it's okay. Um, would there be anaesthetic?'

Boz smiled and shook her head. 'No.'

'Anything for the pain?'

Boz leaned forward. 'Oh, babe, I'm sorry I brought it up. I just didn't want to say 'because I love it.' I'm sorry. I'm disturbing you.'

'No worries, no. You're not disturbing me. Yes, I'd trade. I'd – I'd give up the finger.'

I'd never cut off a finger for hockey. I wouldn't cut off my hair.

I kept going. Boz tilted her head. I wanted to know: how could anyone punch her? I'd tell her the right things, the words that would keep her nodding like that, nodding and nodding and saying 'mm hmm' like I was infinitely interesting, like she understood, like she had fought for this interview with me, this was exactly where she wanted to be.

I told her about Kristjan, about his nickname – Norse Giant – and how he'd gotten it. I told her about that playoff game in Junior when he scored all the goals for his team and then the overtime goal too, and how his picture had been on the front page of the *Kenora Tribune* the next day with a headline reading, *Norse Giant Does it Again*. I told her about all the trophies in the Rec Centre engraved with his name. About how he'd died, the bridge of sticks at his funeral, how Sig told me sometimes people looked like they'd seen a ghost when they saw me as a kid, with my mushroom haircut and boy's swimming trunks. I told her about Buck's lake rinks, the way he measured and scraped them perfectly square, and then more snow came, and he was out there the next morning with his measuring tape, Sig laughing at him out the window but never to his face. I told her about Sig naming me after Isobel Stanley and my suspicions that the original Isobel had been an ankle-bender.

Boz leaned back and examined my face. 'And that's why you play?' I nodded.

She smiled quickly and paused. 'Those are all really good reasons,' she said. 'They are.'

Nodding again and again. Not like she was convinced, but like she was trying to convince me. Patience in her voice as though she'd forgiven me for something.

I knew right then is a bullshit line, as Sig would say. As though a life might be beaded together into a string of gaudy epiphanies, one long, lustrous highlight reel.

Like Sig, I refused to believe in such moments, a goal frozen in a highlight reel, the red light behind the net flooding the ice. Call it a TSN Turning Point.

I placed myself in that tree with Hal and Toad, passing a rock between my hands, the heaviest I could find, waiting to launch it at the boyfriend's skull, but I also felt a brief glimmer I would never admit to. Understanding flung from the branches, a cold and brutal thread of it, out to the crying boyfriend, how he might have wanted to test Boz's forgiveness, the self-mutilating love she could lay out there so calmly – to me, a person she'd sung 'Getting to Know You' to, practically a stranger, who didn't understand, who could watch her gestures of hockey adoration like a play, but never move that way, never speak those words, without acting.

I looked around the room. They were all in on it, all my teammates. Their huge love for the game eclipsed any need for reason. It was simple. I felt far away then, floating away from Boz, from the team. As though I'd been watching them from the stands.

My decision wasn't made right then. But I began to turn, to open toward its possibility. And as possibilities tend to do, it began to grow.

That night, I started to quit hockey.

Sig felt silly, as though she were being tugged unwittingly into ceremony, the dusky shove of the sky, the wind's lean casting the scene around her with a portentous tenor. Of course, it was Grace's fault that such things would even cross her mind, all that spiritual jazz she spouted mixed up now, despite Sig's best efforts, with the eager waves there around the dock, the area she regarded as being as much hers as the jagged square of yard behind their house. She seriously considered, as she shifted the skates in the crook of her arm, disowning Grace.

Of course, her trudge down to the dock, skates in hand, held as much ceremony as did her march down the hallway, magazine in hand, to the bathroom. Truth was, she had no other option. She couldn't just chuck them out with the trash. She'd imagined their presence out there at the dump among the piles of shunned junk, everything irrevocably broken. She would not subject the skates to the noncommittal nosing of the dump bears, one of which Sig had recently seen with a sanitary pad stuck to the side of its face.

Nor could they go to the Sally Ann. They'd be scooped up, no doubt, by some heavy-ankled woman who would buy them because she didn't know any better about skates, and she wouldn't really use them, but they were cheap, so what the hell. And they'd fit the woman's feet like a boy's jacket on a fat man, the leather unfailingly loyal to the contours of Sig's feet. And the woman would be a shrieker, undoubtedly a Bloody Murder type, whooping and flailing her arms like a drowning swimmer as she toddled around the ice.

No.

Sig stood for a moment at the end of the dock and made an effort to hold the skates casually. She allowed herself a final glance down at them, nothing too lingering. With the same discipline, she forced from her mind the calluses on Buck's hands – jagged reefs of skin – passing over the skates' eyelets. Ridiculous to wait when she'd made up her mind. And with every second she stood there the skates gathered to their beaten edges a significance they weren't worthy of.

She heaved the skates with a grunt. They strained away from each other, laces still binding them together, and flapped vaguely, an ugly moth, rusted wings, before dropping. They splashed Sig's shins when they went in, and she felt the lake seeping cold through her pants while she watched them sink, parts of blade untouched by rust gathering green as the algae claimed them. They sank quickly.

She bent for a moment, scrubbing angrily at the spots of water on her leg, avoiding the ripples still spilling out from where the skates went in. Then she turned and limped back down the dock, conjuring a Scotch into her hand and wool socks onto her feet. Straight-armed up toward the house that seemed to shrink and shiver on the cusp of winter like a blue-lipped girl. She stopped only briefly and, without looking back, cursed both the loon and train that were sad somewhere across the lake.

The big red W on the left side of the team winter jacket, over the heart, was supposed to forgive the jacket's lack of fashion. Long and black, the jacket was boxy when the drawstring hidden in the waist wasn't in use. When I cinched it in, the top part ballooned, the bottom becoming triangular. The first day I wore it, I felt big and puffy and hyper-visible, like I was wearing a mascot costume. The Scarlet crest whittled away my anonymity, narrowed me down.

When I walked down to Dr. Spencer's desk at the end of English class to pick up a handout, he noticed the jacket and pointed to me, winked and then mimed a slapshot. I gave him a fake laugh, hurrying back to the stairs, and got stuck behind a guy on crutches. I wanted out. Should I have pretended to be a goalie? Should I have pretended to get hit with the puck? What did he want from me? The slapshot, had it been real, would never have gotten off the ice, would have been a low-slow. His flimsy, professorish arms. Imagining Dr. Spencer as an ankle-bender made me feel sad and apologetic.

As I was walking toward University Centre, a few people gave me looks, or maybe I was making it up. Definitely a double-take from a guy in a Canadiens baseball cap – he caught the crest and then looked back at my face like maybe he knew me. I'd started taking the tunnels to the rink for practice, walking through University Centre, past The Rock, a ledge of the wheelchair ramp next to the Snaxtime where the football guys gathered to drink protein shakes together and look at girls. A couple of them nodded at me as I passed.

'Tough Bruce,' Darius said at the end of their line-up. He stood and swaggered toward me, pants sagging. Raised his hand. 'Touch it.' I slapped his palm. He'd never talked to me before.

'I love you chicks. You tell Boz I say hi, all right?'

'I will,' I said, palm still ringing as I walked.

The jacket had made me less careful. Jacob rounded the corner, coming at me with that careless amble, eyes jerking when he saw me. Wearing an identical jacket. It was the embarrassment of wearing the same outfit to school as a girl in your class – but twisted, like a balloon animal, into a hermaphroditic elephant. I didn't stop. I pivoted on my toes, mid-step, heart thudding in my ears, and walked the other way. Jacob caught up and walked next to me, head wedged down as though trying to pry up my chin.

'We're twins,' he said. I could see his teeth in the corner of my eye.

'Absolutely not,' I said, kept walking.

'Could you stop for a second? I promise – just a second.'

I stopped, body perpendicular to his, eyes on his shoes. The University Centre lights sizzled yellow. Jacob didn't say anything, too close. I took a step back, raised my eyes slightly and caught the birthmark under his chin. My eyes snapped away, and back again into the rink, nighttime, trying to lift the skin of that person who had rolled on the ice with Jacob. Impossible. I could only watch the two bodies, the strange alphabet etched by their limbs; the words my fingers had held were now an impossible story. He was looking at my face, I could feel it.

'I guess I just wanted to apologize?' he said.

I tucked my chin down farther.

'Are you hiding from me?' he asked.

'No.'

'Well, then you disappeared.'

I looked up quickly, down again. Teasing eyes.

'I've been right here,' I said.

'You don't have to be embarrassed – I'm sorry, I shouldn't have left you there.'

'We're not talking about it.'

Jacob laughed. 'Well, how about if we eat ice cream and not talk about it?'

'I have to go to practice,' I said. I looked up as he pulled his wallet from his back pocket, whipped out his dining-hall meal card and flashed it at me like a big spender. Same jacket, same crest, same drawstring.

'Daddy's paying,' he said, straightfaced.

I laughed a bit. 'I'm late already, so.' I started to walk toward the tunnels again.

'Isabel,' he called. I half-turned. 'You've pulled off an impossible feat. Looking beautiful in the team jacket. Just so you know.'

Toad and Pelly walked up to us then, Toad's face lit with an expectant smile.

'It's the lovebirds in their matching shit. You're like one of those old couples on a two-seater bike that dress all matchy, eh?'

'Tweet tweet,' Jacob flapped his hands at his sides, then he did a Michael Jackson pivot and walked the other way.

'Toad,' I said, face hot, as we walked into the tunnels.

'What, accuser-face? Where's your lover pride, eh?'

'He's not my lover.'

'But he's cute,' Pelly said. 'No, he's handsome.'

A small bump of pride.

'You know, you're allowed to like boys, champ,' Toad grinned. 'You have our permission.'

'I know I'm allowed to like boys,' I said. This was the kind of logic Toad inspired.

'So where's your boyfriend then?' Pelly said to Toad.

Toad looked at her like she was crazy. 'What would I need a dude for when I've got all you losers harassing me at all times?'

This made strange sense. We were triplets in our jackets. They'd rescued me from Jacob. I imagined my stride sharper, heavier, calves biting off the end of each step with teeth. Legs that could swagger if I wanted them to.

I went to the bathroom after practice and when I came back, Jacob's hockey card was lying in my stall. A picture of him taking a slapshot, following through, eyes wide. On the back, they'd circled part of his player profile in purple marker: *Premier power forward.* Scrawled below, *Reach for the stars! Dream big! Go for the gold! Yer Lover.*

Toad was grinning at me. '*Premier power.* Like the sounds of that.'

'Come on,' I groaned. Stuffed the card into my backpack.

'I'm telling you, he's handsome,' Pelly said.

'Whatever,' I said. Put my hands up. Surrender: the only safe strategy. 'Okay, whatever.'

'And I resent – ' Toad dropped her jaw as she looked at Heezer. 'Ooh, Nelly! Heez. You getting some action tonight?'

Heezer turned toward us and looked down at the bra, a lacy, rose-pink push-up, a fake diamond heart in the middle nearly eclipsed by the cliffs the bra made of her breasts. The underwear some of them wore beneath their ordinary clothes – under their T-shirts and jeans, their sweats even. Different lives under there, hidden glittering worlds – after they'd peeled off the sweaty bondage of sports bras we all wore under our equipment and to the gym. I was still trying to figure some of it out. The complicated wiring, the delicate bones of Heezer's bras that allowed them to stand upright in her stall, as though on legs. Hal's minuscule thongs, which Toad called butt floss.

'Nah, working,' Heezer said. She shrugged and glanced at her watch. 'Shit!' She turned to her stall and whipped a white tank top over her head, a blur of orange lettering on the back before she threw on a hoodie, quick, zipping it up to her chin.

'Holy shit,' Toad breathed, gripping her chest. 'Whoa. Okay, stop. Back the truck up, Heezy. You're – no – I didn't just.'

Heezer ignored her, throwing a limp handful of gym clothes into her backpack.

'What happened?' Pelly asked me. I shrugged and Pelly rolled her eyes at Toad, who was taking tentative steps toward Heezer, hand outstretched.

'Just take the hoodie off for a second, Heezer. Please.'

'Toad, I'm late.' Heezer turned to face her, cheeks red, her orange hair twisted into a swinging bauble at the nape of her neck.

'What's going on?' Hal rifled a brush into her stall as she walked across the room from the bathroom. She stood, fists on hips, and tilted her head at Boz.

'Just let her go if she's late, Toady,' Boz said.

'Hal. You have to see this. Come on, Heez.' Toad reached for Heezer, and she jumped backwards, pulling her backpack over her shoulders.

'I'm outta here!' she announced, grinning wildly, taking another step back, and Toad lunged at her, grabbing her arms, twisting them behind her back.

'You savage!' Heezer writhed, crimson-faced, giggling manically. 'You heinous fuck!'

'Get the zipper, Hal!' Toad bit her bottom lip as she danced, mirroring Heezer's steps. Hal reached casually for the zipper and yanked. Heezer went still, chin dropping to her chest in defeat. There, across her chest, blazed the unmistakable orange lettering.

'What does it say?' Pelly said, squinting. 'Hal's in the way.'

'It says *Hooters*,' I told her.

Boz gasped and then began to laugh, a long, slow chuckle.

'But, you don't really – ' Toad stuttered, grinning.

'Toad, who cares?' Heezer jutted her chin.

'Come. On.' Hal said, glaring.

'Listen, I've got big guns – may as well use 'em. And, anyways, it's just a job. Chill out.'

'Oh my God.' Hal faced Heezer, arms stiff at her sides, and they stared at each other, a showdown.

'Big guns? Have they seen your other guns?' Toad asked.

'You guys, I gotta run. It's Wing Night.' Heezer backed toward the door.

'Looks like Breast Night to me,' Tillsy called from the deserted South.

Pelly snorted at me. 'Breast Night.'

'You can't do this,' Hal said.

'Already done.' Heezer, at the door, quickly slipped off her sweat-shirt. Back to the crowd, head bowed, she flexed. 'You mean these guns, Toad?' she said and slapped a bicep. Muscle bulged above the neck of the tank top, shoulders popping. *Delightfully tacky yet unrefined* in orange letters on her back. Thrilled laughter. She swaggered out of the room.

'That's too classic,' Boz said.

'I can't believe she's doing this.' Hal shook her head.

'You can't?' Boz said. 'It's so Heezer.'

'It's sick and wrong.'

'Wings anyone?' Toad chirped.

Heezer kicked open the swinging door of the kitchen, frowning at the yellow baskets of wings stacked up one arm. She steadied them with her other hand, the Hooters tank top on display now, dipping low in front to reveal cleavage sculpted by the pink pushup bra, her hair still in the messy, damp nest at the nape of her neck. A pair of orange spandex shorts – not shorts so much as underwear – completed the uniform. She wore flesh-coloured tights underneath, and they had a strangely luminescent sheen, like the tights old women wear for circulation, so it looked as though her legs were plastic. Hard plastic juts of muscle giving her away as a jock.

'Hoots! Hoots! Hoots!' Toad chanted and hit the table with a fist. Others joined. The baskets trembled as Heezer looked up. A look of panic flickered on her face.

'You didn't.' She fought a smile, baskets swaying. 'Oh my God.' She shrugged the wings off her arm onto the neighbouring table, where two men gulped beer from pint glasses that were dripping water onto their ties.

'Cheers to our good friend Hoots. May she find continued success in her new career,' Toad offered solemnly, lifting her glass of water.

'Cheers! To Hoots!'

Heezer shook her head, her back to us, the line on the back of the tank top, *Delightfully tacky yet unrefined*, shouting its bald irony in orange capitals like a neon sign. All of them wore this sentence, the whole team of Hooters servers, and it seemed to suggest they were acting out an elaborate satire, all in on a joke parodying other women who might look like that, act that way, but who were ignorant of the comic masterpiece in cleavage and flesh they were creating, the fetish incarnate. I looked around at the other servers and saw that this had backfired. They were only performing a parody of themselves, unaware. Men were staring, people were laughing all over the place. From my seat, I couldn't separate the looks from the laughter. Heezer pushed the baskets across the table toward the men.

'Hey, Hoots, strong work. Strong wing delivery there. Keep it up, buddy, we're all watching with bated breath,' Toad called. Heezer shook her head and held a middle finger against her back.

'Better not dump those, babe,' one of the suit guys said. 'I been dreamin' about them all day.'

'Jesus,' Hal muttered. 'Fulfilling life.' She crossed her arms and leaned back, balancing the chair on its rear two legs.

My mouth watered as the sharp, vinegar-edged smell of the wings clouded over our table. I opened a menu. 'What are you going to have?' I asked Pelly.

'Wings, I guess,' Pelly said. She shrugged. 'Beer, probably.'

'You like Cajun?' I asked her.

'Yeah.' Shrugged again.

'You wanna share?'

'Yeah.'

A cheer swelled from the room's bass hum, tinny oldies playing in the background. With a motion that resembled the back crawl, a football player danced in the end zone on a TV screen above. Eyes raised, a group of men at a table across the aisle sucked on their fingertips and smiled, baskets climbing high around them.

Heezer came over and leaned across the table, her elbows on one of Toad's shoulders, one of Hal's.

'Three or more of them, they're here for the guys,' Heezer said in a low voice, gesturing with her head toward the two men at the next table. 'Two of them, they're here for the girls.'

'Oh boy! Now, where did I put my dance card.' Toad pretended to fumble in the pockets of her jeans.

'But, Toady, you're not really a girl. Let's be honest. Mama's talkin' real girls.' Heezer shimmied her breasts quickly in Toad's face and then spun off again to visit her tables.

'I'm gonna pop that bra and then what'll she do?' Toad said, an exaggerated shrug. 'She'll be fired – they're like raisins rattling around inside helium balloons. It's all the bra. An optical illusion.'

'Heinous,' Hal said.

Two servers crossed paths next to our table, and the brunette server slapped the blond's butt. The blond shrieked – a high-pitched squeal like a young girl and as the brunette twisted around to smile over her shoulder, her tank top rode up and a meaty rhinestone in her bellybutton caught the light, a quick flash across her stomach, which was a contrived shade of orange-brown. It happened right behind Hal's shoulder and, in that split-second of sparkle across the server's thin, sharp body, colour all over her – orange shorts, brown skin, glossed-pink lips, sunset highlights in her hair – I saw the sudden paleness of Hal's skin, the monotone grey of the team sweatshirt, the disorder of her coarse hair, the bareness of her face. It was as close as I'd come to feeling sorry for her. But everyone at the table wore team clothing – jackets, hoodies, sweatpants, T-shirts. We were all overdressed, we were all bare.

I watched Hal. Her eyes flitted darkly around the room.

'Totsis,' she muttered.

'Speak up, son.' Toad leaned toward her, cupping a hand behind her ear.

'Totsi hell,' Hal said, louder.

'Correct,' Toad said. She shifted into a mangled Australian accent, whispering loudly. 'We have the *thrilling* opportunity here tonight, mates, of observing a pack of *rare, purebred totsis* in their natural habitat!'

Hal laughed. Pelly twisted around in her seat, looking around the room as though for the first time.

'What's a totsi?' I asked her. Pelly turned and stared blankly at me for a moment, chewing on her lip, braces a-gleam.

'Hey, Toad. Toad. Corinne!' she barked across the table. Toad, now in a downstream conversation with Tillsy, looked over, irritated.

'What?'

'Iz wants to know what a totsi is,' Pelly said.

'Just look around,' Toad said with distaste.

'The fingerpainters,' Tillsy piped up.

Pelly leaned toward me and translated. 'That's the figure skaters. The ones with ice time after us.'

I nodded. Heezer bounded by with empty beer bottles in both hands and cracked Toad lightly over the head with one before flying through the kitchen door. Toad touched her head and looked after Heezer.

'Rude,' she said dryly.

'Does that mean Heezer's one?' Pelly asked.

'A totsi? Oh fuck, would that ever be a crime. We lose the strongest farter on the team to the dark side. I suppose we have to be objective about this, though,' Toad sighed.

'Look at her – she's wearing hot pants. Of course she's a totsi.' Hal jutted her chin toward Toad.

'I don't think that makes her a totsi,' Tillsy argued. 'This is work, it isn't who she is.'

'Whatever,' Hal said dismissively. 'Flashing her boobs around like that. You're right, she's the anti-totsi.'

The blond server arrived with pitchers of beer and began to throw glasses around the table. The conversation halted awkwardly as she hovered over our shoulders. When she'd jogged off, ponytail swinging across her back like a metronome, Boz reached over and rubbed Hal's arm. 'Okay, babes, enough of the totsi philosophy. They are who they are,' she said.

'But who they are isn't *right*.' Toad leaned forward. 'The thing with being a totsi is that it's so boring, so predictable. I mean, where's your sense of irony? You know, like if you're going to wear hot pants and have blond hair, at least throw on a Harvard Debating Club cardigan too, or something.' She held up a pitcher, then began to pour.

'Oh no, hon, I'm good.' Boz reached for her glass. 'I have to study tonight.'

'Boz, we're at Hooters,' Toad said. 'It's Wing Night at Hooters. We're here to support our good friend Heezer, who works at Hooters. Exams come and go, but this evening – this opportunity – will never come your way again. It's Thursday. It's been a long week. You're young. Be gentle to yourself. *Carpe diem.*' Toad held her glass up to Boz in a toast.

Pelly turned to me. 'That's totsi,' she said.

'Okay,' I said. 'I think I got it.'

On the ice, we saw numbers. We called each other's names and shifted and joined into shapes that broke and reformed and broke again. Coming together, falling away, trying again. Away from the ice, though, away from the familiar rooms of Sam Hall, they didn't have to be together. But they chose each other. At Hooters, in that room sprayed with testosterone and totsis, I watched them grow together into one giant girl, getting to her feet, spreading her arms, filling the room with her huge voice. Spotlight on.

Toad discovered Newfies. She wandered off to the bathroom and came back trailing a line of guys in baseball caps with goofy, boozed-up smiles.

'Newfies,' she said incredulously. 'Newfies. I go to the can and look what I find. I fucking love Newfies.' She elbowed the round, freckle-faced guy next to her. 'Say something.'

The guy raised his pitcher of beer to his clan and yelled, 'Ayyyyyyyyy!' To which they responded, 'Ayyyyyyyy!' and Toad, Tillsy and Pelly joined in. Everyone pushing their glasses toward the mouth of the pitcher like hungry baby birds. Toad grabbing a pitcher from our table and snapping her fingers at Heezer.

'Garçon! Garçon! Sweetheart, honey, darling – could you be so kind as to bring a lady a straw?'

Heezer flipped her the finger from across the room. Toad shrugged and grasped the pitcher's middle and hoisted it up over her face, throat moving in slow pulses as though her heart were trapped in there. The Newfies going all bug-eyed and cheering Toad on like they were at a wrestling match. As a finishing move, she dabbed daintily at the corners of her mouth with a napkin, shaking her head modestly at the whoops and applause of the Newfies.

'Where have you been all my life, girls?' one of the Newfies said with rapture.

Toad hugged him. 'The feeling's mutual.'

The Newfies scattered to hunt and gather chairs from other tables and Toad sat back down.

'What a find,' she said, belching.

'Toad, you're a shit show,' Hal laughed. 'You're bush league.' She shook her head.

Toad scooped her keys from the table. 'Barbie, you boozing?' she said. 'Yes? No? No, right?'

I wanted to say yes, to turn her assumption upside down. I shook my head.

Toad threw the keys at me in a jangling arc. 'DD. I'll owe ya one.'

I caught them against my chest. 'Yeah, no problem,' I said, feigning coolness. I didn't understand Toad's logistics – what I would do with the car at the end of the night, if I'd have to drive everyone home, how late this all would go, how much worse it would get. But the keychain held a healthy handful of keys and its weight in my hand leaked a sense of purpose.

'Yeah right,' Pelly said, snorting. 'Like you ever drive, Toad.'

Toad thought about this for a moment and spread her palms as the Newfies began to descend, carrying chairs above their heads and raining them down around the table, still in their crooked smiles. Heezer arrived with three more pitchers.

'I'm a professional, sport,' Toad said. 'Somebody's gotta keep the fans coming back. Everyone has their own unique role on this team. Right, Boz?'

'Toady, I'm going. Seriously this time.' Boz lifted her purse from the table.

Toad cleared her throat loudly. 'Gentlemen, my friend here is attempting to flee the premises in order to study. What are your opinions on this behaviour?'

The Newfies erupted into loud, incomprehensible expressions of outrage. One of them plunked a pitcher in front of Boz, who shook her head and smiled politely. Heezer appeared with the straw. I put the keys in the pocket of my hoodie. Sat back and watched the show.

We made it to the Blue Moon on Campus for last call after Heezer got off work. I stood with Hal at the bar and we watched Pelly, Toad and Heezer dance to 'Baby Got Back' as though it were an anthem written for them, all of them shouting the words, faces intense: 'I like big butts and I cannot lie!'

'Our friends are an embarrassment,' Hal said, but she was smiling. Tilting a beer bottle over her face, eyes gleaming a thicker kind of lacquer.

'Heezer should try out for the fingerpainters,' I said as Heezer did a pirouette and then bent over and shook her butt in the air.

Hal snorted and touched me on the shoulder with her beer bottle. I grinned at her and then the lights came on as though we'd been acting in a play.

'Hey, what'd Barbie do with my car?' Toad slurred on the dark path to the parking lot.

'She's right behind you, fuck-eyes,' Hal said.

Toad pivoted messily. She looked at me and rubbed her eyes like a cartoon character.

'Where ya been, bud?' she said.

'Man, Toad,' Pelly said. She hiccupped and hit her chest with her fist.

'I've been around,' I said. 'I saw all your moves on the dance floor.'

'Yeah?' Toad put her arm around me, drew a shaky line from her eyes to mine with two fingers. 'Fucking eagle-eyes here. You should watch my moves, kid, for sure. Fo sho. I gots moves like ya never seen.'

Then she grabbed my wrist and twirled me around once, wrapped my arm around my body and pushed me backwards against her arm into a low dip. She staggered a bit, her face bumping above mine and I shrieked, my head so close to the ground, hair dusting the cement. But she held me there, her Cheshire cat grin through the darkness, breath like an open beer bottle, and I felt a hit of gratefulness. Pulling me through the darkness into her spotlight, our teammates the audience that held us there.

She set me on my feet and smacked my butt, then poked a finger in the air and announced, 'Friends. I gotta whiz.'

'Seconded,' Hal said and we all moved toward the Agriculture Building where Toad whipped down her pants and crouched, slamming her back against the wall. Hal and Pelly followed suit, Heezer standing off casually to the side. My decision was made while Hal bent her knees. I had to go, but I hadn't realized until then, until I saw them crouch, but it was suddenly obvious and urgent, and we were all held together by the darkness, and so I squatted too. I pulled down my pants and slouched against the wall at the end of the line beside Pelly, the dry scrape of brick on my lower back, and joined their collective privacy. I'd never.

'I have stage fright,' Pelly announced loudly.

'Visualize, Pelter. A stream of flowing beer.' Toad pointed accusingly at Heezer. 'Hey! Where'd that beer go, Heez? From before. I'm going to close my eyes and count to ten, you stale scammer.'

'Just hurry up, Toader,' Heezer said beside the bush.

'One, two.'

'Poutine,' Hal mumbled. 'Whopper and poutine. Barbie. Make it happen.'

I could make poutine happen, I could make anything happen in the double invincibility of darkness and the group, our line united by the trickling stream at our feet. The campus shifted then, all of its paths pouring toward us, the drunken braying of a group of guys across the street a laugh track played for us, the flat peak of Sam Hall rising darkly just beyond the Agriculture Building. Ours. The city getting to its knees, then, peering down, looking at me, saying, *There you are, finally. You've arrived.*

The flashlight beam, when it shot at us, pinned me to that wall, to the coattails of that giant girl with her booming voice. The light sealing us together, pants around our ankles.

'Uh, what are you doing?' A man's voice said, uncertain. I scrambled with my pants, still crouching, but trying to yank them up over the hills of my knees. Toad's only movement was the slow rising of her hand to shield her eyes.

'What's it look like, champ?' she said. 'Carry on.'

'Uh, I'm campus security, actually.' We could just see his silhouette around the yellow star of the flashlight, the confused tilt of his head.

Heezer shrieked with delight. 'The name is Corinne – that's C-O –'

'Pull up your pants, please.' The flashlight beam swung to the right, drawing a line of light through the trees before settling in a small pool in the grass at the guy's feet, illuminating the cuffs of his safari uniform pants.

Thrown back to the darkness, we all sprung to our feet, yanking up our sweats, our jeans, our xylophone flies. Toad gave a hushed, desperate laugh.

'Oh shit oh shit,' Pelly breathed.

'What do we do?' I whispered. I felt loose-limbed in the darkness, flight instinct kicking in.

'Well, I mean fuck, what can the guy do to us, really?' Hal said quickly. 'I mean, really?'

'Do we run?' Heezer hissed manically. 'Like, do we just bust it right now?'

This idea struck me as criminal, desperate. I saw handcuffs, jail cells. 'He probably saw our jackets, though,' I said, breathless. 'Don't you think?'

'Shit shit shit,' Pelly intoned. The flashlight bobbed up and down, stabbing at our knees as the guard approached. He stopped and raised the light around our waists; it bloomed a wan green-yellow glow up around our faces. I looked around our circle for cues. Toad's face erupted into a garish grin.

'Evening, officer! How're you doing tonight, sir!'

The guard was skinny with a sad, failed attempt at a moustache, and he looked about my age. I moved in closer to Pelly. He just stood there. Bewildered eyes.

'Why were you doing that?' he said finally. We hadn't expected this – this opportunity for moral reckoning. We shifted, looked at each other. I felt small comfort, knowing that, among them, I wouldn't have to talk. Heezer let a short, uncomfortable giggle spill. Pelly followed with a barked laugh like a tic, then clamped her hand over her mouth, wide-eyed.

'I just mean, uh,' the guard shifted uncomfortably from foot to foot and I felt sorry for him. 'There are ladies' bathrooms all over campus. You know?'

'Yeah, okay, but. Do we look like ladies to you?' Toad slurred the word *ladies* slightly. 'Well, except for Hoots here maybe.'

'Toad, just shut up.' Hal elbowed Toad in the side and Toad yelped.

'Sorry, we're sorry,' Hal said, quick, gruff.

'The point is,' the guard said, his voice growing confident edges in the face of Toad's drunken disorder. 'This is campus property and – '

'And we're campus broads, detective sir. We own this place. Seriously, seriously.' Toad leaned forward unsteadily.

The guard shuffled back slightly. 'I don't think I like your attitude,' he said.

'Yeah, well,' Toad pronounced, 'I don't like your muss-stash.'

I grabbed Pelly's arm like it was the scary part of a movie and she leaned into me. Hal stepped directly in front of Toad.

'Don't listen to her,' she said. The guard touched his upper lip as though expecting to feel blood.

'I see you play hockey,' he said and shone the flashlight on the Scarlet crest of Hal's jacket. 'What do you think your coaches are going to say about this?'

Pelly and I gasped under our breath.

'Please. I know this – ' Hal began.

Toad stepped out. 'They'll be thrilled! Our coaches are pro-peeing! They're progressive!'

I laughed a bit by accident as Toad swayed and Hal shot me dead with the FOAD look.

Behind the closed door of her office, Moon asked that we issue an apology to the team for misrepresenting them.

Toad bristled with indignation. 'Mooner, come on. If anything, it was an accurate representation. It was like a real Discovery Channel moment for buddy. Like,' Toad switched to a teacher voice. 'And today in biology class, Moustache, we'll be learning that women *also* have bladders.'

Toad, as a form of protest, was wearing a T-shirt that said *Guns Don't Kill People. People with Moustaches Kill People*, next to a silkscreened outline of a grinning, moustached man who looked like Burton Cummings. Sober, her political stance had sharpened.

'So, let me get this straight,' Moon said. 'You are pleading ignorance to the wrongness of ... defiling campus property while wearing team issue. You're telling me that what you did was perfectly okay.'

Stan coughed into his hand.

'Precisely,' Toad said. 'I think we should fight this, personally. It's discrimination, this notion that we should have to run around frantically with our knees together looking for the closest powder room, when guys – they just – '

Moon sighed. 'Let me stop you there, Corinne.'

'Buddy,' Hal groaned. 'Buddy, you have to shut up.'

Pelly and I glanced at each other. I raised my eyebrows. Pelly looked scared, like she'd lost some sleep over this, bruised wedges under her eyes. Moon pinched the bridge of her nose, closed her eyes. 'Enough, you two,' she breathed, a weary mother. 'Okay, okay.'

'STOP.' Stan slammed his palms on the desk next to Moon and leaned forward. A vein bulged in his forehead and his face grew red. 'You acted like jackasses. All of you. You were caught. Your teammates know. You have to be accountable. You are ambassadors of this team and of the Scarlet Athletic Program and you have to be held accountable for acting like assholes and getting caught. That's it. Bottom line.'

Silence. Stan rarely raised his voice. Now: *jackasses, assholes*. Our eyes slid like kicked dogs to our laps, slinking down across the dirty beige carpet.

'Ah did not have sexual relations with that woman,' Toad mumbled to her knees. Hal punched her in the arm hard enough that I heard the dull rap of knuckles on bicep. And this sound released in me a startling surge of inspiration. I stepped out, suddenly, from the escarpment of their egos.

'We're sorry,' I said tentatively, looking up at Stan, at Moon. The resonant wobble of that word, *We*. Then, again, louder, with conviction. 'We're really sorry.'

Hal and Toad looked at me as though I'd just broken out into Spanish opera. Pelly smiled like I was a boyfriend who had surprised her with flowers. The horn signalling the end of the ice time before ours sounded through the office wall. The ice just there on the other side. Ed starting up the Zamboni.

Toad dragged her eyes from me. 'We are, Mooner,' she said in a voice as quiet as she was capable of. Hal gave a grudging nod.

And then we couldn't waste any more time. The Zamboni's shining tail dragging us all toward practice.

Toad, Hal and Pelly all seemed relieved to get back to their stalls, climb into their equipment, return to the ice. But I felt like I'd been away for a long time, like I'd been on vacation, and was now forced to go back to school. I didn't want to put on my skates.

'What the hell is Moon doing? That is not a power play – there, okay, that's better, now you're talking. Go, Corrine! Shoot that! Shoot that!' Mo bellowed, pushing himself up from his seat, hands raised over his lap. Sig looked over to Terry and the two chuckled. Eileen, on the other side of Mo, grabbed his jacket sleeve and yanked.

Sig pulled her glasses down her nose and squinted at the numbers around the faceoff circle, the name bars too blurry from this distance. She was starting to attach numbers to names, names to parents. She'd gone for coffee with a few of them after the last game, Mo inciting a cheer right in the middle of Tim Hortons. These parents were different from the parents of the boys Iz used to play with. Chuckling about their hockey-playing daughters, the nicknames twisted roughly from the girls' names they'd given them, laughing about the game-time spars. Pride edged with a kind of vigilance like something might break at any time, blood in their eyes when a daughter got benched or shaken up along the boards, but laughing all the while.

Terry, all bundled in that fleece blanket of hers, leaned in to Sig. 'Iz is looking strong out there tonight, Sig.'

'Not bad at all, you're right.'

A University of Regina player tripped a Scarlet, and Mo leapt to his feet. 'Get your head out of your ass, ref! Here – ' He fumbled wildly in his jacket pocket and yanked out a pair of glasses. 'You want these? Want these? You'll – '

Eileen gave his arm a violent tug and Mo fell hard to the bench.

'Enough,' Eileen hissed. Mo craned his neck at her, spread his hands.

'What? I was just offering – that was bloody Sausage, you remember her? Number Six! She's been getting away with this shit all game – '

'Bloody Sausage?' Eileen giggled. 'Listen to yourself, Mo. For chrissake. It's different when the girls say it.'

'What?' Mo began to laugh.

The Scarlets wove down the ice, passes echoing tightly into the stands, the players' calls to each other blurring into crowlike squawks. Sig watched Moon pace along the bench, pen in her mouth. Her eyes darted from the ice to the tops of the players' helmets to her clipboard, in ticlike sweeps.

A scream.

Movement on the ice sprayed to a quick stop, stilling the bobbing toques in the stands. Breath caught under parkas. A circle of team-mates gathered around a fallen Scarlet player, and Sig murmured, 'What happened?'

Another howl from the ice. Sig had heard the sound before, in countless other rinks. Always made the hairs on the back of her neck stand up. Eileen leapt up, eyes wide, and stepped from side to side. Mo breathed heavily.

'Shit. Shit. It's her knee.' Under his breath. The stands were still, faces slanted toward the trainer slipping across the ice on Hal's arm.

'Oh dear,' Terry said and shifted uneasily.

Eileen sprinted to the stairs, skittered down to the ice, arms pumping at her sides, her mouth a wild arc. Mo didn't seem to notice Eileen's departure, eyes fixed on the circle surrounding Toad, swearing steadily under his breath.

Sig clucked her tongue as she watched Eileen fumble with the gate to the ice, no one helping her. She yanked the handle frantically, and a young man ambled slowly from the penalty box, the one who took the stats, and began to jiggle the handle. Eileen stood back for a second, arms jerking at her sides. He wasn't fast enough, Sig could feel this in the urgent appraisal of Eileen's eyes, remembered the way her kid's, her grandkid's, screams would rip the inside of her ears, rip through and grab some hidden muscle, ancient and red inside her. The kid wasn't fast enough with the gate.

Then Hal reached down, took Toad's arm and hoisted her up. A small cheer moved in the stands as she glided slowly across the ice, Hal helping her along.

'Not her knee then,' Mo said, blew out a long breath. 'Probably just got the sauce knocked out of her.' He turned to Sig, wiped a big hand over his cheek.

'She'll be fine,' Sig said.

'That wife of yours is quick.' Terry leaned over toward Mo.

'Yeah,' Mo laughed incredulously. 'Corinne'll give her crap for that later. Girl's twenty-one and she still has her mom trying to come on the ice when she's hurt.'

'Ah, can't blame her,' Sig said and watched as Eileen leaned toward the stats boy, saying something to him with an embarrassed smile.

'Better go collect her before she slips him her number,' Mo said, grinning, and stood up. 'Buy her a coffee or something.' He headed toward the stairs.

'It's awful when they get hurt, isn't it?' Terry said. 'I remember once when Chris was young, she sprained her ankle in a ringette game – real bad sprain, big swollen lump the size of a tennis ball.' She cupped the shape of a ball with her hands, pink nails poised like claws. 'I saw her go down, and I don't even remember the rest of it. The coach said she'd never seen anyone sprint across the ice like that. And, you know, I can't even walk on ice without falling all over the place. Tried curling once, and spent more time on my butt than on my feet, I think.'

'Well.'

'I don't know what it is.' Terry shook her head. She gazed out at the ice. 'There's something about daughters in pain. Makes you crazy. Crazy and brave.'

The door to the toilet stall was open a crack. Pulling at a tangle in my damp hair, I pushed it open and took a step in.

Hal slumped on the toilet, cheek resting on her knees. Her face whipped up, eyes welted red over the eyelids and down into the darker crescents beneath, her cheeks wet. She looked at me and a sound twisted from her throat. She threw her hands, shaking, over her mouth.

'Shut the fucking door.' A muffled croak.

'I – ' I said. 'Do you want me to – ?'

'Please, just close it.' Hal kicked at the door with her foot. I pulled it shut carefully and then stood for a moment, registering what I'd just seen. Boz walked into the bathroom, makeup case in hand, and positioned herself in front of a mirror, squeezing moisturizer into her palm. I went over to her.

I leaned toward her ear and whispered loudly, fighting the Guns n' Roses coming in through the doorway. 'Boz?'

'Yeah, hon?' she said, unsurprised by the whisper. Hers were ears accustomed to secrets, to confessions.

'Hal's in there,' I pointed to the stall. 'And she's pretty upset.'

Boz cocked her head at the stall. 'Like, *upset*?' she said.

I nodded. She touched my shoulder.

'Thanks for telling me, babe,' she said and moved toward the stall.

I went back to my spot. The room was emptying out in carpool-sized chunks, everyone headed to Boston Pizza for our post-game meal. Next to me, Pelly rubbed her scalp violently with a towel. She journeyed a Q-tip into her ears. She applied vigorous layers of chapstick. Boz came out of the toilet stall eventually. She went to the CD player and turned down the volume and when Heezer began to protest, she shook her head in warning, her mouth a line.

Soon afterward, Hal stalked out, blotches all over her face and neck. In front of the mirrors, she grasped the edge of the counter and leaned forward, shoulders bunched up around her ears. She froze like that and the room didn't skip a beat, the slow swarm of departure continuing, oblivious, while Boz and I watched from a distance. Hal turned her head slowly to the side and rested her mouth on her shoulder. She stared down at the microwave next to her hand. Heezer brayed loudly. Pelly threw a tape ball at the garbage can and groaned as it rebounded off the rim. I caught Boz's eye, then looked back at Hal.

In one quick motion, her arms unhinging suddenly, as though jerking awake, she yanked up the microwave and threw it against the opposite wall, a tinny din. All eyes chasing Hal as she ran from the room. Stung silence for a few moments, set to the hushed, whining backdrop of Axl Rose, then Toad said, 'What in fuck's name?' Her voice dripping wonder. Boz went over to her, said something in her ear and then they both went and, together, lifted the behemoth microwave. They eased it back onto the counter and Toad ran her fingers over its busted wall, gently.

'Bitty!' she barked. 'Get over here. We need an engineer.'

Bitty, pulling an arm into her track jacket in the West End, blushed. 'Toad, I'm in my, like, first year. I don't – '

'Engineer. Stat. Useless or whatever.' Toad bent her face down close to the microwave, brow furrowed, and gave something a forceful poke.

Boz looked up and caught me watching. She came over, brushed my hair back from my ear, bent over and whispered. 'It's Terry. Hal's mom. She's sick.'

Nobody mentioned the microwave at Team Meal, Hal eating her spaghetti, eyes down, at the head of the table. Monday, Toad showed up carrying a gleaming white microwave in her arms. Put it on the counter, plugged it in, went to her stall. We played on.

When we walked through the yellow door to the dressing room, it was easy to believe in the pulse of the room, to change our clocks to the long sweeping circles of the Zamboni. As if nothing could get in.

'Good evening, could I speak to Miss Isabel Norris please?'

I rolled over to my back on the bed, crooked the phone into my neck. My history text fell to the ground. 'Hi.'

'Miss Isabel?'

'Who else would it be?'

Jacob laughed. 'I'm trying to be a gentleman.'

'Okay. Yes, this is Isabel.'

'Brilliant.' He cleared his throat. 'So, I was wondering if you wanted to come over here to watch the game? A few of us are setting up in the common room.'

'What game?'

He laughed. I didn't say anything, his laughter even harder to navigate on the phone.

'Oh, you were serious? Flames and Oilers. Is there another game?'

'I don't know.'

'You coming then? It's going to be a pizza and wings event.'

'I don't watch hockey.'

Jacob laughed. 'You play.'

'Yeah, but I don't watch it. It's boring. Don Cherry's a jerk and always says the same things.'

Jacob paused.

'No offence or anything,' I said. 'I just never watch it.'

'I'm speechless over here.'

'Why?'

'So have you been fooling me? Do you even play?'

'I've always played.'

Jacob gave a surprised snort. 'What next, Isabel?'

My teammates followed the NHL with a mixture of lust, envy and hockey love. Heezer wanted Eric Lindros and also wanted to be like him: 'Did you see that bastard's goal last night? How does he do that? Bastard. Father of my first-born son.'

'Pat Quinn makes me horny,' Toad responded.

They discussed games the next day in the dressing room, dissecting plays and moves and fights. They negotiated trades among our stalls, placed bets, yelled. Scheduled their bar plans around *Hockey Night in Canada* when we weren't playing ourselves.

It was all the same to me, though. Same characters, different teams. Same ending, with Don Cherry rattling on like he was saying something new. I've always known about hockey being the Religion of Canadians. But what about the other side: the hockey atheists, the disbelievers, the half-believers? I played, so I'd never thought to look in that direction. The ones sitting on the fence. Jacob made it sound like I was headed to Hell.

'Here, could you pass these down please, doll?' Boz fished out a noisemaker and passed the bag to Pelly.

'Whose birthday?' Pelly asked. Boz puffed out her cheeks and blew out slowly. 'It's not a birthday,' she said. She hit her thighs with fisted hands, and then stood up, whistled on her fingers as she strode out into the middle of the dressing room.

'Could you guys just listen up for a sec, please?'

The sparse pattern of heads dotting the stalls turned toward her, the room draining to quiet. Practice had been cancelled due to the upcoming travel weekend, so we had open ice instead, no coaches. Some had opted out, some of us had come to shoot around, to savour the rare anarchy of no equipment, no whistles, no drills. Just pucks and skates and sweats.

Noisemakers trumpeted around the room as Boz cleared her throat. 'Well, okay, um, most of you know about Duff and Hugo – about their relationship. There's been a lot of talk. And they know that, so they asked me a couple of days ago to just kind of make it known, so it wasn't this gossip, like, flying around behind their backs. They've kept it quiet for a long time, and that was probably really tough. So, anyways, there it is. But we thought – me and Toad – we thought that instead of just saying it, telling you guys, and then all of us just pretending it never happened, we thought we'd have a little celebration. Just to let them know that, well, that we know, and we're happy for them. And we're here for them. Okay? Um, if any of you don't feel comfortable you don't have to participate, of course. We'd understand. But I'm just handing out the noisemakers now and we have confetti. Toad's with both of them in the gym right now, holding them up, so what we're going to do is, when they come out on the ice, we'll just give them a little surprise. Blow these, throw some confetti, say a couple words. Like a surprise party – '

'A coming-out party,' Hal said dryly, lips curled. She rolled out the noisemaker absent-mindedly with her forefinger.

'Exactly,' Boz said, smiling uncertainly. I looked over at Pelly. She chewed gum placidly, unsurprised. She'd failed me. I'd thought Duff and Hugo were best friends, inseparable, a kind of odd couple: big Duff with her army boots and spiky hair, earrings like nail heads scaling both lobes up into the cartilage. A stay-at-home D, she planted herself in front of our net and flung members of the other team out of Tillsy's way like she was shovelling the sidewalk. Stan called that cleared area the Duffer Zone. Hugo pulled strands of pale orange hair through her cage during games and chewed it like a rabbit. They wrestled, Duff jerseying Hugo after practice at centre ice, delivering flying elbow drops to her exposed stomach. Headlocks in their stalls across the dressing room. Hugo squealing, grinning hysterically, begging Duff to stop. 'Say Uncle,' Duff always said. 'Uncle, Uncle,' Hugo whispered in her kid voice. I pictured them kissing.

'Are you sure they'll be okay with this?' Bitty piped up from across the way. 'Don't you, uh – well, Hugo's so shy. They're going to be embarrassed as hell.'

'Sure they'll be embarrassed at first. But, the point is, we're their team, you know? They shouldn't be embarrassed. I mean, Tillsy came out to us, right?'

She nodded toward Tillsy and Tillsy pointed at herself – *who me?* – and then smiled, clasping her hands victoriously beside her head.

'Okay? Listen,' Boz sighed, looked up at the ceiling. 'They're in love, you know? You can just see it. And what could be better than that?'

She sat back down.

'How is Toad making them to stay in the gym?' Pelly asked her.

'You know Toady. She works in mysterious ways.'

'I can just imagine the stupidity occurring down there as we speak.' Hal snorted, shaking her head.

'Oh – the hats. I forgot.' Boz craned around and pulled another plastic bag from her stall. She handed cardboard party hats to Pelly, Hal and me. The hats bore the faces of girl clowns, different hair colours, winking long eyelashes. Crooked letters in red marker on the backs of the hats read *Duff and Hugo are Gay!!!* Pelly hiccupped a laugh and I touched the writing, red coming off on my finger.

'Subtle,' Hal said.

'Do you think it's too much, babe? I left Toad in charge of decorations and this is what she came up with.'

'She wrote this on every hat?' I asked.

Boz nodded, wincing.

'Boz, you're holding a party to stuff down their team's throats – the team they've successfully been hiding their situation from – that they're gay. You bought a cake. Relatively speaking, I don't think you could say the hats are going overboard.'

'You think we shouldn't do this.'

Hal shrugged and blew on the noisemaker, eyebrows raised.

'There's cake?' Pelly asked.

'No, you know what?' Boz tugged on a skate lace. 'Toad had a good point. She said, what do we do to everyone else when they like someone? We bug them, right? You will get teased if you have a crush. Lord help you. And you know, Toad comes on to Dufresne every time we're at the bar, because he's Bitty's boyfriend and she has to bug Bitty. She just has to. So the fact that Duffy and Hugo have been ignored by us, that they haven't even gotten harassed, that's just – tragic, you know?'

We huddled on the ice beside the gate, about ten of us, ridiculous in the clown hats, noisemakers clutched in our palms. Heezer and Tillsy performed a half-hearted sword fight. Duff and Hugo saw us, of course, through the glass as they walked up to the ice behind Toad. They smiled in a frowning way and Toad smiled modestly, the smug conductor. When she opened the gate and the three of them glided onto the ice, Boz yelled, 'Surprise!' She skated over to them and flung her arms around Duff's and Hugo's shoulders, squeezing them in.

We looked at each other and followed her lead, shouting weakly, blowing on the noisemakers. Pelly, Heezer and Boz launched handfuls of white confetti toward them, but it didn't quite reach, and we watched their faces through the confetti falling in the middle of our circle, slow as snow. Then, quickly, silence.

'I don't get it,' Duffy said. Hugo's eyes flared green against her crimson face. I watched her gaze reach Heezer, who wore the hat on the side of her head, covering one ear, and backwards. I saw her read the red letters.

'Oh my God,' she breathed quickly, as though someone had jumped out at her just then, hand flying to her mouth. Heezer smiled, apologetic, and pulled the hat on top of her head.

'Okay, you guys,' Boz said, releasing their shoulders. 'Okay.' She cleared her throat. Pelly blew on her noisemaker in a nervous succession of lengthy honks. Toad snatched it from her hand and launched it over the boards. I looked to Hal. She stared grimly at Boz, arms crossed, hat resting against her back like a hood. I squirmed and prayed that Boz would make us seem less mean.

'All right, guys ... so we're gathered here today to celebrate the relationship between our girls Hugo and Duffy,' Boz began, her voice ringing hollow against the ice, breath just visible in front of her face. She smiled brightly at them, and Duff's scowl deepened, the tips of her ears flaming red above the nail-head earrings, Hugo spreading her fingers over her mouth until her hand covered half her face. Heezer trumpeted hopefully at Boz's shoulder. But it failed, ringing out like a fart at a funeral.

'Um, I guess we just want you guys to know that we love you both and we're totally happy for you, and – '

'Sorry, Reverend Bozzo, but I feel compelled to interject.' Toad stepped into the circle. 'You aren't marrying them, champ. No offence. Look, this is what it's all about.' She sighed and pulled her hoodie over her head. A pink T-shirt underneath read *Lez-apalooza*.

She did a sloppy figure-skater twirl, and sprayed to a stop with her back to us, legs spread, hands on her hips. On the back of the T-shirt: *Scarlet Gay Pride Day, 1998. 1 on 1 at the Crease.* Quiet as we all read it and then Tillsy clapped her hands and laughed delightedly.

'I want one of those, man!'

Boz's mouth dropped.

'For fuck's sake,' Hal said.

Then Duffy began to laugh. She bent over, hands on her knees, shoulders shaking.

'Oh my God,' she said and stood up, wiping away a tear beside her nose, still laughing. 'Oh my God, Toad. Holy shit.'

Pelly threw some more confetti, and I blew on my noisemaker with everyone else.

Duff and Hugo glided toward us, Hugo ducking her head, a grudging smile. Toad stuck a hat on Duff's head, snapped the elastic under her chin. It must have been the confetti – Hugo must have skated over the confetti. Her skates just flew out beside her, as though she was running across the ice in socks, and she went down, hard. Falling backwards, hands thrown out behind her to brace her fall. Breath hooked in my lungs, I watched her curl forward, clutching a wrist, rocking back and forth in the fetal position, orange hair brushing her knees.

'Shit,' Boz breathed, and it sounded strange to hear her swear. Duff crouched beside her, frantic, Hugo breathing deep in a disciplined pattern, gliding through the pain. In through her nostrils, out through her mouth, a rapid meditation. Rocking. We bunched in around them. Duff had her face down next to Hugo's and was whispering something. When she turned to look up at us, her eyes were wild.

'Someone do something! Please! Get someone!'

She held Hugo's limp wrist carefully on her palm, just balanced it there in front of her, as though it had been given to her, while Hugo rocked, head down. Tears slid fast down Duff's face.

'Get someone!' she shrieked again, but Boz had already gone. She tucked Hugo's hair behind her ear, and stroked her back with clumsy jabs.

'It's okay, baby. It's okay,' she whispered. How quickly it all had broken. Toad shivered in her T-shirt. She crossed her arms over the words and watched them, off to the side, with tired eyes.

Hugo had fractured a bone in her wrist, but she returned to ice the following week with a blue playing cast. It matched Segal, who'd been wearing one since the beginning of the season, hers now ratty, trailing tattered pieces of cotton around the fingers like an old security blanket, giving off a smell of sour milk and rotten socks. But the point was, they could still play, Hugo and Segal, the casts fitting perfectly into their gloves. Segal came in with a new one, red this time, and she told me that while the plaster was setting the doctor got her to hold a stick in the palm of the cast, so the cast dried in that position, her broken hand frozen around a hockey stick for weeks. I pictured this, Segal clutching the stick in the doctor's office, those long, meditative moments while the plaster dried. Like some misguided act of worship.

The team boasted an impressive roster of broken bones, pulled ligaments, strains, sprains, aching backs and knees. Our athletic therapist, tiny Greek Tamara, came in after games hauling a cooler full of ice packs. She stood in the middle of the room and threw them around the stalls like she was delivering newspapers. She laid players out on towels in the middle of the dressing room and pummelled muscle cramps into submission with sadistic nonchalance, her small hands finding the pain. There, there. Moans like a torture chamber, a brothel. Players were drawn to her, dragged themselves to her office whining like kids, seeking out her motherly aptitude, that calming ability to draw circles around the pain and then plaster over it.

In a scrum around the puck during practice, someone's blade nicked my calf, just above the heel of my skate boot, right where the shin pads leave the well-being of your legs to fate. On the bench, Tamara snapped on latex gloves from her kit and wiped away the garish blood with impatient strokes of gauze, looking for the real story. In her sprawling kit, she located the perfect size of bandage.

It was the same colour as my skin and, when she smoothed it over a reddening wad of cotton – a soothing undulation of fingertips – it disappeared into my leg.

I couldn't believe Hugo came back so quickly. But they always came back, as quickly as they could, sooner than they should have. As though playing with pain might somehow make the team stronger, this act of limping back with the hurt parts displayed, proving their messy love for the game, for each other. The team shifting its shape around them, over the torn muscles, the fractured bones. Healing the hurt parts.

I tested myself: What would I do if I broke my arm? Would I make a comeback with the playing cast? I didn't know. I'd probably go home.

Had I known that dressing-room geography would make my destiny for the rest of the year, I would have sat elsewhere, in the far corner with Duff, Hugo and Roxy, maybe, in the area Toad called Mime Village – it wasn't that they didn't speak there but that they spoke in normal volumes rather than the megaphone-for-mouths brand of communication favoured in our end, the vocal-cord work-out demanded by the CD player that sat at Heezer's feet. The Mime Village horizon seemed to shimmer like an oasis through the shower steam after practice. A haven, mellow and neat, their move-ments saturated with casual lethargy, or so it seemed from the North End, our tilt-a-whirl side. Our end remained loyal to each other, in restaurants, cars, buses. Hal and Toad could probably take or leave me, I thought; it was Pelly who had cemented me in.

'Iz! Here!' Pelly's voice pierced through the thick morning air on the bus. Near the back, she waved a magazine in the air. I pushed through the aisle, stalling as my teammates in baseball caps and toques shoved their backpacks above the seats, everyone moving in slow motion, falling in next to their stall partners. They mumbled sleepy greetings as I passed.

Hal and Boz spoke quietly in the row Toad called Prime Real Estate, the only row of three seats, very back, next to the bathroom.

Someone had transferred the No Kicking It sign – like a No Smoking sign, but with a boot instead of a cigarette – from the dressing-room toilet stall to the bus toilet door. I'd thought that *kicking it* meant dancing when I first started, and could easily imagine the reasoning behind the sign – Heezer getting carried away and dancing on the toilet one day after practice, slipping and getting a booter. This scenario grew edges, became logic, the boot entered my swelling dressing-room lexicon. Heezer dancing on the toilet could have happened; it was getting harder and harder to weed my own memories from team legend.

'Shitting,' Pelly had said to me out of the blue one day. 'Kicking it is to shit, you know?' I'd nodded like I knew. When Pelly offered me these morsels out of the blue – *Shitting* – I felt strange gratitude, a small seizure in my stomach.

Hal and Boz didn't look up as I slid in ahead of them, next to Pelly, who was acting out a drama involving a bottle of Aspirin, her Scarlet water bottle and head pain. She moaned as pills spilled over her hand, into her lap, and rubbed her temple while she scooped up the excess.

'What's wrong?' I asked as she whiplashed the pills back. Toothpaste spit chalked one corner of her mouth.

'Got my braces tighten yesterday,' she grimaced. 'They're a bitch. But I'll look this way when I'm done.' She pointed to Julia Roberts's horse teeth on the cover of *Cosmopolitan*.

'Yeah, I can see it,' I said.

Moon's whistle scissored open the team's morning drone. She was small at the front, her track jacket wrinkled like she'd slept in it the night before.

'I had the worst dream ever last night,' Toad had said a few days before. 'I broke into Moon's cromulent lair, and I was all excited, like, right on, let's have a lookie here, let's break some shit, whatever. But I get to her bedroom … and I look in the closet … and hundreds – thousands! – of track jackets fly out at me, like – like bats! And I go through her drawers, and there are these, like, self-renewing reserves of track pants, layer upon layer, no end. An infinity of track suits.' She'd shuddered.

Moon's eyes drooped. Stan handed her a Styrofoam coffee cup from the front seat and she took a hard swig.

'Who're we missing?' she called. Pelly raised her eyebrows at me and formed a T with her hands, raising it high above her head. Moon's cheeks dropped and she scanned the back, then heaved a disgusted sigh, flicking out her wrist to look at her watch.

Toad jogged in, holding a partially eaten doughnut out like a baton. The bus lurched away from the rink as she staggered oblivious down the aisle in flannel Barney pyjamas.

'Prime Real Estate!' she enthused, eyeing the empty seat at the back.

Hal snorted. Pelly and I angled ourselves around casually.

Toad struggled to fit her backpack overhead. She offered the doughnut to Boz, who shook her head, smiling.

'Oh, I almost forgot,' Toad clapped her hands. 'Happy birthday, champ.'

'It's tomorrow,' Hal said.

'But the presents can't wait!' Toad pulled the backpack down again.

'Oh Jesus,' Hal breathed.

'Why don't you save it for tomorrow, Toady?' Boz said.

Toad looked down at Pelly and me and waggled her eyebrows as she rummaged through.

'Morning, youngsters. What's wrong, Pelter? You look constipated.'

Pelly glared at her. 'I got my braces tighten – I'm getting a migraine.'

'That sucks – oh, here.' She pulled a newspaper from the bag and flipped through, folding it back with a grin. 'Hal's first modelling spread. Happy birthday, totsi.'

Hal studied the paper for a long while, the crease above the bridge of her nose deepening, shadows thrown down over her eyes. Boz rested her chin on Hal's shoulder to look, an unsure smile wavering on her mouth.

'You're kidding me. Where did you get this?' Hal glared at Toad.

'It's next week's *Press*, I just got it at U. Centre. What's your problem?'

'You're kidding me,' Hal repeated.

'What is it?' Pelly said urgently. 'Let me see.' She snatched the paper from Hal's hands and I read over her shoulder. The headline, *Scarlet Hockey Makes Its Mark*, was bookended with an action shot of Ben Hardy, captain of the men's team, a small triangle of tongue poised at the corner of his mouth, body leaning nearly parallel to the ice as he cut a sharp corner. In the neighbouring picture, Hal wore a black, low-plunging dress with jewel-studded spaghetti straps, her face and chest flushed red, eyes lidded down with dark eyeshadow, lips shining a hard gloss. Her hair was pinned up in dark snarls of curl, and a strand had escaped along her cheek, lending her a look of unravelling as she stared, smiling absently, away from the camera.

'Is this from the athletic banquet?' Pelly asked. Hal shook her head at Boz, speechless.

'It's a gorgeous picture, babe,' Boz offered.

Hal was slipping into a mood, you could feel it coming off her. 'It would have been *so hard* for them to get a shot of me on the ice,' she said quietly.

'At least it's not a picture of you at morning practice or something – all zitty and pale. You know?' Toad offered.

'You're a hottie.' Boz rubbed Hal's back.

'Hardy will love this.' Hal gazed out the window, chewing her bottom lip.

'Fucking rights Hardy will love it,' Toad said. 'He totally wants you, Scotty said – '

'Stop telling me that,' Hal spat. 'I don't care.'

Toad blinked rapidly, silent for a moment. 'I just want – '

'For my birthday, Corinne, I would like you to *not talk*.' Hal shook her head, staring out the window.

I elbowed Pelly. 'Did you get the card?' I whispered. I'd wanted to get Hal a birthday card but didn't want the responsibility of choosing it. Pelly rummaged around in the backpack at her feet, then shot back up, grinning. She threw the card onto my lap.

'Sign it,' she said.

The front said *To a Special Grandma* in flowing letters. A lengthy poem inside mentioned babies, butterflies, sunshine, cookies and God. Pelly's signature already scrawled at the bottom.

'I'm not signing this,' I said.

Pelly shrugged. 'Best card ever.'

I signed it. Hal was turning twenty-three.

'Heezer!' Toad hollered across the aisle after she'd attempted a few seconds of silence. 'You got that present?'

Heezer popped up like a gopher, a few rows up. 'Oh yeah, happy birthday, Hally!'

'It's tomorrow,' Hal said.

'It's all week! Gestation period!' Heezer shouted.

'Vile,' Toad said. 'Who says *gestation* at seven in the morning?'

Heezer came down to Prime Real Estate and handed Toad a folded sheet. Pelly and I angled ourselves over the backs of our seats, dangling like moons above the heads of Toad, Hal and Boz.

Hal opened the paper, a certificate that read *Welcome* (*Chrissy* written into the blank in confused-looking scrawls, like Toad had written it with her left hand) *to the Silver Salmons Water Club!* and had a picture of an apple-shaped, white-haired woman cannonballing off a diving board, a group of grannies laughing and frolicking – in that stiff-necked, vaguely panicked way older, permed women have – in the pool below her.

Hal smirked. 'Yeah. Fuck you very much,' she said.

'They'll be expecting you at the New Horizons Senior Centre on Tuesday,' Heezer drawled. 'Just so you know.'

Toad took the certificate from Hal. 'I'll take care of that. Wouldn't want it to accidentally get thrown in the garbage in some fit of dementia. This is Wall of Hein material.'

The Wall of Hein was getting out of control, growing across the wall beside the bulletin board – the board already overcapacity with unflattering drunk photos of players, magazine cut-outs of men's underwear ads, and sketches of Peter Mansbridge, also in underwear, that Heezer drew as presents for Toad during her Women's Studies class. Spreading like a rash toward Mime Village. I hadn't made it up there yet.

Pelly dropped our card into Hal's lap. She picked it up with a look of distaste.

'Pelly chose it,' I breathed quickly.

'Who's a thoughtful Barbie?' Toad said as Hal tore it open. I watched her eyes move in lines and held my breath. She looked up.

'I hate you all,' she said finally. But then she started to smile and I tumbled back into my seat. Out the window, the highway ran a gash through endless brown fields. Boz brought out the cake. It was eight in the morning. We all sang.

Grace's arrival on the deck sent the blue heron into flight from the big rock on shore. Its slow form a shade darker than the sky. She was wearing one of her sweaters. Grace didn't follow a consistent pattern when knitting, preferring instead to improvise. She let patterns and colours bleed into each other, tracking a confused palette across her shoulders, another around her middle.

'Jesus, Grace,' Sig said and then wouldn't look at her any more.

They sat in silence the length of two cigarettes. Jack shifted lazily, splayed in a patch of feathered sunlight coming down through the branches of the birch. A bird in it somewhere that wouldn't shut up.

'When will you tell her?' Grace said finally.

'Never.' Sig jutted her chin skyward.

Grace sighed. 'You don't want her finding out from someone else.' Climbing into patience. 'You know this.'

'What? You're going to advertise it in the paper? You're the only one I've told.'

'Oh, Sig.' Grace's voice was tight and thin, stretched across a distance.

The girl was in a new city, surrounded by a team of girls. She was laughing.

'Not yet,' Sig said.

Luigi, of Luigi's Restaurant in Regina, put together a custom buffet for our team. Wearing a white chef jacket, he lead us into the back room, throwing open the door.

'Eat, eat, ladies. All for you!' he sang proudly. I saw Pelly's eyes widen as we approached the table, which must have been several tables lined up end to end, but a gigantic green tablecloth tricked the eye into believing it to be a table of epic proportions, smothered in every manner and ethnicity of carbohydrate imaginable. Toad approached the table, arms outstretched.

'God love ya, Luigi,' she said.

'This isn't right,' I told Pelly.

'I think I'm going to ralph,' she said.

Buffets sparked a particular brand of team joy and bonding. I grabbed a plate and jumped in, sink or swim, everyone jostling up against each other in line, shouting recommendations, exclaiming over finds, comparing this buffet to buffets of road trips past. *We got macaroni salad. Dessert! I'm talking chocolate cake here. Steer clear of the broccoli salad, for the love of God. Best buffet ever. Better than Holiday Inn Saskatoon.*

Plates grew pyramid-shaped and players spilled off toward the tables for Round One. I went heavy on the perogies, fished from a vat of melted butter, their tubby bodies emerging with the rainbowed gleam of oil patches. Lasagna. Potato salad. Fried chicken. On my plate, I pretended I was fearless and so maybe at some point I'd become the person who'd attack a buffet in this manner, who'd put together a plate like this. A self-fulfilling prophecy. Moon always told us visualization was half the battle. I'd been trying out this theory on the ice – pretend to be in love with the game like everyone else and maybe the love would come.

I sat next to Pelly at one of the long, cafeteria-style tables. Heezer brought up some buffet legend from last year. The last-year stories were unending. Their first season together. This seemed unfathomable – that they hadn't known each other. I tried to imagine the mass chemistry experiments that must have gone on in corners of the dressing room, during the long highway hours, layered together in motel beds. I could hear it in their voices, the excitement of those legendary days, the rapture they'd felt when they found the perfect groupings, when they all began to fall for each other.

That inaugural season was a test run for the university and so the team had been on welfare, as Toad described it, paying a fee at the beginning of the year, buying their own jerseys, paying for their meals, taking passenger vans on road trips instead of buses, staying in cheap motels with depressing names.

The athletic program had begun to throw the team more money my year – still not as much as the other teams, but enough to get us out from under the poverty line – so I'd missed this depression. There was collective pride among the ones who'd weathered it, though: the solidarity of a family of poor kids done good, sharing the hilarity and perversity of their meagre beginnings. The more ridiculous stories incited a kind of avalanche, everyone shrieking out pieces, different versions, tumbling their voices in.

I considered the rubbery texture of the lasagna with my tongue as Tillsy brought out the one about the news crew from Birtle, the segment they did on the team. All of these stories with their doors shut against me.

When Toad intervened with a Perogy Challenge, I was relieved. Eating myself into the conversation offered itself as a possibility.

Moon let it all go. We had the room to ourselves, so she didn't have to remind Toad and Heezer that they were representing their team, their university, their city, their nation, their gender, their generation, like I'd seen her do at other points during road trips. She sat with Stan at the far side of the room, her back to us, wilfully oblivious. And so Toad and Heezer, already stuffed from Round One, rolled on the ground to the buffet table for the next round of perogies, a form of protest and appreciation for the buffet's fascism.

I made an obvious competitor with my pre-existing stack of perogies, so all I had to do was raise my fork slightly when Toad sent out her call for participants. Heezer wrote all our names on a scoreboard napkin.

I didn't have time to think. The first five went down pretty smooth. Pelly signed on as my manager – brought a pitcher of water to our table and kept my glass full, then massaged my shoulders in between five and six when fork-to-mouth motions began to slow. Going bite for bite with Toad across from me. Boz folded early on. Booed for her poor effort. Roxy spiked her napkin at seven. My stomach began to carousel, telling me to give up. That's when I decided I wanted to win. Duff gave up, groaning. Tillsy toppled off her chair. I held Toad's gaze as she chewed ten in slow motion. Pelly dabbed my forehead with a napkin. The carousel sped. Spectators gathered around our table. It was down to Toad and me and so they cheered for me. Stomach spinning up into my throat. Eleven down and my swallow mechanism short-circuited, my throat sprained. Systems shutting down. Something larger than the sum of the perogy parts rising now. Coming up. Thirteen and Toad making a sound like a sick cow. Both of us lifting fourteen at the same time, biting the wan, rubber heads off, their skin the texture of formaldehyde frogs in science class. The perogies becoming these living, crawling things. Their esophageal creep.

The moment of reckoning. Toad gave an unconvincing growl. Our eyes locked. Don't look away. They were all watching, rapt, cheering me on. I breathed deeply. I saw her about to do it, the decision made in her eyes. As she threw her fork – which speared that remaining fraction of perogy – against the plate, she was the older sister pretending sudden weakness in an arm wrestle. Letting me win. She put her hands up in surrender and I swallowed my last bite and swooned suddenly under Toad's unexpected generosity and the hot release of nausea.

'You heinously obese sow,' Toad said, grinning.

It came to me. I was practically in a perogy coma, but it felt like a spell. 'Well, champ,' I said. 'Pain is temporary. Pride is forever.' It just came to me.

You imagine yourself into the game and then you force your stomach to get behind you. I looked at Hal. She was examining me with a surprised smirk. Pelly screamed. Tillsy said, 'We have our front-runner for Rookie of the Year!' Toad shook my hand and Heezer took our picture.

I ran to the bathroom and fell to my knees.

'You play hockey?' the punk-rock guy next to me said out of the blue. We were learning personality types in Psych class and Dr. Hurlitzer kept whipping the overheads off before I'd finished copying the notes, panic accumulating with each one. It was starting to feel competitive. I looked over and, next to this guy, I felt like an extreme jock in my Scarlet hockey sweatshirt, which was hoodless, my number, 5, stitched on the arm. He had black bedhead and his thumbs hooked through holes in the cuffs of a black hoodie, slouched in his seat.

I didn't have time to chat. 'Yep,' I said and then Dr. Hurtlitzer was snapping away another overhead.

'You don't look like a hockey player.' He wasn't even holding a pen. He smiled and shoved his hands into the front pouch of the hoodie.

'Okay,' I said, insulted and flattered, my pen racing. 'So what does one look like?'

'Not you.' He grinned, a chipped front tooth.

The rest of the class, I kept catching him looking at me. Sig might have called them bedroom eyes.

Dr. Hurlitzer told us there are two main types of personality: Type A and Type B. Each with its own collection of traits. You're one or the other. I was finding it hard to believe in this division, but then I walked into the dressing room and all I could see was As and Bs. I went through the stalls and labelled them, each of my team-mates. Split them into these two teams, and they didn't even know. It felt like a trick.

They all looked like hockey players.

After practice, I sucked in the humid dressing-room air and yanked hard on the zipper of my jeans. I blew a quick breath out and then inhaled again and did up the button, elbows bent in a tight angle from my sides. The jeans – an old pair normally sagging at the rear, the knees – fit tightly across my thighs, my butt, digging in at the waist. I thought the bloating must be due to the coffee I'd been drinking twice a day, before class in the morning, before practice. I'd gotten hooked, like Jacob said I would. The shrill buzz ringing through my body, my mind gaining speed, hands springing alert. I would have to stop.

When I turned to grab my jacket, Toad grinned at me from her stall, eyebrows raised.

'Having some pant problems, Izzer?'

'Yeah, I'm bloated or something.'

'Bloated, eh?' Toad snorted. 'Bozzo! Iz's pants don't fit.'

'Did you call me?' Boz's voice strained over the music that churned from the CD player. Wearing a sports bra and basketball shorts that dangled down past her knees, Boz juggled tennis balls. Her six-pack danced, mirroring the movement of her arms, eyes steady on the electric green arcs. She moved in closer to Toad. The balls didn't flinch.

'Iz's pants don't fit.'

'Oh, you're getting junk in the trunk, Iz,' Boz said encouragingly. She nodded in my direction, but didn't look.

'Junk in the trunk?' I said.

'Let's see,' Toad pushed me into a clumsy half-pirouette so I faced the opposite wing of the dressing room

'Very interesting,' Toad said.

I squirmed under her scrutiny. 'What?' I turned.

'The ass fairy has visited you, child – you are truly blessed.'

'Are you talking about Barbie?' Hal said over her shoulder. She stood in front of her stall, arms pretzeled into the middle of her back, hooking her bra. She turned to face us, the bra lace and blood-red. 'Impossible.'

Boz retreated to her stall, tennis balls bulging in one hand.

'Yeah, you do look like you've grown a bit. You're getting some legs,' she said, an approving nod.

'Really?' I looked down. 'No, I don't think so.'

'I wouldn't believe it if I didn't see it with my own two eyes,' Toad said. 'We got Pelly last year. Another success story for the Scarlet Eating Disorder Clinic. We should make a brochure, eh? Iz on the front, before and after shots – "Send your skinny children to the Scarlet Anorexia Clinic at the WU Ranch, success guaranteed."'

'If they don't come back with junk in the trunk, we'll give you your money back,' Heezer said, without skipping a beat, Toad's Hype Man, always.

'And, a special limited-time offer – if you call now, your child will receive a lifetime membership to Club 160, made up of several illustrious members of the Scarlet hockey organization! Just ask Iz, one of our satisfied customers.' Toad held an invisible microphone up to my face.

I smiled, mind grabbing at any words they might want. 'I won the perogy-eating contest,' I offered, bending toward Toad's hand, their laughter turning in my chest.

'She's still skinny.' Hal applied deodorant emphatically, her eyes pointed at my legs.

A piece of looseleaf winged up in front of my feet as I opened the door to my room. The paper had a ragged edge, torn from a notebook. At the top, three scrawled lines of Psych notes, crossed out. Below this, a sketch: feathered lines in ballpoint pen. An outline of a girl with a ponytail, a side profile of her face and then a smiley face where her heart would be, its mouth open, a wave pouring out.

I walked over to St. Mark's, the third floor, knocked on Jacob's door. His head reared with surprise as he opened it.

'Wow,' he said. I'd never seen him blush before.

'Are you the artist?' I asked, holding up the picture.

'Ah, you got it. Excellent.' He laughed, stepped back from the doorway. 'Come in, or – ?'

I nodded my head, stepped inside. The room smelled like week-old towels and Old Spice. An unmade bed, the same plaid comforter all guys in Rez had. A couple of team photos on his bulletin board. One of him as a kid, crouched in a snow fort, sticking out a purple tongue, a sucker held in his mitt. An autographed poster of Ted Nolan when he played for the Penguins above the desk scattered with notebooks and pens and textbooks. Sports Psych. Rocks for Jocks. Religion. A couple of sticks poked out from under his bed and he had a running-shoe fetish. A pile of laundry climbed the wall in the far corner.

Jacob yanked up the bed covers, grimacing, and stuck the desk chair on top of the laundry. It teetered, legs off the ground.

'Uh, we're getting up to laundry time here, so…' He stood with his hands behind his back, scanning the room like he was the one who had just arrived. 'Oh! Have a seat.' He gestured to the bed and I sat at the far end.

'Do you mind if I – ?' He pointed to the other side. I shook my head. He sat and looked at me like I might hit him.

'Awkward,' I said. And then we both started to laugh a bit. At first, we were laughing to punch a hole through the tension. Then, we stepped through this hole, laughing in relief. Then laughing because we hadn't stopped laughing yet. Laughing because we couldn't stop. Jacob's shoulders shook. He tossed his head helplessly. I bent over my knees, tears hot in my eyes. Tipped upside down like a jar. Laughing in rewind, back through matching jackets, Rookie Night, Rocks for Jocks, tequila, Flames, Oilers, awkwardness, Don Cherry. Laughing at the terrible drawing. I held it up.

'I have no idea what this is,' I said, wiping my face with the back of my hand.

Jacob made a moaning sound as he calmed. 'I made it in class,' he said.

'What – Arts and Crafts for Jocks?' My face still frozen in a smile. Jangly shoulders.

Jacob yelped. 'Touché.' He took the paper from my hand, tilted his head as he examined it. 'You don't get it?'

'What's this?' I pointed to the wave. It looked like the smiley-face heart was throwing up.

A confused squint. 'It's the lake,' he said. 'It's you.'

I grabbed the paper from him, looked again.

'So what – I have two heads?'

'No. Your real head is the – ' He laughed. 'Yeah, I forget.'

'I think my real head should be the lake, if anything.'

'Your head's a lake?'

'No.'

We studied the picture.

'I had this theory.' Jacob chewed his lip. 'But I forget it. I'm sorry, I'm a nerd.'

'You can't be a nerd,' I said. 'You're a hockey player. But you're a terrible artist.'

Jacob fell back on the bed, clutching his chest. 'All my hopes and dreams – what will I do?' he said.

'This doesn't look like me in the least.'

He jumped up and grabbed a pen, took the sheet, held it against the desk and scribbled something. When he gave it back to me, there were skates on the girl's feet.

'Even worse,' I said.

'Harsh.' He sat back down, closer. The silence between us had changed shape.

'Hey,' I said, quieter now. 'Did I scare you that other night?'

'You mean with the Flames game?'

'No, not that.' I paused. 'The other one.'

'Oh – well, okay. Yeah, a bit.'

'I'm sorry.'

'No, it's not a bad thing, it's – you're scaring me right now, actually. Sober. It's a good thing, though.' He glanced at me quickly and smiled.

I could blow over buildings then, and I couldn't imagine a time I hadn't felt that way. I was giant. As big as Hal.

Then, in the next breath, the next held breath, I shrank. Jacob put his hand on my knee and I could hear my bones folding, small, into a compact version of me, one he could slip into the breast pocket of that old blue dress shirt, right next to the pen leaking a tiny map, and I'd smell his sweat and ink, and be incubated like an egg by the bramble of hair over his heart, by the hot plate of skin.

I didn't want to feel small.

I took a deep breath and moved my knees slowly toward him.

University of Brandon. Bunch of thick-necked players and they played the body like it was going out of style, their homer refs hit with these sudden attacks of blindness whenever a Bobcat elbow or knee slipped. Breaking the puck out of our end, attempting the push down to theirs, was like swimming out from the dock in a Small Craft Warning wind, muscular crash of white caps against your bones, the relentless beatdown.

Bitty stopped behind our net, dribbling the puck for a couple of seconds, looking for the play that would get us out of our end, we needed out, finally, please, someone, and then she stepped out, skating through the middle, sailing the puck over to Pelly near the blue line for the break-out and I skated up through centre ice for the pass from Pelly, but the ubiquitous Number Ten had already stepped in, cleanly, quickly, squishing Pelly along the boards – I heard the breath siphoned from her lungs, an urgent *oof* – and then Pelly struggling with the puck, arms squashed up against her body, Ten's embrace from behind, Pelly's stick moving like some crawling animal on its last legs, the puck jittering around at their feet. I went at the puck, trying to extract it from their legs, Ten kicking it back into their mangled feet, going for the whistle, and the ref – their ref – more than thrilled to accommodate Ten, as she had been the entire goddamn game.

Whistle.

'Uggghhhhhh!' Pelly warbled. 'Fucking get off me, you cow!'

'Grow up, baby girl,' Ten sneered as she slowly, slowly, peeled herself off Pelly.

Hal and Toad skated up. The ref moved in nervously, hands up, ready to catch bodies.

Pelly took off a glove, grabbed the front of her own twisted jersey, straightened it out with a grimace.

'Yeah. Yeah, okay,' she said, turning toward our bench. Then, over her shoulder, 'Your girlfriend's straight, shitface.' And she skated off.

Toad emitted a sound of undiluted delight. She grabbed my shoulder, pulled me toward her, and touched her cage to mine. An astonished grin glowing beneath the cross-hatches.

'Did that just happen?' she said. 'That burn? From our little Pelly?'

'It did, it did,' I said. 'She's good.'

Toad backed away, shaking her head. 'Top ten proudest moments.'

We skated to the circle.

'Awesome calls, ref,' Toad said as we passed a linesman along the boards. 'Top-notch work you're doing here this aft. Fucking art.'

'Watch it, Two,' the linesman barked.

'We'd say the same to her, but we know that's not happening,' I mumbled to Toad. Toad snorted. We were in the second period now and a slow boil had been building in my chest since the beginning of the game. U of B throwing their bodies around like gymnasts, amputating our plays, the refs rewarding their cheap elbows and hip checks with blind eyes. The viral spread of frustration among my teammates.

Toad and I settled into our posts at opposite sides of the circle, Hal bent over in the centre, stick braced across her thighs, shoulders hunched. Boz and Duff behind us on D. I lined up against the drag-queenish Ten, who must have been close to six feet, the lanky bulk of her legs, submarine skates. She spit through her cage onto the ice.

The ref lumbered down into a wide stance and raised the puck, then paused for a few teasing seconds, as though posing for a picture, Hal and the other centreman jerking out a false-start scrabble with their sticks, then settling back down, pretending patience, Ten wheedling her elbow into my side. I moved away from it, jabbed her forearm with my glove, and then the ref dropped the puck, flicking the switch, all of us moving at once, a giant wind-up toy, Brandon's centre winning the draw, throwing it back to a D who chipped it along the boards, dumped it back into our end, no icing call. I caught up to Ten and glanced off her side like a car against a guardrail, letting her know I was there and nothing was going to happen between her and the puck, tying up her stick a bit. Then Duff dove in for the puck in the far corner and I moved away, looking for open ice, Duff moving up along the boards and running into their winger. Duff sent it back along the boards, behind the net, knowing Boz was there even though she didn't look. Knowing that Boz would be backing her up. I looped back again, back toward our net, toward Boz, looping up around the boards, looking for the opening, eyes slicing out a clean angle to Boz, hands ready. Boz scooping up the puck behind the net, deking around their centre, flowing up along the boards. Open.

Whistle.

Hal and Ten were pushing each other, back and forth like a seesaw, just beyond the blue line. A strong matchup, both of them big. The coil visible in Hal's arms sent a cold chord up my spine, the ref sprinting over. All of us, skating toward them, Moon bellowing 'Chris!' from the bench.

'Come on, bitch,' Hal was saying, straining against the ref, Ten turning a bit, like she might be backing down. 'Where ya goin', eh? I got lots, I got lots.' A mean twist of a smile that jerked adrenalin into my throat.

'Enough!' the ref said.

Boz pushed back gently on Hal's shoulder. 'It's okay, Hally. It's not worth it.' All of us crowded in so close we could feel the hard push of each other's breath. Ten turned back. Her eyes settled on Boz, a smirk cracking open one side of her mouth.

'Whatever, nigger,' she said.

Our circle smashed. Toad and Hal leapt at the same time. Hal spiked her stick and gloves to the ice almost before the word was all the way out of Ten's mouth. She lunged forward, eyes wide, mouth a gash in her face – 'I'll take your fucking head off!' – but Boz was still blocking Hal, Toad getting a quick blow in to Ten's chest before the ref wrangled her roughly around the waist and Toad staggered to her knees on the ice – 'If that's how we're doing it, you fucking cunt, if that's the fucking way!'

Ten started her cruel laugh as Boz pushed Hal away.

'It's not worth it, Hally. Not worth it. Let's go,' Boz hummed quietly.

Chest hardened, I looked at Hal's face and saw my own pulse of anger. Her eyes were flashing and she looked like she was trying to hug Boz as she struggled to get her arms around, to get leverage, to get away so she could kill Ten, but Boz had her skates dug in, knees bent, and held her back murmuring, 'No, Hal, don't,' as though placating a child. But that look around Boz's eyes, that injured look like she'd pulled herself inside.

Ten laughed again and went to her bench, then Boz let go of Hal and skated over and picked up Hal's stick and gloves and brought them to her as Hal gestured violently in the ref's face.

'You're kidding me!' she said. 'You're *kidding* me.'

The ref shook her head and pointed to the box. 'You want more?' she said, brightly, like a server offering another beer, and Hal skated to the box, shaking her head, violent strides. She wanted to cut the ice to the bone.

I skated to the bench, last man standing on my line, and sat for a moment, sucking back the cool air, trying to force breath through my coiled throat, examining the closed hunch of Boz's shoulders, wanting to reach into her eardrums, to pluck out that word, to give her back the game for which she would cut off her finger.

Playing on the boys' teams, I'd felt a certain kind of anger during games, an adrenalin-shoved cloud of it blooming thick and red behind my eyes. But it was always held in place by a knowing fear, fear that watched this anger, that kept it contained, kept my bones safe, prevented me from doing anything that would get me hit by a two-hundred-pound train. But I could feel the edges slipping now, that hot path through my chest, down my legs, rising in my throat. Its heat pulled from Boz, Hal, Toad. Passed between us, flowing outward, losing shape.

Moon put me on Penalty Kill. Ten was on U of B's power play. I hit her the way a person might try to break down a locked door. Heard the crunch and felt a shudder echo through her, the horrible intimacy. A gasp, a sigh, a clattering swoon. The hit an act of honesty, motion stripped of pretence. The clarity of violence. Pure intention.

I began to skate to the penalty box as the ref whistled a quick hard burst like an outraged shriek, skating toward Hal and Toad before she'd even called the penalty, looking to the bench, Moon frozen in a pose of frazzled disbelief, Stan smiling a bit but trying to hide it with his hand, my teammates' faces shadowed behind cages, Boz there at the D end of the box, beside the door, face unreadable.

'Way to go, Iz! Way to go, buddy!' Tillsy called down the ice from the net. Every breath of mine still a roar, thick and scorching, a back-draft through the burning house of my chest. And in the centre of this heat sat the hit, a stone I might retrieve with my hands and give to Boz, to Hal.

Toad opened the box for me and I settled in next to Hal as the U of B trainer crouched over Ten's fetal curl, the three of us cramped, shoulder to shoulder on the small bench. Toad let out a quick, crazed giggle. Hal looked straight ahead. From behind the scratched glass of the Sin Bin, we all watched, like a silent movie, the pain in Ten's slow movements.

The audience buzzed concern for a couple of stretched minutes. Then Ten got up and, leaning on a teammate, one leg dragging behind, she skated back to her bench. The trainer trailing in their wake, running on tiptoes. The crowd made their applause into an act of aggression against the three of us and players on both teams banged their sticks on the ice for Ten. We, the captured, didn't move.

'Heinous,' Toad said quietly. 'I wanted to hear ambulance sirens, no?' She elbowed Hal, but Hal didn't respond. Instead, Toad turned to me. An accusing look, like it was my fault Ten had gotten up.

The bow-tied announcer played a little Doomsday tune over the loudspeaker to herald my penalty. Then he played it again. And again. Hal stood up.

'Hey!' she shouted over the glass wall dividing our box from his. He looked over, surprised. 'Enough,' Hal said. 'Stop it.'

He shrugged uncomfortably, paused for a moment, then leaned into the microphone. 'Scarlet penalty! To Number Five … ' he drawled.

Hal looked at me. 'It was good,' she said quietly. I shook my head.

Then we sat, silent, caged in together, watching our wounded team limp on, down three men. Five on three. Nothing we could do. The silent reckoning demanded by the Sin Bin: we'd hurt our team, ourselves. The refs like tongue-clucking playground monitors. The rules were there to keep us safe, keep us in the lines. Keep it off the ice. Hockey: the same story told over and over. All of us, trying again and again. Never getting it right.

Sig had picked up Terry in Winnipeg and then they did the three-hour trip together to the afternoon game in Brandon. Sig felt her shoulders loosen as the Chevy's tires buried the grey jungle gym of downtown in the rear-view, the old road-trip feeling. Just to Brandon, but still. They ate a bag of jelly beans and then giggled like sugar-shocked kids at some perverted joke on the radio. Sig glanced over then and saw the smile fall quickly from Terry's face, sharpened fins of cheekbone pushing out, her eyes dragging along the highway out the window. Pulling that huge jacket in tighter. She looked at Sig and gave a tired wink.

They sat on the bench just behind the Scarlet goalie, huddled in for warmth, muscles clenching the tension they saw in their kids' movements, thighs vibrating against each other. Sig read the anger in Isabel's strides toward Ten and she grabbed Terry's arm, steadying their bodies in the moment before impact. Then, Ten clattering to the ice while Iz stood above her, legs strong, looking down at the wreckage, and Sig gasped out her held breath, loosening her fingers against Terry's arm, thumb reigniting its flutter-beat, kneading Terry's soft muscle.

'Pow,' Terry whispered. 'Pow.'

'His birthday today!' Ed shouted from his office as I walked past. I ducked my head in. He was sitting in his chair, hands in his lap, TV off.

'Whose?' I said.

'Who'd you think?' Ed snorted. 'Norse's.'

'Today?'

'Same as my sister's. Today.'

'Oh. Okay,' I said. I thought about this. 'He'd be thirty-eight, I guess.'

'Nope, thirty-seven,' Ed said.

'Really? No, that can't –'

'Yep. Same as me.' Ed nodded.

I did the math. The year I was born – the same year he died. His age then, and my own age.

'It should be thirty-eight, then,' I said. 'He was nineteen, right, when he –'

'He was eighteen,' Ed said. 'He was eighteen. Positive. We were the same.' A deep nod. Small sadness around his eyes at this mistake of mine.

Value Village, beside the 7-Eleven just off campus, smelled like our attic back home. All that unaccountable taste and dust in the pockets, and I wondered, as I pawed through the rack of men's coats, how many of them belonged to people who'd died. I felt the smell coming off on my hands. A woman wearing the Value Village red smock came up to me while I was peeling off the hockey jacket.

'Here, I'll hold that for you, hon,' she said. Smoker's voice, *hon* rattling like a coin down a drain. She looked about Sig's age, her hair dyed pinky-orange, in a ponytail that was too high. *Elsie*, her nametag said. The white parts of her eyes were bloodshot a milky pink colour that made the blue parts look like they were lit from behind.

'Thanks.' I handed her the jacket and pulled on a black peacoat. It jutted from my shoulders, dangled past my hands. Next to us, a teenaged girl modelled a puffy football jacket, some unknown team, *Ned* stitched on the arm. She catwalked down the aisle, sucking in her cheeks, and the guy who was with her laughed.

'Wicked,' he said. '*Ned*. That's hot.'

Elsie shook her head at the coat and took it from me. I pulled on a leather jacket. It was mottled brown, like a fall leaf. When I zipped it, the smell of an old baseball glove wafted up.

'The one,' Elsie breathed, as though I'd been trying on wedding dresses. She pushed me toward a mirror outside the change rooms. The collar was worn and ragged like a dog's ear, the waist hugging in a bit, a zipper the colour of pennies. I took a couple of steps. Watched my legs, their bulk. I pulled the elastic from my ponytail. An aviation patch the shape of an old-fashioned plane was stitched on the sleeve. The arms all scratched. This jacket had flown.

'You look like a movie star, hon,' Elsie said. 'I'll ring you up.'

Sleep fought me in my Rez bed. I thought of all the sleeping bodies behind the walls, Gavin's gravelly snores that had disgusted me at first and then began to lull me to sleep. Strange orphans, we were, in residence. Playing grown-up, playing house with a Rez boyfriend or girlfriend for a while, but always going back to our old beds, back to borrowed cars and little sisters. Pretending bravely to be gone for good, and then making that decision that was never really a choice – to go back. Sig always said home is where you lay your head, her view a biased one. She'd lived in Kenora her whole life. She didn't know what it was like to live in a building that smelled temporary. The huge recycling bins in the lobby full of paper, the remains of classes. Every test, every class, every essay, a gesture toward focusing the lens that would capture a blurred, older version of myself, that would eventually slice her out in angles and light.

I pictured Sig on the deck in the lawn chair – hard to picture her anywhere else in the house, alone, impossible to picture her sleeping. She was an orphan herself now.

The building slept, and I watched Kristjan. I'd probably known his real age at some point, but it had slipped a year somewhere along the way. A small error, considering the uselessness of numbers when skating against a ghost. Kristjan's vapour trail, always a different version to dredge up, to match to the current edition of me.

He leered at me from the wall, drunk as hell. A boy. He could have been my younger brother. For close to a year, I'd been outgrowing him. I hadn't known this – that these lines could jump, blur, dissolve to static. I looked down, spread my fingers wide. The fact settled in among their small bones: I'd outgrown his hands.

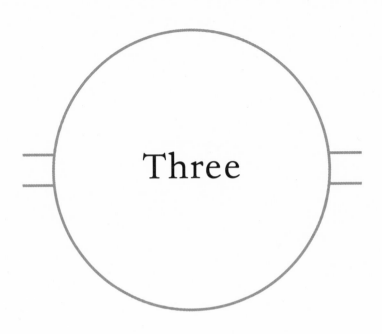

Three

Highlight reels are a lie. A hockey game writes its own Coles Notes, this much is true. It's like it's manufactured in an ephemeral package, ready to be butchered and filleted into three clean chunks, then chopped further, this massacre, then strung together in highlight reels – for those who missed it, for the illegitimate fans who believe that a hockey game is a list of the goals and fights, nothing else.

A TSN Turning Point is a different story. A book could be written about every one. The Turning Point is often shown in slow motion. It occurs when, say, the puck is stolen somewhere around centre ice, the other guy not careful enough, a little cocky, while his team is changing lines, that chance crossing of variables that leaves the offensive end gaping and bare like the toothless open mouths of your teammates. And you're the goalie, alone, and if you had time, maybe you'd feel abandoned by your teammates, maybe you'd feel pissed off and a little scared in the manner of a kid slingshot from a tube into the middle of the lake by her grandmother's deranged boat-driving. But you don't have time to feel any of this because this guy, this twenty-year-old phenomenon, whom they're calling the second coming of Christ on skates, is a sustained flash of jersey and legs and stick, but not of puck, because it's already behind you in the net, even as you're lunging for it.

But, wait. Rewind. The Turning Point isn't the puck rattling the crossbar behind you. Watch. Watch as the kid steals the puck. That *play*. Something will happen – he's moving, he's turning toward you. He'll score, he won't score, you'll defy laws of whatever and open your glove and the puck will be in it, the puck will spill off his stick and the new defenceman will collect it, sheepish and grateful, the crowd will make a peeved noise at the kid like one giant parent.

Something will happen. But in that vibrating moment as the puck swaps sticks, the ice is empty, waiting, and the kid is moving, turning. He's opening toward you.

Jacob and I shifted around in my bed, slipping into the routine for sleeping we'd stumbled out those nights when we'd play cribbage in my room until late. He'd just stay over instead of walking back to his room on the other side of campus. The routine was this: we'd both start on our backs, overlapping a bit like crowded teeth on my narrow mattress. I'd start to turn, Jacob would follow, and we'd both end up on our sides, facing the same direction. All this in silence, or whatever muffled thumps and music stood in for silence in my end of Rez that night.

Sometimes we kissed. Jacob pushed my shoulders, like he did that night at the rink when he told me no. He'd kind of push me away, even while he was kissing me harder. I panicked when he did this, opened my eyes up fast, but he didn't notice, his own eyes squeezed shut, eyebrows drawn in together like he was trying to remember something important. I moved into the space he created between us.

Sometimes we just slept.

I could feel his hands clasped together against my back, the small hairs on his knees brushing the damp backs of mine. Gavin was listening to Madonna – he'd been listening to Madonna all week – and 'Like a Virgin' buzzed through the wall, Gavin chiming in once in a while, a flat falsetto: *Like a virgin ... hoo!* Jacob laughed, a surprised huff that caught me just below my neck.

Then they were there: Toad, Boz and Heezer dancing to 'Like a Virgin,' Heezer's favourite song, in the dressing room after practice, wearing Jill straps and sports bras, the Jill straps doubling as chastity belts. Toad had cut a toilet paper roll in half and stuck the pieces inside her bra. The three of them leaping around the room, Toad doing Elvis pelvic thrusts and Heezer dumping baby powder into her hands and throwing it in the air like confetti, the North End getting all hazy, the sweet grit in my nose, on my tongue, and Boz collapsing on the ground beside her stall, hand on her heart, laughing her head off, 'Oh goodness. Oh my goodness.' Toad making hand motions around the toilet-paper-roll cones like she was focusing camera lenses, her face dead serious.

'Do you think,' Jacob said, his voice loud. 'Do you feel like, well. You know. You and me. That we're growing?'

He pressed his palms against my back and I tried hard to understand this vaguely Hallmark lingo that he had a supply of. *Together,*

we shall grow our love. Bigger it shall get, every day. Amen. I pictured our
bodies oozing together, a tumour all hair and teeth and tissue,
expanding like a lump of bread dough.

'Well, if you're asking me,' I said carefully. 'I don't know if you ...'

'I know about me, Isabel. I'm asking about you.'

What about me?

We went to a movie, a chick flick he'd chosen, the audience full
of middle-aged women clutching Kleenex in their laps, and I was
pretty sure that was a tear on his cheek when the lights bloomed at
the end, but he didn't touch it, and so I got antsy and couldn't look
at him and raced ahead to the bathroom. Another night, he reached
into the pocket of his fleece and pulled out a handful of tube jigs,
little rubber lures that looked like worms. 'Nice, I haven't worn this
since the summer – I was wondering where these all were,' and he
stuck one in both of his nostrils. I was embarrassed at first, but then
there was something about the tiny wobble in the jigs as he nodded
his head, frowning, that made me laugh like a five-year-old. And the
next morning, the jigs scattered across the floor next to my bed, my
Rez room looked more like home.

I let his question ring through my body like a doorbell, my teammates still dancing around to Gavin singing *Hoo!* Jacob's hands on
my back, but my teammates' bones, their springing muscles, somehow closer. Right there.

'We're going to visit Terry in the hospital tomorrow,' Sig said
when she called.

'What?'

'Chris is a teammate of yours. This is what we do.'

'I don't think so. I don't think I can – I've got tons of homework.'
The excuse pathetic even in my ears.

Hal had been missing practice frequently. Players brought in
casseroles, lasagna, muffins, and Toad and Boz dropped them off at
Hal and Terry's house.

'Left them on her front step,' Toad would say the next day, and
that would be all. No one mentioned it. They just brought the food,

hidden modestly in bags, Hal's empty stall bristling with plastic, kitchen smells setting up home in our corner of the dressing room.

'Isabel, you don't have any choice in the matter. This is a team-mate of yours, and a friend of mine, and you will show your support. I know it's not an easy thing to do, but I don't have to remind you what it's like, do I? Isabel. You will go.'

Hal sighed, disgusted, when players – on the other team, on her own team – went down in a game, propping her stick up dramatically on the boards, eyes rolling, as though we were in for a long haul. She was impatient with the frailties of others, dismissed them as though they were all contrived.

So, I clung to the possibility that Hal wouldn't even be at the hospital. I imagined her navigating the halls, steering herself full-tilt through gurneys and wheelchairs, head fakes around nurses, her eyes on a muscular pivot, ducking in on her mom's room for a few quick words, spoken without losing momentum, then gliding out again, the door shot open with a seamless twitch of her wrist, all stealth and held breath. I could see this – Hal fleeing out the hospital doors as Sig and I arrived.

Sig's eyes shifted nervously over the light grey hallway. 'I hate this bloody place,' she muttered to me out of the corner of her mouth.

I nodded. Skin and bones. My hospital weapon, a mantra in my head. *Skin and bones.* This was how I navigated the hallways. I had a knack for picturing people sick, could read the blueprint of bone structure and then go from there, an inverse architecture, knocking down flesh and muscle. Preparing myself for the worst.

'Whoops – this is her number here,' Sig said, backpedalling stiffly to the closed door. She knocked.

'Yeah?' Hal's voice rang quick, gruff. Sig opened the door a crack, and I stood behind her, crouched close to her back. I could still run. I'd take the stairs, beat a straight line to the revolving door at the front, the slow-motion suck of the door, and then I'd be out, I'd be gone. I'd prepared myself for Terry, but Hal – there was no way to prepare for Hal, no rules I could possibly flatten myself to in this place, that room, the door opening, and that yellow smell coming out into the hall, Hal in there with it, taking it on.

'All right if we come in?' Sig said. I was still against her back, and then Sig moved, stepped inside. I was left alone in the hallway, and I had to go in. I pictured Hal on one of those black and steel chairs by the windows, her knee jerking an impatient rhythm. By the window, Hal could look outside, she could plan her next move – even while she was in the room, she would always be on her way out. And so, that was my backup. Skin and bones, and Hal in that chair, about to leave, legs ready.

I never pictured this: Terry so small in the bed that she barely took up a fraction, and Hal next to her, under the covers, huge, legs drawn into white mounds, dominating the bed with her wide shoulders, and Terry slumped like a sleeping child against her side, her body trailing tubes across Hal's lap, TV flickering silent on a caged perch near the ceiling.

I had her. I had her pinned.

Hal glanced down at Terry's head, the mouth gaping in drugged sleep, then looked up at us, a defensive jut to her jaw.

'Hi, kiddo. We thought we'd just drop by quickly, say hi. But we don't want to wake her up, so … ' Sig gave a half-wink, abandoning it in the middle.

'Well, she's been sleeping for a while, so maybe I could – '

'No, no, Chris, we'll just stay for a quick chat, and then – just let her sleep.' Sig, whispering now. 'You been getting any sleep, kiddo?'

Hal shrugged. 'Not tons. Enough, I guess. Not as much as her.'

She looked at me, and I combed her stare, watching for any signs of challenge. Nothing, just tiredness.

'Moon bag-skated us yesterday,' I offered.

'Yeah?'

'Yeah, she was mad at Toad, I think.'

'Of course. Anyone set Toad in her place?'

'No. Pelly tried.'

'Pell. She'll never get it.'

A white machine hummed an insect tune next to Hal. Terry's chest moved under a nightgown patterned with snowmen. The smell twisted between my teeth.

Hal didn't move until Sig said we should go. Then she gathered the tubes carefully in her hands, slowly, as though picking up icicles, and lowered herself out of the bed, propping a pillow next to Terry where her body was. Terry's shoulders jangled loosely. Hal followed us out into the hall.

'Well, you try to get some rest, girl,' Sig said.

'Okay. I'll tell her you stopped by.' Hal's face twitched, and Sig and I stepped down the hall.

'You're the only one who's come here,' Hal said. 'From the team.'

I half-turned. 'Yeah, I didn't know if – ' I looked to Sig.

'Hope you don't mind us stopping by,' Sig offered.

'No, I didn't mean that,' Hal said. 'Just – the rest of them. They're chickenshit, I guess.' Her jaw muscle pulsed.

I thought of the anonymous casseroles stacked in her stall.

'They probably are chickenshit,' Sig said. 'You bet they are.' She reached over and squeezed Hal's forearm, her knuckles blue against Hal's skin.

'She's a tough one,' Sig said as the truck reeled down Pembina Highway, the fast-food fluorescents, the flower hut in the Sally Ann parking lot, the couple necking on the bus bench, all tumbling past in a reckless blur.

'Yeah,' I said.

'Mo says she's been sick for so long, and I didn't even guess, didn't have a bloody clue.'

'Oh, you mean Terry's tough.'

'Well – and Chris too, mind you. Of course. Jesus, of course.'

'No one knows what to do.'

'Well.'

We stopped at a red light and a pack of teenaged girls in a hatchback next to us were laughing – the dulled sound of it came in through our closed windows with subdued explosions of bass. I looked over and they were all decked out for some party or the bar, all in a uniform of straight, long hair and darkened eyes. Their red, laughing mouths seemed ignorant and cruel, and then the light turned green and they sped off.

'Brave,' Sig said, her eyes twitchy, jumping from the rear-view mirror to the road to the mirror. Her thumb beating ragged percussion on the wheel. Sig had turned the radio off in the hospital's parking lot as we were leaving, a frustrated sigh as the polished, perky tones of an announcer came barrelling out when she turned the key in the ignition. Silence tightened around our seats in the close-walled truck.

'Pardon?' I said.

'Your friend. She's damn brave. All alone like that,' Sig said gruffly, checking the rear-view again.

I looked at her. I thought about that word, *brave*. No. She didn't know Hal. To mistake her weakness for bravery. What I saw when I walked into that hospital room: Hal giving in. The room, the smell, the indifferent hum of the machines, Terry's hard, bald head, all seemed to exist because Hal had let them. Climbing into the bed with Terry was an act of permission, a flat-out abandonment of battle. She placed herself in that bed, climbed right into the centre of it, and so the room spun around her heavy axis, a slow orbit, and with it came the gradual shedding of light. Furious disappointment flooded my chest. Hal had given up.

I started to take the long way back to Rez from the rink. Out the front doors of Sam Hall instead of the rink door by Ed's office. I didn't visit him Tuesday after practice. On Thursday, he caught me walking out of the dressing room, down the hall toward the front doors.

'Heya, Iz?' He called at my back from the opposite end of the hall. I pretended I didn't hear him.

'Norse!' Louder now, the clatter of his footsteps on the rubber floor. I kept going. 'I found this other picture last night, thought you'd – ' A desperate edge to his voice. He called Kristjan his brother, but he'd only known him for a season. His best season. I couldn't help him find it again.

I pushed through the doors, out into the cold.

'Come on, sweetheart, you can do better than that,' Toad yapped at Pelly, the two of them in the faceoff circle. Moon faked another puck drop and Pelly squirmed against Toad's shoulder in that unsure moment when the puck could be there, it could be in their feet, but they just didn't see it drop.

'The disc ain't even there, honey,' Toad said. 'Whatchoo gettin' all up over me for?'

'Corinne, could you be serious, please?' Moon said, hovering the puck above their sticks. On the board side of the circle, I shifted my elbow over Woo's, impatient, my limbs all twitchy with the false starts. Woo layered hers back on top, poked me in the ribs with the butt of her stick, and giggled. Our skates stuttered gasps as we dug in, limbs poised with waiting, ready to guess.

'Toad, come on,' Hal said, crouched on the opposite side of the circle.

'When am I not serious?' Toad said, and Moon sighed. She shook the puck slightly, as though weighing it in her hand, and then dropped it. Toad's elbow darted into Pelly's stomach. She pivoted, bringing the puck back into her skates as she pushed Pelly off, and I watched, blocking Woo's path to the puck with my side, Woo ramming me with her elbow, a jolt in the ribs that I vaguely registered, watching the black line of the puck to Heezer along the boards, and then Heezer going with it, around behind the net. I abandoned Woo, pushing off from her side with a half-turn, and headed toward the boards, Heezer approaching, head up, looking for someone open. Calling – 'Heezer, here! Heez! Heez!' – lifting my stick off the ice, up to my waist, a flag, open, Heezer sailing the puck along the boards, and I flicked down the tip of my stick, licking up the puck as Woo heaved against me, spine-first into the boards, and I twisted, but Woo was still there, grinding me in, chest crushing, and I put a glove out on the glass to steady, kicking the puck with my feet, and – 'Iz, Izzer, atta girl, Iz, feet, feet, Woo, Woo, here, point, feet!' – whistle.

'Christ, you guys, what's up with the whistles?' Hal said as we jostled around the circle again, the opposite one this time.

'See, this is our problem, ladies.' Moon held the puck up near her face like a bribe. 'This is what we keep running into. You gotta quicken up those hands. Nat, that puck should have been out of your hands as quickly as you got it. None of this lollygagging around the net, okay?'

Heezer nodded vigorously. 'I just didn't see anyone open, so – '

'Iz was open – see, there's a window of opportunity that we keep missing with slow hands, ladies. Okay? I want you concentrating on that. We don't need any heroes – you play around with the puck and you lose it. I see it happening over and over.'

'Did yooooou ever know that you're my heee-rro … ' Toad sang in the middle of the circle.

'Toad, zip it,' Pelly said, bent over, stick across her thighs.

Toad sent her an exaggerated air kiss.

'Corinne! Maybe we should get some fresh legs out here … ' Moon looked toward the bench. Helmets shifted along the line as players' legs coiled, ready to jump the boards.

'No way,' Woo objected under her breath, and I looked at her in agreement, our helmets almost touching, arms locked tight again.

'We just got on. Toad, shut up,' Hal said.

'I'm on mute, Mooner, I'm on mute,' Toad said. Moon shook her head and raised the puck.

'Okay, let's go.' And, as though trying to shatter it, she spiked the puck to the ice.

Toad, on it quickest again, didn't get as much of an elbow up on Pelly, and the puck dribbled weakly toward the goal, Hal lunging toward it, on it, skating behind the net, and I sprinted down and up through the centre, Woo's stick on mine, glove on my back, and then I broke away from Woo, open, and – 'Hal! Hal! Here!' – the puck on Bitty's stick along the boards, and me lurching, breaking past the blue line, watching Bitty, Bitty dropping the puck down the boards, behind her, and Hal picking it up, looping back again, back along the boards, behind the net, buying time, more time, and I skated back over the blue line, cutting toward Hal's boards, and Hal looking up, wheeling around Tillsy, looking toward me, but not at me. Behind me, past the glass, outside the ice, looking, and then a quick glance at the scoreboard – the rehearsed tic, reckoning with seconds, as though it might give her a clue to improvise – and she fell down, on her knees, on her stomach. And I picked up the puck still gliding the arc of the boards, bolted forward, but wait, wait. No one was skating with me.

I stopped, the puck dripping from my stick, and turned, looked past the glass, into the stands. Mo and Eileen stood at ice level, Mo's arm around Eileen, the two wet-cheeked. Eileen covered her nose with a Kleenex, buried her head in Mo's shoulder. I stood for a moment, watched Hal, unmoving, watched the semicircle form slowly, confused, Boz crouched next to Hal's head, Toad skating to the gate, leaping off the ice toward Mo and Eileen, and then coming back on, slowly. I heard her say that one word to Moon, *Terry*, and then, 'Fuck, fuck,' as she skated past me. And I glided toward them, players from the bench draining onto the ice – 'What happened? What's wrong?' – and then the words from Toad, passed from helmet to helmet, down the crooked line along the boards, passed to the players still on the bench, waiting for Hal to get up, she never stayed down long, even that time she tore the shit out of the tendons in her ankle, she never stayed down.

And then we all fell. That second Hal hung her eyes on the score-board must have balanced us there, all of us strung together like a giant, moving mobile, before it crashed down, that second the clock couldn't shuck away, and didn't we all fall when she did, as teams do, as families do. And there should have been a crash, we should have heard it, the hollow gunshots of our shin pads hitting the ice all at once, the thunderous crack of helmets colliding, of equipment cracking open and scattering across our ice. But, instead, a sound none of us had heard with each other before, a hovering emptiness that was more than quiet: as Hal fell, she inhaled all of our voices, all the swearing and insults and calls for the puck, all the laughter – sucked in with her breath as she fell, as we all fell. And we didn't know when she'd breathe it out again. When she'd let us play on.

I watched, from the circle, Hal's head not moving, her legs not moving, everything still. Watched Boz take off her glove, put her hand on Hal's back. Toad kneeling down beside, sneer twisted underneath her cage, throwing her glove, violent, against the boards, and placing a careful hand on Hal's arm. I watched five, six, seven bare hands fall down onto Hal. Then I put a hand on too. The hard shell of shoulder pad underneath my chilled fingertips.

The horn went and Ed hovered confused beside the Zamboni, watching us through the glass. He needed to flood.

Quiet, and Hal pinned to the ice under our hands.

My funeral would be casual – none of the God stuff, some of my favourite music, and maybe a picture of me at the front next to the casket, an appropriate one. A hockey picture, an action shot, maybe – my face wouldn't even be visible, it would be one of those blurred photos, my body streaking out behind me like spilled paint, and it wouldn't matter what my face looked like, because I would be flying. And there would be another picture next to it, an action shot of Kristjan – I knew exactly which one, I had it in a scrapbook at home. A picture almost identical to the one they'd have of me, and people a few rows back wouldn't be able to tell which one was Kristjan and which one was me.

I'd be wearing a white jersey in the picture, and with my arms streaking out at the sides, I would look as though I had wings – this would be for the people who needed some nod at God for the whole thing to be right. *She's with her dad*, they'd say. *They're playing hockey together, right now, finally.* This last statement would unleash the tears.

And Sig would be happy with my picture too, because it would be tough, it would be ferocious. And my teammates would be in the front pew, maybe surrounding Sig on both sides, Sig in the middle, and the players forming a kind of protective wall, stand-ins for me in my absence, the whole greater than the sum of its parts, and all that.

Most of this, of course, would be bullshit. My teammates, and probably Sig too, would find it hilarious, the bullshit. It would be important they find it hilarious. The only way I could even begin to make it up to Sig. My leaving.

Some people I couldn't picture at a funeral. The team would be there at mine, of course, but I couldn't see it. What games could they possibly play? I pictured them passing a note down the line, written on a Kleenex maybe, an appropriate disguise for the quip written in Toad's slanted capital letters, something perverted, and Pelly would have to run from the room to laugh. I pictured them playing dodgeball at the end of the service with a balled-up program. All the mourners shuffling down the aisle, and my team-mates ducking among the pews, crouching away from Heezer's wicked overhand throw, disguising their laughter with their jackets pulled capelike over their faces.

That they would all be there, quiet and still, seemed an impossible fiction.

We filled the left side of pews five and six at Terry's funeral. Hal's tall head jutting in the front. The line of faces slanted diagonal down from me, eyes cast down into their laps.

Pelly forgot the last notes of the song, we could all tell. Momentary panic chased across her face, fingers still moving on the keys, and then she pulled out those last hesitant notes, an improvised offering leading in the wrong direction – a kind of downward slope when the song should have gone up – as though it just fell away from her. And then the amplified silence following it, the hush edged with sharp sniffles, coughs choked into hands.

I looked at Sig across the aisle, sitting next to Eileen. Big Mo cried, shoulders heaving, eyes clenched. Eileen held his hand. Sig clutched the peach purse on her lap, her funeral purse, and it looked old.

Toad leaned her head slightly toward me, her hair bent at awkward angles against her head, untethered from the usual pony-tail, her eyes bloodshot and antsy. She leaned against the silence as Pelly found unsure steps off the platform, and said, voice husky, 'Pell fucked up, eh? Shitty. I can't believe it.'

As though this mistake outweighed the bad coincidence of all of us there, serious for once, the too-white casket at the front. As though it outweighed the fact that Hal hadn't looked up, not once – I knew this because I hadn't been watching the piano either, I'd been watching her. It was the small mistake of Pelly's fingers, instead, that sent a frustrated tear reeling close to Toad's nose. She'd been holding it back the whole time, her face twitching in almost comic spasms with this restraint. She shoved the tear across her cheek with the back of her hand, pissed off in all her misplaced grief.

'Jesus, of all the times to fuck it up. Of all times.'

Parts of Kristjan's funeral had been filmed by a teammate's parents and given to Sig and Buck afterward.

The footage bore a vague indigo tint – eye sockets sunken in the blue air outside the church, concrete swallowed by shadow. Close to the camera, a woman stood in profile. When she raised a Kleenex to her face, it was Easter egg blue. The pall bearers shouldered Kristjan's coffin out of the church, blue flood of shadows beneath their eyes. They would be teammates, maybe. Although there was nothing athletic about their jerking movements, legs under the coffin awkward, the film speeding slightly. They eased the coffin down the stairs, passing between two rows of young men in black-blue suits who raised hockey sticks in the air to form a bridge. The young man closest to the camera squeezed his eyes shut, mouth jumping, hair waving across his forehead in a girlish cowlick. Thinking back: those wincing eyes. It was Ed. Sticks swayed lightly as the coffin passed beneath.

Sig and Buck followed, less grey, less stooped, but the same. My grandparents, younger and moving across the screen, Buck with his barrel chest and slow amble, hands dangling helplessly below his cuffs, jacket arms too short; Sig, curly hair and sharp face. They both looked bewildered as they stepped into the indigo sunlight – probably the sun was just too much after being in the church, but their squinting seemed confused, as though neither knew how they'd gotten to that church on that day.

Sig and Buck moved under the bridge of sticks, a few feet apart, Sig slightly ahead. As they reached the end, Buck seemed to stumble slightly. Head bowed, as though guiding his feet with his eyes, he grabbed Sig's arm. She didn't flinch. Face clenched like a fist, Buck held on to Sig's arm as though he was walking a tightrope, and he might fall if he let go. The camera followed them and then Ed was gone.

Sig told me that Kristjan looked like an old man when he was born, his hair so blond it appeared white, face lined. His eyes were set into pockets, wrinkled and deep, she said. She told me this as though it were a beginning, the part of a story that followed once upon a time. But I knew this beginning was wrong. Kristjan's story was born there, in that indigo afternoon, somewhere in the sign language of grief.

Even when he was quite young, Kristjan's hockey equipment had always given him an air of bravery, of fierceness – that hefty bulk of shoulders, the muscular glove fingers, the boxy shins under the hockey socks, the thick, fast feet. Layering on that equipment, dressed for a game, he distilled to the essence of who he was as a boy. And so Sig had kept him in that equipment. She'd left his skates on, handed him down to Iz in this package. It was Sig's duty and so she made damn sure the boy was given a legacy and that it was passed to his daughter and then she'd given Iz hockey itself, put her in the equipment, in the skates, dressed the girl with her own hands.

Iz went through a period as a kid when she was obsessed with Kristjan. It seemed to be some sort of a hobby, like the godawful sticker collection she arranged and rearranged.

'I'm going to write a letter to Kristjan,' she said one morning, sprawled across the living-room floor on her stomach, skinny toes burrowing into the carpet. Shards of blue construction paper were strewn everywhere, the massacre of paper her latest craft.

'What?' Sig's attention torn from the news flickering on the small set above Iz's head. 'What did you say?'

'I'm going to write a letter to him. For Father's Day. Everyone's writing letters in my class.'

Iz was compiling scraps of Kristjan now, mounting them in haphazard order. Sig could only imagine what she saw.

'What are you going to say to him?' Sig croaked, her mouth dry.

'I want to ask him about hockey – like how to do a slapshot and stuff.'

'Can't you ask your coaches that?'

'They don't know how. And Kristjan was better than them at hockey anyways – you said.'

Sig could pretend she didn't hear the girl, leave the room, make a pot of tea. But she felt in this flight instinct a trigger of selfishness, the familiar click, and she knew about duty. 'Why don't you write a letter to, uh – Walter Gretzky?'

'Who's that?' Iz looked at Sig over her shoulder, eyebrows furrowed.

'That's Wayne Gretzky's dad.'

'Why?'

'Because – ' Sig stammered, grasped. 'Because he'd be able to answer you back, kiddo. You know Kristjan can't answer your questions, right?'

'I know.' Iz turned back to the construction paper, considered a toothy hole.

Sig's philosophy from the beginning had been that the girl should know Kristjan, she should know him well, and that this knowledge would keep her healthy. She wasn't prepared, though, for the questions.

'And if anyone's a hockey dad, it's Walter. He's *the* hockey dad, Iz.'

'Okay,' Iz said.

'I'm sick,' Sig said on the phone. 'There. I said it.'

I thought a cold. I thought the flu.

'You don't sound it,' I said. She sounded the usual.

'Well, it's not cancer, not the big C, so don't you worry about that,' she said, an embarrassed laugh. I laughed too because I was thinking a cold, the flu. Sig was silent.

'What are you talking about?' I said.

'I'm sorry about the phone and all,' she said. 'I just – I didn't want you to hear it from – I didn't want anyone else to say and – '

I saw a white casket. The back of Hal's head. Hands falling over the ice like snow. A bridge of hockey sticks. I heard a whistle. A slamming gate.

I sank down into the couch draped with an orange and green afghan. Hal's eyes skated my face, then slipped off around the living room, with a kind of embarrassed confusion, as though noticing for the first time the pictures of her on the mantel, baseball bats propped gigantic on her shoulder, ringette team photos with uniforms like pink and purple leisure suits, as though just noticing now that the flowers in the vases, all of the dark fistfuls, had wilted.

I twisted my hands in my lap, weighed the bruised moons under Hal's eyes, the rash splashed across her chin and neck, the way her skin hugged her cheekbones a little tighter, shoulders diminished. Fat or muscle or both, lost.

I'd practised on the bus on the way over. *I just wanted to say*, I'd begin. I needed a beginning; the rest of it would move on the heels of those first words. But in the muffled air of Hal's living room, that voice in my head sounded stupid. I should tell her about the basketball instead. We'd taken up playing before practice every day, because most of us were bad – and this was hilarious to us, all the clueless mistakes, the blind, mid-court collisions, the ball drops – and because we kept getting better.

'The blind leading the fucking blind,' Toad said, shaking her head, but I marvelled at the improvisation fumbled out by our mapless limbs. I could tell Hal that Toad had claimed her for their team.

'She's just MIA,' Toad said, a term that, from what I understood, excused drunken wanderings, hockey injuries and other miscellaneous breaks from play. Hal might like this.

'So,' Hal said. I unfroze then, with that challenging lilt in her voice, smaller, but still there. I moved.

'I just wanted to say,' I said, and Hal flinched, as though I might hit her. 'I just wanted to tell you that, um … that I have this – my dad, he died. I just wanted to say that – with your mom and everything.' I wouldn't say Sig's name, her sickness. This wasn't an option.

Hal's brow furrowed, and she looked again at the mantel, at all the girls that were her. I edged carefully around the turned curve of her face, my eyes skimming the patches of rash. What did I expect, really? I had no strategy.

Hal leaned back on the couch then, hair caught like a web on the afghan, and folded her hands over her stomach. She tilted her chin toward me.

'Barbie,' she said levelly. 'I worry about you sometimes. Listen. Shit happens. This kind of thing happens and it's shitty. But that's it, you know. You go toe-to-toe and then you move on. That's it.' She shook her head. 'I'm just tired – that's why I'm not playing. I can't play when I'm tired.'

Her face overly casual, a kid pretending to be bored.

'That's not it,' I said quickly, quietly. Sometimes I didn't concentrate on words, didn't measure.

'What?' Hal's neck made a sound like a twig snapping as her eyes thudded over my mouth.

'I mean, do you even care?' I said again, and anger came that second time, a surprising shove behind my ribs. I wouldn't say Sig's name.

'Have you lost your fucking mind?' Hal sounded as though she were dead tired of asking this question.

Lone Ranger costumes, cowboy music, girls with too-big teeth that were all her.

'Do you?'

'Barbie, seriously, get a grip.' Her voice still tired, but a flicker around her mouth now, that old hunger for fireworks. Hal's bloodshot eyes spun wildly around the room, over the pictures, all of the chubby little girls holding baseball bats and ringette sticks, trying to look tough in hockey gear but failing, with the botched perm in one, the braces in another, the sparkling eyeshadow in another, girlish girls never getting it quite right. *Choose*, I wanted to say.

'You just – ' I said.

'You're kidding me right now, Iz. I mean you come here, you come to my house, and then you … ' Hal drew on her thighs with her forefingers, digging furrows through the muscle, face drawn, as though trying to map the skewed trajectory of my words.

Don't guess, I thought, *because you'll be wrong too much. You'll be wrong most of the time.*

Hal blinked then, hard. She sucked a breath like she'd been underwater too long, pulling up her shoulders, and turned to me.

'Why don't you just leave,' she said quietly. 'Just leave me alone. You've never lost your fucking *mom* – ' She blinked again hard, jaw dropping slightly. As though this fact had been handed to her just now, and there it was, she could see it. She shook her head. A chuckle spilled from her mouth – dry bones of laughter, just the creaking intake of breath over and over – and she turned to me again, eyes cruel and beaten. 'You have no fucking idea. Just leave. You've got no game here.'

A phone began to ring, shrill and hollow, in another room. Hal didn't flinch. She closed her eyes and her face cracked into that smile again. I hadn't recognized the larger silence in the house, the muted roar of it beyond the living-room walls, until the ringing began. It rang ten, a hundred, a million times. The silence, when it stopped, stung my ears.

'Got rid of the answering machine,' Hal said like she was starting a joke, eyes still closed. 'Probably Visa again. I like to know that whatever fucker's on the other end of the line is waiting. Waiting for me to answer like I'm waiting for them to hang up. Win-win situation for me. Visa – they call and ask for my mom, but – here's the best part – they fuck up her *name*. Ask for Kerry.' She began to laugh. Pushed her hands into her thighs and laughed forever. '"Oh, *Kerry*," I tell them. "She's gone to Disneyland!" Every time. *Disneyland*. They don't even have the fucking decency to get her name right. They ask when's a better time to call, when she'll be back. I tell them she fell off Space Mountain, and they're still looking for her. Or, if the guy's a real dick about it, I tell him she only meant to go for a week, but then she met Peter Pan, and now they're getting married. "That Kerry's a flighty one," I say. Hey, there's a ghost for you, Barbie – Visa. You wanna be fucking haunted, talk to them.' She breathed hard for a moment, then looked at me sharply like she'd just remembered something. 'Why don't you come back for this little chat when you've had to answer for your dead mother's debts?'

I don't often cry. I have this reflex – like a gag reflex, I suppose. It started back when the boys were outgrowing me, shooting up above me so quickly, like scrawny, pimple-faced Incredible Hulks. And I'd take this really hard hit and be down there on the ice, and there would be the boy who hit me, looking all sorry, but there'd be something else in his face at the same time – worry, like he was just waiting for the tears. I couldn't stand that waiting. So I'd make my eyes suck the tears back up. They never existed, hanging there in the corners of my eyes, threatening to incriminate me. Or maybe this began much earlier. With Uncle Larry. *Keep it off the ice.* Regardless, I knew how to take it like a man.

But with Hal, it happened too quickly.

'You're right,' I said. 'You're right.' I pushed down hard on the corners of my eyes, frustrated, digging sharp pain into the bridge of my nose, as though I might stop the flow of tears with my fingers, the way you stop blood spilling from a cut. Hal watched me cry, her unsurprised face deformed through the tears.

'I haven't lost a mom,' I said, and then I began to laugh – I could, because she had – the sheer ridiculousness of it all hitting me, nonsense words jangling around in my mouth like loose change. 'I have a lost mom, but I didn't lose her myself, I guess.' Out – the ridiculous, unsolvable riddle. My nose had begun to run; I wiped it recklessly with a sleeve, inhibitions gone, drunk on pathetic tears and on the words out there in the room now, already wilting like Hal's sympathy bouquets, grown smaller with the plucking, with the offering. Exotic in my mind, but unremarkable in that room full of girls and petrified flowers.

Hal watched me with guarded wonder and disgust. She reached slowly to the table beside the couch, then held out a Kleenex box, carefully, as though offering food to a wild animal.

'So you know – ' I snorted into a Kleenex. 'Maybe she's in Never-Never Land with Kerry.' I hiccupped another laugh, sobering. 'But how did we start talking about – I was talking about Kristjan.'

Hal laid the box in her lap. She balanced fingertips on two corners, and then began to press down, skin blanching around the cardboard. She pressed until the box began to cave in, watching it carefully, chin down at her chest.

'Toad was telling me the other day some bullshit story about her great-aunt Gertrude dying a couple of years ago or something.' Monotone voice. 'And I didn't know what the hell she was talking about, and didn't really care, to be honest. But I think what she was trying to do was kind of join in. Like, get in on the action, the death action – everyone who knows someone who's died join hands, and we'll all do a square dance or something, and it'll be okay. We'll all live happily ever after.' She began to push in the remaining two corners of the box, her hands slow, methodical. I had to lean in to hear her, Kleenex tourniquet pressed to my eyes. 'But what you all don't seem to understand is that I'm so tired. I'm tired of people talking to me. I'm tired of the phone ringing. I'm tired of the stupid dance. So, I'm thinking, Why don't you guys leave me out of this. Go throw a pity party for each other, instead. A hugely tragic pity party, with all of your unbelievably heartbreaking, imaginary grief.'

The box began to cave in again, and Hal's shoulders sagged, as though lamenting this feat. She inhaled through her nose, deep, fingers frozen into the collapsed caverns. Then, in one smooth swoop, she launched the box from her lap. Out toward the mantel, toward the pictures, a perfect shot – clinical, Stan would have said – the box sailing over the stone corner of the ledge, then sliding like a curling rock against the picture frames, a grating sound, cardboard on stone, and the frames crashing into each other, all the girls plummeting, their frames shattering into crystalline shards.

The phone began to ring again. That endless bell.

I stood in the hallway on one foot after school, cold venting from my snowsuit, yanking at the laces of a boot. The low growl of Sig's voice and the higher lilt of Grace's knitted together as they slid out under the kitchen door. They hadn't heard me come in – Sig didn't shout at me when I closed the door.

Stepping from my boots, I crept toward the kitchen, avoided the creaking board just outside the door. I'd stood there before, listening, and regretted it. Their raw, unpeeled voices, and the things they said – Sig employing all the swear words, in various creative forms – had given me stomachaches.

I leaned in.

'– big old house in Virginia. But it came back again just the other day, no marking on it – like I'd sent the goddamn thing to myself. They're cavemen down there, I hear. They'll go their entire lives pretending she doesn't exist, I'd bet, if they can pull it off. Stinking rich Neanderthals.'

Grace made a clucking sound. 'Well, how did you get the address in the first place?'

'The father used to fly into the camp to fish every summer – how the little tart got the job in the first place. Father'd fly her up. Probably thought he was keeping her out of trouble.' Sig snorted.

'Which camp again?'

'McNabb's.'

'Well, maybe they've heard from her, maybe she's kept –'

'Jesus, no. A stupid thing, but if she hasn't done a bloody brilliant job of falling off the face of the earth.'

'Well, she was mourning, I suppose, when –'

'Oh please, Grace. Spare me the bullshit. She was already gone in her mind while she was farting out those crocodile tears. Mourning. Please.'

'Well, I suppose there comes a time when you just have to, well – close the book. Wash your hands of the chase.'

'Amen to that. I'm too old to be playing hide-and-go-seek with a weak-kneed kid. Amen.' Sig sighed. 'What a dizzy girl. What a dizzy, dizzy girl.'

On the top shelf at the back of Sig's closet, behind the clothes on hangers, I'd found the photo album, a pocket in the back cover of it housing hidden pictures. I knew I wasn't supposed to see them. One was of Sig in the bathtub, a younger Sig. Her palms were raised toward the camera, fending it off half-heartedly, but she was tilting her head back, eyes closed, mouth a giant, laughing oval. Whenever Sig told stories about when she was younger, I pictured her with the laughing mouth, that tingle aching in my stomach again. The second picture was of Kristjan, hair white-blond against his tanned, squinting face, and a girl with long, dirty yellow hair that looked black in the places where it waved in closer to her body. Kristjan had his arm pulled around her tight, and her small shoulders crumpled into his chest. She was squinting as well, one hand poised tentatively at her forehead: she could have been wiping away sweat, or trying to shade her eyes, or hide her face. Kristjan was grinning with a kind of sureness that made the girl's uncertain smile – like she wasn't convinced her picture was being taken in that moment – wilt.

This was the dizzy girl.

As the purple light seeped into my skin outside the kitchen door, then past my skin, a drip of darkness into my stomach, I closed my eyes and imagined the dizzy girl on the dock, summer, that time of day when the sky is so blue you can practically see through it. She twirled around and around, arms out perfectly straight, face tilted up to the disappearing sky. The lake lay in front of her. She twirled until she was a blur, and you couldn't see her smile through the yellow umbrella of hair. She twirled until you'd think she couldn't go any faster, it was impossible, and then she twisted off the dock and into the lake, and afterward the lake didn't even move, so it looked like the dizzy girl never fell in.

As the shadow bloomed an aching tumour in my stomach, this was where I put the dizzy girl: under the lake. Everywhere and nowhere.

Sig's knees felt as though they'd been taken hostage, the blunt edge of a knife dug in to the bone, threatening her not to move, or else. She groaned as she lowered herself to sit on the edge of the dock, her parka and snow pants crumpling like paper in the cold. Her ankles, then knees, then hips, then the old bones of the dock, each creaking in turn.

She brought the rod onto her lap and opened the tackle box, the lures' tangled silver only a small gleam in the stifled light. She sighed as she tied the lure onto her line, as though she'd been forced down from the house, forced out into the cold. But she wasn't forced to do anything these days. She could do bloody well whatever she pleased.

She cast stiffly out toward the open water, the lure kinking hyperactive in the air, a show of yellow feathers, before dropping with a ripe plunk. The water pleated into metallic edges around her line and then smoothed.

She'd been fishing away boredom the past few days. The waiting involved in fishing she could stand. The other waiting was what got to her, the hours crouched at the feet of the next scheduled event: lunch, tea, dinner, cards with Grace. Even while she did nothing, sat there slack-jawed in the veranda, cigarette burning a lazy retreat between her fingers – without the girl around, she'd begun to smoke inside, each cigarette one step closer to Hell – she was waiting, her neck muscles coiled.

With fishing, the waiting at least contained itself, held itself together in the taut thrum of the fishing line. This was sport, this drawn-out freezing of ass and nose. Sig would be an athlete, then, in the long winter hours.

She felt a nibble, like a sneeze caught in her palms. Again. She didn't hesitate, yanked the rod quick, up and back, its skinny head recoiling. And then: a new heaviness on the line. She chuckled to herself as she began to reel in. Such satisfaction in the *Wheel of Fortune* clatter of the reel. Such promise. Arousal fluttered like fingertips across her skin, beneath the layers. Greed.

The pickerel thrashed angrily over the open water, Sig's arms mirroring its movement with a loose-skinned wobble. Jack appeared at her shoulder and whined anxiously, fingernails dancing on the frozen wood. Sig gave him a sharp elbow.

'Outta here, mongrel,' she growled, manoeuvring the rod toward the dock like a crane. The fish flopped sluggish against the wood, mouth hinging open and closed. Its tail drummed a ragged beat. Sig looked at its grizzled face, the flat eye. The mouth opened and closed, the tail slowed until it moved with trancelike drowsiness. It would give up if she wanted it to. She felt a sudden shove of disgust for the creature.

She unhooked its mouth and heaved it back to the water. Cast out again, and waited. Nothing. Her fingers had begun to freeze up, gloves taking in the cold like sinking boats.

She began to reel in the line for another cast, but the line resisted. A snag.

'Friggin' Jesus.'

She glared out at the water. Her eyes dropped below the cobalt surface, down. Followed the razor-drawn fishing line to its snagged conclusion, the yellow feathers peeking out from – what? Where the hell was she caught?

She grunted and tried again, careful. There. A bit of give to the line. Not a rock, then. She kept going, slowly, wincing as though she were extracting the lure's hooks from skin. Whatever the lure had found, it was heavy; the line might snap at any time, the yellow feathers fluttering defeated to the bottom of the lake, her favourite lure lost. Jack watched, ears up.

'Not a fish,' Sig said, pushing against him with her shoulder. 'Quit breathing down my neck, you bloody slob.'

What the hell had she caught? She'd hauled up a variety of objects in her day: sunglasses; Coke bottles; a dead turtle, its flesh dissolving like Kleenex; a woman's old-fashioned cigarette holder. None of these objects had been as heavy as the weight tugging the end of her rod down now. She was getting close, the rod nodded this fact. Closer. A few more tugs, and then.

A blade broke the surface first, like the fin of some cocky fish. Reared up. Then the disembodied toe of a boot, the lake still claiming the rest. It glistened in the air, a gummy brown eye. Sig choked as she pulled up. Choked as she eyed the yellow feathers cradled there in the nook between the blade and the boot, the toe-end, nestled so smugly. *Will ya just lookie here*, the lure seemed to be mocking. Like some prankster friend showing up on the doorstep of your own goddamn party with someone you despise.

She yanked up on the rod, breath still webbed in her throat and, Jesus, there was the other one, trailing behind on wet umbilical laces, seaweed bleeding from them, limp. My God. She hauled them over to the dock and Jack danced backwards, then hovered behind Sig's back, whining.

It wasn't until the skates were slumped crooked on the dock, leaking a slow puddle, the arrowed tips of feather peeking out from underneath, that Sig found her breath, pulled it from her throat like an afterthought. One silent howl, out. She touched the skates with her eyes, careful, there and there. The lake had soaked the leather into a deep brown, old lesions blooming into fleshy forgiveness, blades polished, dust from the shed dissolved, absolved. They looked young again. New.

Sig began to chuckle, a slow roll out from her stomach, heat spread through her chest. She took off a glove, reached out a finger and touched the heel of the closest boot, its leather a cold, stiff musky pelt. Had she ever heard a joke as great as this?

'Hello?' Jacob said sleepily.

'Hey, it's me.'

'Hello, Me,' he mumbled. 'My favourite Me.'

'Hi. Um, I was thinking of coming over there. Okay? I'm bored.'

'I'd be upset if you *didn't* come over. I'd cry myself to sleep.'

I didn't want hockey. So when he opened the door and he was wearing a Scarlet Hockey T-shirt, I asked him to take it off. All I knew was that I didn't want hockey. But then he thought he knew what I wanted, his eyes flashing this idea, and maybe he did know.

We crashed and rolled against his mattress, and I wanted to laugh because we were suddenly different people, throwing each other around like wrestlers, these brawny characters with brash, grandiose names, and I wanted to laugh at this and because my shirt got hooked on my nose and my hair caught static and because we were so serious, that scowl of concentration on his face as he rubbed his cheek stubble across the skin of my chest until it burnt, but I was scared to laugh because I was travelling far away on that pinprick pain.

He grabbed my hips and pulled me over beside him, his fingers fumbling the button on my fly, and my arm got caught, mangled underneath me. I yanked it out, caught him in the rib with my elbow, and he jumped and gave a surprised *oof*, our eyes cracking open.

'Oh,' I breathed, and we regarded each other warily for a second like strangers suddenly crushed together on a bus. Then he smiled.

'Two minutes for elbowing,' he said.

I hurtled back into the room then. Slammed into the bed with the plaid comforter that smelled of scalp, next to the desk scattered with practice schedules and his teammates' hockey cards and, above it, the signed Ted Nolan poster. My bones crunched and sighed against the mattress and my eyes fell into the gaudy bruise on my forearm, dark purple and the smeared shape of a puck. Hit by Duff's shot in practice a few days ago while going in for a deflection, and the colour had deepened since; it had grown a nearly black heart.

'I have to go,' I said.

I dangled my head over the side of the bed. Blood blushed heat toward my scalp as I scanned the floor for my shirt. Jacob was silent. I looked over at him as I pulled my head through the shirt and he raised an eyebrow, his mouth still.

'It's not that you –' I stood up. 'It's just that I have to go.'

His face didn't move, eyes shrunk. I'd watched him play at Sam Hall a couple of times, and by the end of those games I'd been able to anticipate his moves: deke to the left when breaking past the defenceman, shot to the top right – the goalie's weak glove – quick twirl against the shoulder of the other D, in for the rebound. A clinical reading, like a practice drill, its narrative laid out on the white board beforehand, this destiny of our bodies. But, still, it was so satisfying, the transparent intention of his limbs, their signal reaching to me high up there in the stands. Off the ice, though, with that distance removed – in the dining hall, wandering the cold trails through campus, in my room, his skin mapping a path against my own – his moves were impossible to anticipate.

Jacob, however, was becoming more confident in his reading of me. He had an ear for details – the names of dead pets, family members, Sig's sayings, brief childhood memories I allowed him when he insisted. He was delighted with the scraps I threw him, a little more, a little more, nodding his head happily, as though I'd confirmed something he'd been guessing at. As though these small facts of my life occupied the bricks of a crossword puzzle he was working on. One more bridge filled, leading to the next blank bridge and the next. An organized jungle that was me.

He'd begun to guess. I didn't set him straight when he was wrong, when he was beyond wrong. Every time he made a bad guess, I felt my skin growing another layer. But he looked at me with disbelief, admiration, with hope, as though he'd begun to see my organs glowing dimly like underwater lights.

Jacob hopped off the bed. He plucked a shirt from the mound of laundry in the corner, then grabbed his jacket from the back of the desk chair. Quick, like he was trying to beat me. Thrust his arm through a sleeve and opened the door.

'What are you doing?' I asked.

'Taking a walk.' He didn't look at me, examined the zipper on his jacket.

'Why?'

His eyes scraped across my face.

'Okaaaay,' I said, buying time. 'What – are we breaking up? Why are you acting so...' It kind of started as a joke, but dribbled away from me, my voice cracking a bit at the end. Scared of his face.

'Isabel. There's no such thing as breaking up.' He sounded tired. He paused and looked at the door. 'There's this conversation, there's me taking a walk, there's us sleeping in our own beds tonight. And then there's tomorrow.' His bulldozer eyes on my face again. 'Seems to me you look at your life, Isabel, like you're looking through a telescope. Through one end, things are huge, they're giant, swallowing your life. And then you flip the telescope over to the other end and everything you're looking at's microscopic, it's so small you can almost pretend it doesn't exist, you can almost convince yourself.'

I wanted to force him to stay now, close the door. I wanted to tackle him to the bed. 'That sounds like a breakup,' I said.

He hovered at the door. 'Your world,' he said finally, shrugging wearily. He shut the door quietly behind him. The surprising fact of his disappearing back, like a body spasm upon entering the May lake, cannonballing, and the ice gone out just hours before.

I wasn't sad yet.

I told myself this: when he guessed at me like that, he was just plucking out another rib of his own, leaving spaces open like doors. Doors anyone could walk through. I told myself: he's the one who's going to get hurt. My skin was growing layers. It was my world. I didn't feel any pain at all.

Sig stood in the doorway to the living room and watched the skates. They lay on their sides across a blanket of newspaper, in front of the fireplace. The boots now dry and stiff, mummified brown. She sighed and went over, ran her fingers down the rows of eyelets.

Just beyond them, next to the couch, sat Grace's old blue duffel bag. Sig hesitated, then pulled the bag over, opened the zipper. A shaggy nose poked out, dirty grey fur and the musty, ashlike smell of a fur coat left forgotten in a trunk. A taxidermy eye, luminous brown, with a liquid, lacquered centre. Mouth open in a friendly grin and, at the back of its throat, the screen through which you looked.

Grace had dropped the bag off before she left for Thunder Bay to visit her grandkids. The wolf costume was part of her gig as mascot for a hockey league for kids on a couple of the neighbouring reserves. The kids bussed into town once a week and Grace put on the wolf costume and danced around like a fool and they ate it up. Grace thought it might be good for Sig to fill in for her while she was out of town, a reason to get out of the house, to give back to the community and all that, and Sig had given that a firm no – her exact words being 'Hell no, woman. You've lost your frigging mind.'

And yet there was a kind of suppleness around the joints of the day, a pliability that made Sig feel like hockey. Throwing the duffel bag into the back of the truck was not a commitment. When she walked in the arena's back entrance, past the closed dressing room doors, and the tiny room was wide open, she thought, what the hell, she might as well try it on. Trying it on was not a commitment.

She worked the heavy suit on with some difficulty, already beginning to sweat, her right leg refusing to slip into its place at first, pawing the air like the hoof of an agitated horse. When she pulled the costume slowly up over her shoulders and zipped the front, it cloaked her body with surprising weight. Her steps felt suddenly athletic, this flexing of forgotten muscle, every movement meeting a reckoning. Her body became deliberate.

When she put on the head and looked at herself in the mirror through the screen in its mouth, the embarrassment she'd antici-pated was there, absolutely. But it felt detached somehow, this separate thing that existed outside of the costume's layers, beyond the small cross-hatched stitches filtering her vision through the wolf's mouth. And so she was able to take a few steps down the hall. She wasn't responsible for this beast. It wasn't her.

Nothing happened. The game went on, the players' knock-kneed enthusiasm spilling them all over the ice, a few parents laughing and shouting in the stands. Kids in winter boots chasing each other around the periphery of the rink.

She made her way slowly to the stands, gripping the outside edge of the boards, dragging the anchored body along. As she approached the stands, glances began to accumulate. One mother bent over and said something to her kid, pointing at Sig. A little boy with a runny nose stopped running mid-stride and stood stock-still, a few feet away, staring with a furrowed brow, as though trying to make the choice between laughter or tears. Sig could have turned around then, gone back to the dressing room, but she was almost at the stands and she needed a rest. She glanced up at the scoreboard – that automatic eye stutter tattooed into the brain of a lifer hockey parent – and sat on the bottom bench. Second period. People were staring now. This was ridiculous.

After Kristjan, after Buck, she'd been suddenly, entirely visible. Her head blown up with her own gaudy grief and other people's sympathy, swelling into cartoonlike proportions. A garish boo-hoo face that everyone could see coming from a mile away. And yet, strangely, mercifully, the trick: she was hidden. They hadn't seen her shrink. But there she was. A kernel buried somewhere under the padded layers.

They started to trickle over, the kids. Tentative at first, fingers thrust in their mouths, eyes rolling up her body to the shaggy face. Unused to this position – the prostrate, seated mascot. A pigtailed girl with chapped, wind-burnt cheeks shuffled up, paused, then leaned over and poked Sig in the gut, an experiment in bravery. Sig felt the poke like a touch on scar tissue: not the specific touch, but the numbed idea of it.

She got to her feet then, a bit unsteady, and they giggled, all these brown-eyed kids – five, seven, eight of them. Watching her carefully, their eyes dripping fear and anticipation, looking to each other for cues. They had her penned in on all sides. There was nothing else she could do. She raised her arms. She growled.

The kids screamed in surprise and relief. This was what they knew. Not Sig, but the wolf. She'd give them the wolf. They shrieked laughter and threw themselves at her. Sig shook her hands in the air. She shifted from foot to foot. She taunted them more and more, so they came at her harder, flinging themselves at her legs.

And there. There. She could almost feel it. Their little hands.

We went back the Thursday after Terry's funeral. Moon had cancelled practice for a couple of days, her way of flying the Scarlet flag at half-mast. Plastic bags overflowed from Hal's stall. No one mentioned the buffet's cancerous growth since Hal had started missing practice, well before Terry died. It grew out of a sense of team duty, pack mentality, the bags marred with inadvertent competition – no one wanted to be that person, the only one who hadn't contributed. Maybe it grew from collective confusion too. We'd been programmed to look at food mathematically, converting calories into time, distance. How long would a meal last us – how far to Regina before our fuel ran out, how many shifts into a game. One road trip, we'd arrived at the hotel restaurant to find Moon had ordered us all the Low-Cal Breakfast by accident: a minor stem of grapes, saucerful of Special K, small glass of orange juice. Outrage bristled the tables, some calling the waitress for menus – they'd pay with their own money if they had to – and Toad pounded the table with her knife and fork, bellowing, 'Where's the fat at, yo?' We had a game to play that morning; the Low-Cal Breakfast wouldn't last us even until warm-up. So, once the buffet for Hal was initiated, we didn't know when to stop; the distance we were fuelling was unfathomable.

Smells layered our corner: cinnamon, garlic, yeast, melted cheese, broccoli, chocolate, hockey gloves, baby powder. Our hands conducted wafts as we pressed on shin pads, pulled haloes of tape around our knees and ankles, plastered Velcro straps, threaded skates – all this with awkward speed. Too much quiet, so we dodged it, ducking into our boxes, the upper shelves of our stalls. This quiet was a dangerous brand, the kind that comes after you crash your bike, while you're still counting the scrapes.

'You know that fucking prof I was telling you about?' Toad said, fingers all twitchy on her shoulder pad straps.

'Yes?' Boz said, her head down near her knees. She pulled a sock out from the lip of her skate.

'He's being a total dick again – you should see this essay I just got back. A massacre, these huge red slashes all over it – it literally looks like the pages have been stabbed to death. I'm thinking he might be asking for a flaming bag of shit to come the way of his front step.'

'Oh, babe, maybe you should just ask – '

'No, I've had enough of this bullshit. If he's such a fucking Einstein, he can figure out how to put out the fire without getting shit all over his urban-ghetto sneakers. I refuse to go kiss his scrawny ass – that's probably what he wants – to see if he can get the hockey chick down on her knees. Jesus, it's not my problem I have bigger muscles. Maybe if he fucking *extricated* himself from the library, and *supplanted* himself into the gym, we wouldn't have this red-pen *issue*.'

Boz opened her mouth and closed it again as Woo walked over and pulled a plastic bag from her backpack. The careful way she plucked the handles, pulling up and out, nestling the bag carefully into Heezer's stall. We all made our eyes busy with our equipment, as though Woo stood there stripping for the shower. More garlic, with a hint of hot mustard.

'Ewww,' Pelly said, wrinkling her nose. 'It reeks over here.'

Toad snapped a look over at her, irritation bristling on her pale face, but Pelly wasn't looking.

'I had piano before this?' she said to me. 'And my piano teacher, he had this really bad bret? Like, so bad. Like, what's it called – heliprosis?'

'Halitosis?' I offered.

'*Heliprosis* – what are you, Icelandic? Fucking Frenchie,' Toad grumbled into her shoulder pads as she pulled them over her head.

'Like, his bret was bad. And I was thinking, what if I had heli – you know. What if I had it too? Would I even know it? Like, can you smell your own bad bret?' Pelly looked at me sideways as she tugged on her laces.

'Um, I think you'd know,' I said.

'Okay, but would you tell me if – ?'

'For fuck's sake, Pelletier! Shut up and throw me some tape!' Toad flicked out a palm, her lips in a thin line.

'What's your problem?' Pelly instinctively hid the tape behind her back, her voice quavering nasal.

'Fuck you, that's my problem. You're being a totsi. Tape!'

Pelly looked like she might cry. 'Why are you being so mean?'

'Here.' Boz rummaged around in her box and handed Toad a roll of tape. 'There you go, Toady. It's all good. Don't worry about it, Pell.'

'But, like!' Pelly looked at me, the whine transferred to her eyes.

'Jesus fucking Christ, this tape is out. Does the universe not want me to have fucking tape?' Toad barked, spiking the empty roll onto the ground.

'Oh, babe, maybe you should – ' Boz put her hand out to touch Toad's arm, but Toad slid from her reach, up off the bench.

'And you know what? These – ' she pointed to the mess of plastic bags ' – are fucking tacky. Doesn't anyone see this?'

She pivoted sharply and began ripping containers from the bags, flinging them behind her. They fluttered drunkenly to the floor, the air folding new smells into our corner.

Toad clattered Tupperware and casserole dishes and cookie tins into Heezer's stall. The lid of a margarine container came off and brownies tumbled into a pile of brown rubble. My mouth watered, my stomach rumbling hunger or warning. When I walked in, I hadn't known if it was them, the external lean of grief I'd felt at Terry's funeral, or if it was me. These boundaries were becoming harder to trace, like the garbage in the dressing room, the stalls all bleeding together – harder to tell where their mess left off and my own began.

Toad turned and began to gather the bags in her arms, shoulder pads shifting awkwardly as she crouched, head comically small above the huge equipment. Glaring, she looked up and took stock of our faces. Her eyes settled on me like Hal. That look that said you were about to be enlisted, useless to try to escape. Toad wasn't as good at it, though; there was a kind of listlessness around her eyes. Her mouth was softer – a joking mouth even when she was furious, the threat curled in her lips that they could break at any time.

'Iz, grab the rest, eh?'

I nodded quickly and crouched next to her, grabbed at the slippery skins and wadded them into the crook of my arm. Pelly watched me, frowning.

I followed Toad out into the hall, past the garbage can in the dressing room. We'd both already put on our skates, so our walk down the hall was a tandem waddle, bouquets of bags blooming ghostly from our hands. The garbage can inside the door to the rink was overflowing with ketchup-smeared cardboard baskets, Styrofoam cups, banana peels. A ripe, hot stench clouded around it.

Toad grunted in frustration. 'Apparently no one works in this place.'

She stalked off around the perimeter of the ice, following the curve of boards to the back door, the one past Ed's office that led to the parking lot. She flung it open and looked over her shoulder for me. At her back, I peered past the bulk of her shoulder pads, out into the combined grey of the parking lot and the night filtering in.

All hockey players have been instilled with the healthy fear of concrete; we've all imagined the sound our skates might make against it if we dared venture past the islands of black rubber. The intolerable scrape, fever-dream screech, fingernails against a chalkboard. Blade edges lost in a heartbeat.

We were trapped, Toad and I, marooned by our blades. Toad threw the bags overhand from the doorway, like she was pitching a ball, and I watched their white edges catch at the orange sky as they winged away on the breeze. I shut my eyes. I threw the bags like that, with my eyes closed, and when I looked again, they were scattered at the foot of the door, scuttling small tics across the pavement, the wind holding its breath.

A hockey game is the same story told over and over again. Shift the plot around, switch the characters, change the ending a bit, but it's all the same and we already know how it will end. Even if the scoreboard doesn't give you what you want after the last seconds have fallen down over the players' helmets and the final horn has bounced off the ice, you'll still be okay. It's just a game. A safe place for people to put their hope. The promise of trying again and again. This is what they tell us.

U of A loped slow arcs along the boards toward the net, yellow and green, sprinting up around the red line toward the sloppy line of us waiting at the gate. Hard slow hard slow. The hammered blare of AC/DC and the announcer clearing his throat into the microphone.

'Here come your Winnipeg University Scarrrr-lets!'

Flooding fast onto the ice, finding our rivets under the crowd's eyes, quick circles.

The same circles. A few hours earlier, I'd written a history exam, a hundred of us hunched over identical booklets, all those blue lines, digging at the pages with our pens as though we might gradually unearth some buried machine, some system to initiate us into action. In Sam Hall, we skated these blue lines. We dug at the ice with our blades. We weren't finding anything.

Spilling ourselves around the circles. The dull thunk of pucks against Tillsy's pads. Warming up, revving our legs like snow-stunned cars, forcing the blood thaw.

The same circles, but Hal wasn't there. It wasn't like the whole team was injured just because she wasn't playing; teams are adaptable, shapeshifters, growing over the holes, the hurt parts, inventing new ways to thrive. Hal was our captain and a ringer, but the team could reinvent itself around her absence for one game, Heezer taking her position on the first line, the line shifting, stretching, a different ladder of hands reaching toward the goal.

She wasn't just MIA. Her absence, that loss into which she'd disappeared, had enacted a violence on each of us. You couldn't see it, but it was there, as though we'd all gone out on our days off and gotten into a gigantic scrap, each of us limping back to the ice, to this game. The evidence hidden under our equipment, in the shadows of our helmets.

Our legs weren't in it. Moon could see this before we even hit the ice. She'd tweaked our line combos, hoping this minor disorientation might jolt us awake. She wanted us chipping the puck past the trap. She wanted the 2-3 Press. She wanted.

'Listen,' she'd sighed in the dressing room after laying out our strategy. 'I know we've all had a rough week and we're worried about Hal.' Here, she'd tried to goose up her tone a bit. 'But we've gotta just get out there and give it a hundred and ten. Play every shift like it's your last. And just … keep it off the ice.' No one said anything afterward, the silence pointedly empty, as though it should be filled with a gaudy *Amen*. Her words held a brassy quality, a Don Cherry monologue delivered by a bad actor. They weren't hers.

'Just imagine,' Sig said once as I hovered in a snowbank next to the lake rink Buck cleared each winter, terrified of the ice's deep-bellied percussion. These sounds seemed to come from the dark purple fissures threaded through the ice, bruised mouths that might creak open at any time, swallowing me whole.

Sig stood in the middle of the rink in her prehistoric skates with the long, sabre-toothed blades and she told me to imagine that the same family of giants who bowled in the sky during the summer – the ones who made thunder – moved south in the winter and there they were, playing, far beneath the ice. Instantly, I could see this: the sky-sized ice ruled by giants. She tapped her stick and shrugged and the ice sounds shrunk suddenly on that small jerk of her shoulders. With one touch of her hockey stick.

Moon wanted us to imagine. Imagine the ice was a safe place to put our hope. Imagine Hal and Terry never existed, just for one game. Keep it off the ice. I looked around the room at my teammates' faces. We didn't believe.

'Fuck!' Toad yelled as her shot got away from her during warm-up, grazing the goal post and then rebounding with a high-pitched gong off the glass behind. I skated in on her heels, took my own shot, Tillsy licking out her glove hand, folding the puck quick into her catcher, then dropping it by her feet, ready for the next. I glided up beside Toad, into the lineup along the boards.

'This is such bullshit,' she grumbled, holding her stick upside down, picking slush off the tape on her blade.

'Yeah, it is,' I said and she looked at me sharply, like she'd expect this from herself but not from me, her thin eyebrows arched beneath her cage.

'You okay, bud?' she said. 'You look kinda shitty.'

'Yeah,' I shook my head. 'I just don't feel like playing.'

'I'm with ya,' she said and then it was her turn again to get a pass. The Horseshoe drill, it was called.

I'd forgotten which U of A players I was supposed to hate. Some of my teammates held a hit list, a catalogue of numbers and names and all of the sins they'd committed against us. But I'd only played against U of A once at the very beginning of the season and so I'd lost my grip on any violence I might have held in my teeth a million years ago. You play against enough girls and they begin to lose their faces, like the endless students I passed on campus every day. They become just another set of hands and legs moving toward you, forcing you to make a choice about how you're going to tell the next part of the story. And, anyway, we all know how it will end.

The puck dropped. We played the game. We skated to open ice, called for the puck, found new angles to invest in, but our passes wilted around the edges. Our legs weren't in it.

Toad and I leapt onto the bench, line change, both of us hauling breath, Toad gasping furiously.

'Fuck, you guys,' Toad said to no one in particular. 'You're killing me with the shitty passes. I'm fucking breaking my legs to get to your shitty passes.'

The last bad pass had been from Duff, obvious in its shittiness. Duff leaned backwards in the D end, her face crimson.

'Get in your fucking position then,' she bellowed down to our end.

'Hey!' Moon barked behind us.

'Oy,' Pelly breathed. Wary glances exchanged down the line. We were turning on each other. I leaned on the boards, a red tickle at the bottom of my lungs, gulping air. Looked at the scoreboard. Sixteen minutes left, still in the first. It occurred to me we wouldn't make it that far, and then that I didn't want to make it. A simple fact, sharpened by the blade of my breath. I didn't want this.

Sig walked in then, along the stands across from our box. I hadn't seen her since Terry's funeral. I remembered, my pulse revving again. She walked past the canteen, slow, leaned on the railing for a bit like she was taking a break. Then she began to make her way again, her hand still dragging along the railing, toward our offensive end where the other Scarlet parents were clustered. She was so small. How long had she been humouring her knees like that, tottering along like an old lady? Days, weeks. Years.

Thrown back onto the ice before I could think. We were bouncing off each other like bumper cars, our two teams, a lack of conviction in our roughness. U of A could smell our weakness maybe and decided to save their own bodies; we weren't going to put up a fight, they'd just outskate us. And anyway I'd forgotten who to hate, skating up the far boards, looking over my shoulder, Toad clamouring for the puck Duff had rung around the boards behind our net.

It wasn't a hit or an elbow or a stick. I was alone along the boards, trying to get open. But my movements were becoming unglued. I tripped. I did it to myself, my right blade catching the ice, just the tip, as though I was a figure skater digging in my pick, about to launch my body into something beautiful. But, instead, I could feel the ugliness, falling out of myself, my limbs turning to liquid, boards leaping toward my head. The thunder of my helmet shook my eardrums and a spool of red light unravelled from my head down my neck. I crumpled to the ice on my side. Turned over onto my back and closed my eyes to feel it, every inch of that light, to float down its hot path.

I heard the whistle and the approach of skates, the quick, panicked rasp of blades, and I heard Toad's voice dropping over me.

'Iz, Iz, come on, buddy, you okay? You're okay. You okay? Come on, buddy.'

But I kept my eyes closed. Gathering the words together in that ringing white space behind my eyes. To tell them. Because they needed to know this, that Hal was playing when Terry died and how could she? And that Sig was sick and hockey is the same story told over and over, a safe place to put your hope but what is hope and we already know how it will end. And that eventually we won't come back to the dressing room, to that giant girl who's fearless and brave, and we'll skate off the ice, go to our separate houses, we'll be as small as we are in our own beds at night and then how will we be brave? And that Hal was playing when Terry died and we couldn't keep it off the ice and I couldn't find Kristjan and Sig was sick and hockey was the same story.

I opened my eyes. My legs, my arms, sinking like swamped boats, down into the ice. Tamara, the trainer, her long black hair falling over me like poured oil, thrust three fingers at my cage. The faces of Toad, Pelly and Boz crowded next to her, the curves of their helmets sharp against the fluorescent lights above them, the edges of an eclipse.

'You okay, hon?' Boz said. I let the question roam through my body. The pain had retreated. Or maybe there hadn't been pain at all. I couldn't remember it. Someone had opened a door in my head and fresh air had flooded in.

'I'm okay,' I said. Then, 'Three.' And I swung myself up to the clucked objections of Tamara and got to my feet. I skated around my teammates – Pelly offering me her arm for support, confused face – and jumped through the gate, off the ice. I walked around the perimeter of the rink, past Ed in his office. He looked up and just stared, open-mouthed, quickly adjusting that thin raft of hair across his scalp once again, and I saw a wary kind of pain around his eyes; I think it had been there from the beginning. Like it was me, not Kristjan, who had broken his heart. I wanted to tell him I couldn't pay Kristjan's debts, I didn't have enough, I'd run out. But I just kept going until I reached the door. Then I pulled off my skates and walked out into the indigo night.

I didn't have a lot to pack. In Rez, they like you to make yourself at home in the most refugee way possible. Just threw my clothes into the two suitcases, left all my books on the desk. Left the photo of Kristjan up on the wall with its Milky Way swirl of tack holes, tiny memorials for all the photos that had come here to be lost, hundreds of them over the years and none of them had lasted. Then I ripped the picture down and put it in the pocket of my jeans because I didn't want the wall to win.

Sig was sitting outside Rez in the truck when I walked out with the first suitcase. I peered into the truck briefly and saw the pale glow of her face in the shadows and then I hoisted up the suitcase and levered it carefully over the side of the truck bed. When I went around to the passenger door, I heard the click of the automatic lock. I pulled on the handle but the click had been Sig locking me out. The window yawned slowly down. Sig glowered at me through a cloud of cigarette smoke.

'None of us know what this is about. But if you aren't broken, you aren't getting in this truck. And all I know is that you walked out of there on two legs. Now. Are you hurt?'

I shook my head.

Sig gave a deep nod. 'You finish what you started, girl. Get your bag out.' And she rolled up the window.

Snow began a slow descent as the Greyhound lurched toward the outskirts of the city, the snowflakes tentative, polite. Barely there in the darkness. Somewhere along the line Winnipeg had stumbled into winter.

A hockey game is nothing if not finishing what you started, but that's not what Sig meant: me walking out in the middle of the game. She meant the team and school and the season, this supposed holiday hockey had visited upon me. But I hadn't started any of this.

A girl had taken the seat next to me, although entire rows of the bus were open. She had acne scars around her jaw and ragged fingernails and was maybe around my age, but with the senile, caved-in look of an addict, eyes skipping absently around the bus, out the window, over to me. She pulled a ball of red yarn from her purse and began to knit, the needles pulsing robotic. Between her wrists, a thin scarf dangled, spotted with holes like moths had already destroyed it.

'You going to the States?' she asked. I shook my head. The bus was headed east through Ontario. She shrugged like it was my loss and I turned back to the window and watched two teenagers at a bus stop, the streetlight behind them illuminating the snowflakes that were almost invisible in the darkness, so it looked like they were on a stage and the snow was fake and fell only on them. The girl leaned into the guy, who was wearing a leather jacket liver-spotted with age and, sitting there in the bus, I could smell the wet leather and knew the thick squeak his arm would make as he pulled the girl in closer and the way she'd suddenly stop feeling the snowflakes on the top of her head as the guy looked up at the sky and then moved his own head over hers.

They call it the hockey season as though this is the natural order of things and we should time our lives to its clock, all of us, moons hung on its frozen orbit. It's just a game, but I couldn't remember ever leaving the ice.

At the rest stop near Steinbach, my seatmate asked me if I had a quarter. I offered a couple, but she accepted just one, her fingertip chilled as she drew the coin from my palm. She stood for a long time at the vending machine, head cocked, the hole-filled scarf bleeding from her hand at her side. She pressed a button and a Sweet Marie chocolate bar tumbled down, a yellow flash behind the glass, and then she walked out into the snow.

As the bus rumbled back onto the highway, I saw her walking along the gravel shoulder toward the hunched, dimly lit outlines of Steinbach. A small Mennonite town far from the States. She pulled her hair into a ponytail and stared blankly at the bus as it passed. I wondered if I'd see Pelly again. I tried to watch the news on the tiny flickering box perched five seats up. A blond meteorologist in a pink pantsuit forecasted more snow. I heard Toad say, *How do you get a totsi's eyes to sparkle? Shine a flashlight in her ear.* And so I went to sleep.

'Un-friggin-believable,' Sig said when I walked into the living room. Reclined in Buck's armchair, Peter Mansbridge mumbling on the TV. She fumbled angrily along the side of the chair for the handle, then cranked it, shooting upright. She blinked hard and pushed her glasses up the bridge of her nose as though I might be some sort of optical illusion. 'I'll be frigging damned.'

'Nice greeting,' I said.

'Are you pregnant?' she barked.

'No.'

'Depressed?'

'No.'

'Well, what in the hell, girl?'

I sat on the couch, unwound my scarf, arrows of cold released from its layers. Sig still staring like I'd just returned home with a sex change.

'Well, don't make yourself too comfortable,' she said, wide-eyed, gesturing for me to get up. 'It's not like this is your place any more.' She shook her head, examining the TV as though it might give her a hint. 'Anyway, I've rented out your room, so.'

I looked at her wearily. 'To who?'

'Vlad,' she spat.

'I'm sorry,' I said and headed to my room.

I woke in the middle of the night to the sound of freezing rain on my window, a jarring sibilance, and I thought for a moment it was summer. I moved my leg carefully across the mattress, stretched it out over the side of the bed, and a flush of pain seeped down, hamstring to calf. The endless leg workouts in the Gritty Grotto. Jump squats, dead lifts, lunges, calf raises, hamstring curls, leg presses. Stan had told us our muscles were injured through exercise, the strain causing tiny tears. The way an earthquake leaves fissures in the land. Lesions, he called them too, as though the tremors of pain were a result of our own catastrophic negligence. He told us muscle grows only as it heals. Tissue paving over the wounds, layered bravado above the hurt places. The others knew this already, or didn't seem to care, the subliminal musing of their bodies as unsurprising to them as their fast legs, their clean-angled slapshots. But I was shocked.

Sig mumbled in her sleep on the other side of the wall, a dream translation in jibberish, then fell back into the amplified breaths that soaked the darkness around my bed, that made the air full and heavy.

I moved my hand up under my head, clenched a fist beneath the pillow, and a small strand of pain unravelled the length of my neck to my shoulder. I thought about how long it would take for my muscles to start shedding their layers. If I'd feel myself shrinking. All the small violences playing out in our bodies as we slept.

The silent treatment started the next day, Sig limping past me down the hall, chin down. As I stood at the fridge, she stared through me like a window. She held the phone out to me without looking when Pelly called, but I didn't take it. Twice. Then she stopped answering.

I ranked in my mind all of the worse things I could have done. I monitored Sig's legs, noticed for the first time the strange jerking of her thumb and how did I not notice it before? I offered her scrambled eggs. She turned her back to them and went to the bathroom. I listened to the answering machine, my teammates' disembodied voices floating over me – or me, disembodied, floating over their voices. I'd walked out of hockey and become a ghost. *What's the first thing a totsi does in the morning? Looks in the mirror. Introduces herself.*

Beep. 'Oh, yeah, hello, Iz? Uh, this is Aline Pelletier? Like from hockey? (Toad in the background, laughing: 'She knows who you are, you loser!') Anyway, uh, sorry, that was just Toad. Anyway, I was just calling to, uh, to see, like, when you're coming back? Because, uh, your stuff's still here, and so, we thought – well, uh, we were hoping – I hoped – you'd be back soon? Because your stuff's still here – in your stall, like. So we thought you'd, uh, you'd come back to play maybe. (Cleared her throat.) Uh … okay, bye.' Click.

Beep. 'Oh, hey, babe. Hey, Iz. This is Cheryl Bozzo calling. Just calling to see how you're doing. Hope you're okay? Um, Iz, I just wanted to say that if you ever want to talk about anything, or just hang out, or whatever, then just call me, okay? Anytime. I mean it. We miss you. Seriously. Okay, talk to you soon, babe?' Click.

They were descending mysteriously from their nicknames, one by one, first names outstretched. Cautious. Breathing down my neck. I was scared: that they'd never leave me alone.

That they'd leave me alone.

I perched on the edge of the dock, next to Sig. She looked like a man, like a miniature version of Buck wearing his old red toque with the ragged pompom, his garbage mitts stained with fish blood, the army green parka. The clothes swallowed her. She held the fishing rod in one hand resting on her thigh, and a smoke in the other. Didn't look at me when I sat down.

'Goddamn Northern Light garbage,' she said, jutting her chin upward. I looked. Streams of green and yellow writhed back and forth, desperate banners. She watched the lake where her line went in, blowing smoke out the corner of her mouth, away from me.

I jumped right in. 'So, I quit.'

Sig licked her lips very slowly. She smiled with one side of her mouth. 'Quit what?' She snorted. Like a thirteen-year-old boy, Sig's signature move in uncomfortable situations was deflection.

'I quit hockey. It's fine. I'll be fine.' My departure had become a solid thing, all of the pieces I'd run from melded together into this sharp mass of ice and paper and skin lodged in my legs, and I thought that once I'd handed it to Sig I'd be okay. If she would just take it from me, I'd become light again.

Sig blew out a long cloud of smoke. She looked at the cigarette as she crushed it on the dock, next to her leg, then threw it out into the hole in the ice. I'd never seen her do that before, throw a butt into the lake.

'No, you're not, girl,' she said levelly.

'Well. But I am. I've already decided.'

'You finish what you started, Isabel.'

The way she dismissed my words with a cool flick, like ashing her cigarette.

'It's my choice,' I said.

She pivoted her head toward me slowly, smiling like the Buddha statue next to our toilet that Buck's sister had brought back from Thailand. 'So what're you going to do then?' She gave the rod a forceful twitch, her lips retreating.

'I'll get a job.'

'All right, then.' Cleared her throat. 'So, no university education to speak of and she goes and gets a job slicing meat at Wally's Supermarket and rots away the goddamn winters with a senior citizen while all the rest of the kids are away being drunk and loose at school. Excellent plan.' She gave the rod a bounce. I could see more sarcasm gathering in her face, a hot swarm of it around her mouth. I had no defence against this. Sig had her beaten-up flask nestled against her thigh, so I grabbed it and swigged, a diversion tactic, a smoky burn on my tongue, down my throat. I coughed and pressed on my mouth with the back of my hand. Sig looked at me, incredulous.

'You're drinking Scotch now too? Anything else?' She gave a rough snort. 'Anyway. You already have a goddamn job. You have the dream job, girl. Playing hockey and going to school and being a kid. There's your job. If Kristjan'd had ... '

She swallowed the rest of her sentence with the Scotch. Slammed the flask down between us, a challenge. I took it again. I'd go drink for drink with her, so she knew I could. Buoyed up on the hot cloud rising in my stomach, up through my chest. I had the sudden desire to knock her off the dock.

'He'd have *what*?' I demanded.

'I thought we did a better job on you,' she said, resuming her watch of the fishing line.

'What?' I said. 'Kristjan – what? But he – '

'Oh, never mind,' Sig sighed dramatically. 'You wouldn't listen anyways.'

'I don't – '

'If Kristjan'd had the opportunities you did, but there you go, taking it all for granted. Shitting on the team that was falling all over itself to – '

'Sig. I don't think so.'

'Oh, I see. You have something to say on that front, do you? Well, by all means. Enlighten an ignorant old lady. Go ahead.'

'Just – all those stories. I didn't ask for. I mean, okay, he was good at playing and all that. But what people seem to forget is that he, you know. He was a kid. And he left you with his *mess*. But those stories you told me. I never wanted.'

Sig had been nodding her head rapidly, mouth twitching, in some satirical imitation of a person who might agree with my scattered words. Hauling on the reel of the fishing rod like she'd caught something. But then the blue lure came up from the water and dangled above the ice for a few empty moments. Sig released it again and the lure dropped back beneath the black surface with a ripe plunk.

'This is all very interesting,' Sig said finally. 'This is frigging fascinating. Pardon me while I just get my mind around the disaster we've made of your life, this war-torn country that is Isabel Norris.'

'I didn't say – '

'Drink the hooch and shut up!' Sig barked, thrusting the flask in my direction. I jumped and took it. A huge, burning gulp, my throat clenching a fist, tears bunching clouds in the corners of my vision.

'First off, don't tell me about my goddamn son. You never knew him.' She didn't look at me, mouth drawn in tight. Her eyes darted quick around our dangling feet. My shoulders started to shake. 'Secondly. You aren't a mess. You've never been a mess. You're a good girl who's acting like a flake.'

Sig felt the front of her jacket for her smokes, then pulled them out, rested the rod on her lap. Lit up. She blew the smoke upward, chin jutted, eyes locking on the sky, and I could see her relax, shoulders dropping in the nicotine lullabye. She held her cigarette toward me then, waggled it between her fingers.

'Might as well take up smoking now too. Go all the way. Like the delinquent you are,' she said.

Her usual peace offering: a joke. But she had the cigarette right in my face and the slow turning of the Scotch felt like anger. I grabbed the smoke from her hand and drew my arm back to launch it on to the ice, but then I changed my mind mid-throw, shoved it deep between my lips, clamped my mouth around it, breathed it down like Sig always did, like it was her last breath, and I could feel the specific shape of the smoke as it flooded my lungs, every burning wisp, and then a larger shape, sharp-edged, and I panicked and hacked, tears streaming down my face, turning to cold.

'What the hell?' Sig said and I coughed until it felt like I was bringing up my stomach, bent double over my knees. Gasps like sandpaper dragged through my lungs. When I could breathe again, the air had become ice. I lay my cheek on my knee, facing Sig, watching the small jitter of her rod, the quaking glove. The leg of my jeans wet under my cheek.

'But what will you do?' I said. 'How will you.' I didn't know the questions. 'How.'

Sig was quiet for a long time. Then she reeled in her line, rested the rod on the dock, inched over toward me. I could feel warmth leaking from Buck's old jacket, the cigarette smell in its layers hardened by the cold. She reached her arm around my back then, grabbed my shoulder and pulled me toward her, a move my body remembered from when it was small. Not gentle, but like she was a wave, gathering me in on her arm's current, that rough tug. It felt too strong to be her, she felt strong as me, and my muscles melted down. I folded across her lap.

Sig watched Iz step carefully from a snowdrift onto the patch of ice, trailing threads of snow behind her small blades. The girl looked down at her feet, and Sig wondered if she could see a thing, the balaclava pushing her eyebrows down, the parka's blue hood belling around her face. Without looking up, Iz put her mittened hand back behind her and moved it around, feeling for Sig. Sig chuckled and grabbed her hand. Iz took two steps on the ice as though walking.

'Here,' Sig pulled Iz's arm into the crook of her own. 'You hold on and we'll glide like this.'

Iz gave an excited shriek as Sig pulled her along. They glided toward Buck's hockey stick that stood like a flag in the hill he built while clearing the rink.

Buck thought that Iz should play hockey. He didn't say why, just said she should, as though it was the natural thing for a little girl to do, and Sig didn't question him, although she thought, *We're older now.* And with Buck off at the mill all day, the ice too dark by the time he got home, the sky grown too cold – who was left to teach the girl?

'Remember the last time, Iz? Remember how you push out with your leg, like this?' Sig let go of Iz's hand and glided slowly, one leg frozen out behind her like a figure skater, looking back at Iz.

Iz nodded. She bent her knees, looking down at her legs, and pushed a foot out behind, jerking a small line across the ice.

'You're a natural, kiddo,' Sig said. 'How are your legs doing?'

'Good.'

Iz had been having growing pains. Sig, too, had felt searing fingers gripping her legs recently and believed these were shrinking pains. Cruel joke played on these bones of theirs. Sig imagined she was relinquishing her height to the girl, their pain feeding off each other like the heads of candles held together, a spiralling flame.

Iz pushed out again with a little more force and her blades creaked against the ice.

'Look how fast,' she said. Her snow pants crackled static, then she stopped.

'You're on a roll,' Sig said. 'Keep going.' She began to skate beside the shelf of snow ordering the ice, uneven strokes of Buck's shovel still visible. The corner that he'd angled into a smooth arc. She studied the path ahead of her as she moved, cautious, over the unpredictable surface.

Buck tried to smooth the ice down, sanding it with the shovel. He brought out watering cans and filled any holes he found. But he couldn't beat the lake's mazed desires – it shifted even as he covered its tracks, barking taunts under his feet as Sig watched him search.

Iz, across the ice, lifted her leg and took a step again.

Sig skated up. 'Okay, bend your knees now, kiddo,' she said and pressed lightly on Iz's shoulders. Iz bent, leaning forward, and Sig pulled her shoulders back a bit.

'Now just push like we practised before. Push your leg back with your knees bent just like that, okay?'

Iz pushed and glided a shaky line. She looked at Sig, concentrating, face drawn in. She stuttered out again, moving faster now, head wobbling. She kept going, and Sig watched her, eyeing the ice ahead.

'You're a genius, girl,' she said. Iz shuffled along, and then she tripped.

Sig moved as soon as Iz's knees jerked, small mitten swatting the air down as though closing a lid – she moved, blades cutting. Iz, falling in her direction, and Sig's legs fast, unthinking, and then her hand grabbed Iz's elbow, Iz still falling, and Sig's other hand catching the shoulder as it dropped like a stone.

Iz falling heavy – she wasn't light any more, legs lengthening every night, ripping muscle, injuring themselves to grow like this, to grow heavy. And Iz's shoulder falling down into Sig's palm, and Sig dropping too, bending. They bent.

B_{eep.}

'Izzer, this is Toad – hang on ... (a muffled, static sound) ... so that was a birthday fart going out from me to you on this most gassy – I mean happy – of occasions. Oh shit, shit – ow, don't, totsi! Ow! Ow! Okay, fine! O-kay! Right – Hal appears to be somewhat perturbed that I held her phone to my ass. She finds it erotic, deep down. Anyways – okay! Like I was saying: Haaaappy – ' Other voices chimed in. ' – biiiirthday to yoooou. Haaappy biiiirthday to yooou ... '

I'd never heard the Birthday Song slaughtered so badly and so deliberately before. Someone sang opera-style, Duff performing her infamous offbeat beat-box in the background. Another player deliberately made her voice crack, like a pubescent boy, while someone else – Heezer, maybe – rapped, going off on ridiculous riffs, which ignited a violent laugh attack from Boz, her throaty laughter unmistakable. Toad rang out clear, probably the closest to the phone, and her voice was surprisingly good, smooth and high, hitting every note, a jarring intimacy from her among the symphonic carnage. They finished the song spurting laughter – each other's biggest fans, always.

A birthday can make or break a person, Sig often said. *Best just to celebrate with Jack Daniel's and let him forget it for you.*

Then Boz came on the line: 'Hey, babe. Hope you're having a good one. Miss you, doll! Kay, I'll hang up now. We love you.'

Click.

When I was a kid, Sig, when giving me Eskimo kisses good night, called me her favourite broad, her Girl Friday, her funniest friend – names that made me feel the way I thought a movie star must feel: heavy with the admiration and envy of millions, a huge, open-ended love. I had no need to be placed, alone, on the bull's eye of that word, the maudlin L, violent scythe of V, carving its precise tattoo.

But as soon as Boz spoke those words, I felt a reordering of lines. New definitions were required. Now, a flash of heat underneath my skin. I hadn't needed to hear it. I'd never craved, never felt owed. But suddenly, inexplicably, I was lit, lying back on my bed across the tangled blankets, Jacob burning away, telescopes falling to ashes in his hands – *Through one end, things are huge, they're giant, swallowing your life. And then you flip it over...*

No such thing as telescopes, only the specific life of these eyes, these ears. Everything else a distortion.

A birthday can make or break you, kiddo.

I stood at the opposite end of the ice from the circling pack. They wore long skirts and hats, like the players in the Isobel Stanley picture, their uniforms all white. They skated that circle over and over, heads down, skirts billowing out behind them like sails. We were at Sam Hall – the same boards surrounding us and the yellow boxes there to the side – but the rink swelled with sunlight, buttery all over my shoulders, as though the roof had been removed. I called for a pass from Pelly, and she looked up, began to skate over. Closer. Fear solidified in my legs – Pelly's face was gone, her features smudged like the photo of Isobel Stanley, like a burn victim. Her mouth indistinguishable. She couldn't speak. I tried to laugh it away, Pelly's face getting closer, and swirling, smearing, as though some invisible hand were wiping it off. She offered me a stick of cinnamon gum, and somehow I knew she was sad.

The rest of our team circled like seagulls at the other end.

I heard the slur of tires on gravel behind the house and then Sig came into the living room, twisting her hands together. She cleared her throat. 'Well, Grace is here,' she said, glancing over her shoulder. 'We're, uh, going to a hockey game and I figure since you are in the midst of this divorce with it you probably didn't want to, you know.' She laughed a bit and then coughed into her hand. 'Leftovers for supper if you want 'em. All right, then. Toodle-oo.'

Earlier in the afternoon, Sig had been involved in a whisper-fest with Grace on the phone. Now these over-the-shoulder glances and half-assed jokes, like a minor heading out from her parents' place to the bar. I didn't have anything else to do. Got in the old truck and took the long route through our neighbourhood, the roads that held hands, all leading back to each other, shoved up against the lake.

I didn't see Grace and Sig at first, so I climbed to the top of the stands to look for them. The kids on the ice were young, wobbly, falling all over themselves to get the puck. Parents in the stands laughing at the sloppy proceedings. A horn ended the first period and then I saw them, wandering out from the bottom row of the stands, Grace in an orange and red clown costume, her long, white hair flowing down the back, a red foam nose, pulling on the hand of a less-willing wolf. Who was undeniably Sig. Sig's gait. Her old, cracked running shoes. Grace pulling her toward the ice. I held my breath. They took a few tentative steps onto the ice, grasping each other's arms, heading toward the teams that had now gathered at centre ice. A shooting contest. Grace said something and gestured to the group and two of the little skaters came forward and offered Sig their arms. She went slipping along between them to the far net.

When the contest was over, Grace produced three medals and Sig draped them over the kids' helmets, patting each one on the shoulder in turn. The teams skated off and music flooded from the loudspeaker. Sig and Grace shuffled back toward the gate, gripping each other's arms, as the Zamboni backed out of its bay. A small group of kids who'd been climbing the stands when I'd first arrived now clamoured around the gate, waiting for the mascots. Grace stopped. She grabbed Sig's arm and pointed to the kids. One of the kids squealed something and Grace broke into dance. Her signature bounce and snap, grinning wildly at the kids and then looking over to Sig, who had stopped when Grace did and now was standing very still.

A mascot. I should have been embarrassed. I would have been before. I would have bolted. But instead, I hung there in the stands, a nest of astonishment suspended in my throat. The dizzying generosity of this person on the ice. A wolf. Some character in a story I'd never heard.

The children giggled and shrieked. Grace threw her head back and pumped her fists in front of her. The wolf head tilted upward then. There was a hole in the depths of its grin where Sig's eyes would be. This hole pointed at me now like the barrel of a cannon. I thought I could see the glint of Sig's glasses. I raised a hand, unsure, down at my hip, just flashed my palm. But maybe she hadn't seen me. The head lowered again. It angled toward Grace. Then, slowly, Sig began to move. She threw out her arms. She swayed side to side.

They began to clear a skating trail on the lake behind our house a few years ago, always right before the winter festival. One day, the lake's a giant pulse of snow out the window and the next there's a ribbon winding through it, like some Zamboni had run a marathon in its dreams, an ink-blue ribbon appearing overnight, in the distance, the heads of skaters swimming down it, shouts deadened by the snow. It had appeared every year for five winters, but I'd never skated it, didn't even know how far it went. There was no point to skating this skinny hallway of ice when I was playing hockey every day.

I sat on the snowbank next to the trail and pulled on the old skates I'd unburied in the shed. Stepped onto the ice. Gunshot echoes scattered beneath my feet as I picked up speed, leg muscles uncoiling, the clenching creep of warmth. Needled wind wrapping around my head, eyes pricking tears. I looked back across the lake, toward our house, small and unremarkable in its lineup of other tired, weather-whipped houses on our street. As I skated, they stirred slightly in my eyes, a string of flags. Sig small as an ant behind. Faster. Muscle of winter straining, taut and lean, against my shoulders, pushing back on my knees.

Past Clementine Beach and the blue-lipped ghosts of swimming lessons past, the chipped sign on the boardwalk daring me to swim at my own risk, the weary, shuttered canteen. Picking up speed, nothing to stop me, how cold fast could get.

The trail ended at a boathouse, a lonely brown shack with a slip for some memory of a boat. The frozen beige and white froth of a public beach holding it in place. I sprayed to a stop inside. This slip ice, covered by the boathouse roof and so close to shore, was a different beast, a bright, translucent green, and I could see to the bottom, the sleeping sand. Huge bubbles were frozen into place across a backward glow, as though light were breaking up from the bottom, through all that oozing bottle green. Lightning cracks slashing their way down to the sand.

My legs rang confusion now in the sudden stop, the quiet. They'd grown bigger, craved more. The ice creaked outside the boathouse, the lake's impatient shifting. The lake and its million restless dreams. The ice changing its story. In the stillness of the boathouse, I turned.

I needed to play.

I did know the story. The one about the wolf. About how we're lucky. That one set of hands can set the point on which a game turns. To be able to play through the static of winter. To have a safe place to put your hope. To try again and again. To know how it will end. I made it up myself.

I skated back.

'What's this?' Sig slid Kristjan's picture from the counter, held it up a couple of inches from her face and squinted.

'Ed gave it to me. He played Junior with Kristjan.' Drinking coffee at the kitchen table in a patch of snow-spangled light.

Sig frowned. 'Boy looks friggin' drunk.'

'Probably was. Ed says it was at some party.'

'Who's this Ed person?'

'He played with Kristjan. Junior. He's the Zamboni man at Sam Hall.'

'I've no idea who that is.' Sig grunted and threw the photo back on the counter. 'That's a terrible picture. Boy was never photogenic. Always ended up looking like a troll. But there was always a little troll in him anyway, I guess.'

'Hey.'

'What?'

'Are you saying I look like a troll?'

Sig glanced at me with surprise. 'Not in the least.' She paused, examined her hands on the counter. 'You look more like your mother now that you're older.'

We couldn't look at each other. I went to the answering machine, its red light blinking like a channel marker. I pressed the button and Jacob sighed. I grabbed the counter.

'This is a message for Isabel. Or Iz.' He laughed. 'Whoever you are.' Laughed again. 'This is Jacob. I hear you're back home. Say hi to the lake for me. I was just going to say. I have these two tickets. To a play. I thought of you. Thought you'd be a girl who'd like to see a play. Anyway, I'd wear a tux. We could find you a tiara or something.' Laughed. 'Tickets are in the nosebleeds, but we'd still be like people at a play.' He paused here, sighed again. I saw these people then, the two of us high in the balcony in our fancy clothes, feet up on the seats in front of us, folding the program into a paper airplane, sailing it down to the front rows and the people down there would look up but never know where it came from. 'This doesn't make any sense, does it? See you.'

I turned around.

'You could borrow my tiara,' Sig said.

I followed behind as Sig pulled herself along the railing, up to the top, and moved toward the door. She looked back at me and grinned.

'Jesus. What took you so long?'

She opened the door and stepped aside to let me haul my suitcase through, into the hallway. A red tinsel garland strung sloppily down one wall. Gavin's door was open a crack and he had Marilyn Manson cranked.

'Garbage,' Sig said toward the music as I got the keys out. When I opened the door, my books were still spread across the desk, pen angled over a half-full sheet of notes.

I heaved the suitcase onto the bed and unzipped it. Sig and I dug into the stacks of clothing with our hands and carried them to the dresser until the suitcase was empty.

Later, when she'd fallen asleep in her hotel room, snoring quietly, her eyes without glasses shrunken into impossibly tiny lines, I sat in the dark before heading back to Rez and watched highlight reels on TSN. One announcer explained that a member of the Calgary Flames had lost his father that morning. *Lost*, he said, as though the father had gone missing somewhere in the red throngs of fans. The player scored three times, a hat trick. 'Keeping it off the ice,' the announcer pronounced valiantly. Then the player's three highlights in a row, his body frozen into ice for a second at the end of each, when his teammates swarmed him, throwing themselves at him like reunited lovers, the player ducking his head modestly, a bashful six-year-old grin, both front teeth missing. Two of the highlights froze him in this violent embrace. The last goal, he fell to his knees in front of the net, cross-checked from behind by a fed-up defenceman on the other team. In this highlight, they froze him there, puck in the net behind his kneeling figure, peering up, arms spread as though in rapturous prayer, toothless mouth forming a reverent O.

I fell with him then, to my knees on the beaten plum carpet of the motel room floor. Sig's breath rattling through the room.

This must have been his plea to the refs, cross-checked from behind after the whistle, and what injustice, him down on the ice, a hit borne of frustration, of envy. But the highlight froze him there, before any call was made, there on his knees, so he could have been protesting, or celebrating. He could have been mourning. Impossible to tell.

I saw Hal on the path as I walked across the parking lot to Sam Hall. She pushed out with one foot and slid along the icy downhill parts, the soles of her runners grinding against silence hung in the trees. She wasn't wearing a hat, and her ears flamed red as she slid, rough hair lifting out behind her.

We met by the pines that led to the rink, a straight row of tall ones that dropped into a staggered line with the legacy trees closest to Sam Hall. Her face began to flush when she saw me, two red bulbs setting light to stars of freckles up across the bridge of her nose and down to a brightened scab at the tip. The bruises under her eyes hadn't shrunk since the last time I saw her. But her face was tighter, dipping a sharper slope beneath her cheekbones, chin whittled down, so her eyes emerged with tired awareness.

'Iz,' she nodded.

'Hi.'

We walked together for a bit. Hal snorted as we neared the end of the trees and jerked her thumb toward the smallest one. A stone block at its feet was inscribed with Terry's name. It was a Charlie Brown tree at best, with denuded, crooked branches, and a slight hunch, as though favouring a geriatric spine. Hal stood in front of it, hands on her hips. She snorted and shook her head.

'Shittiest tree I've ever seen,' she said with wonder. It was.

'Pretty bad,' I said.

'I'm going to come one night and cut it down – it'd be a hilarious Christmas tree,' she mused. She turned and walked toward the rink door, propped open with a pylon, where Toad and I had released the grocery bags.

I sucked a breath as we walked in. The ice surface had been transformed into a messy triage chamber, littered with tangled hoses and rusted machines. Melting had begun, small puddles spitting out dead ringers of the lights overhead, hanging the surface with a dim chandelier of jumping bulbs. Mouths of the hoses lay directed into the hearts of puddle. Vague sucking sounds vibrated off the remaining boards – they were being taken down, missing parts here and there as though some small bomb had left these random wounds. As I watched, frozen in the door, the puddles grew. Those near the hoses diminished. New ones bloomed, slow and luminous. On the far side of the rink, Ed was bent over, his back to us, examining one of the machines, prodding it with a long finger.

Hal looked over her shoulder for me and stopped.

'They're taking the ice out over Christmas, doing some renovations,' she said. 'It's about time.' She walked over a square of board, inert, in her path and stood still for a moment on the small platform, looking through its portal onto the sweating ice, and then back to me.

'Good thing we like it messy,' she said and barked a single laugh. She raised her eyebrows and waited until I began to pick my way across the fallen boards behind her.

The rink smelled like spring at home – choking, blooming air full of old ice and new water, a smell signalling the death of outdoor shinny, and the promise of diving boards and cannonballs. Ed straightened slowly, a hand on his back, and turned. I put up my hand and he nodded his head, started to smile.

I followed Hal into the drafty hallway. It echoed with voices, laughter, from behind the shrinking line of doors, box-car dressing rooms vibrating invisibly beyond. The noise bloomed as we neared the dressing room: bass swelling voluptuous, hum of voices growing, Toad's crowing laugh breaking through it all.

I'd thought they'd have gone already for Christmas holidays, scattering into corners of the city, or down identical white highways to towns I'd never been to – towns people passed on the highway but never visited: Birtle, Deloraine, Headingley, St. Rose. They had other, unimaginable lives there that waited for them – like Sig and Jack and my small, worn bed still waited for me.

Hal checked over her shoulder, hand on the doorknob. She smiled a bit, as though trying to fight it, and opened the door, their voices spilling out. I stepped into the doorway behind her.

Someone had been throwing baby powder into the air again, a dressing room ritual now for any celebration, and the air was still hazy.

I stood there in the doorway, on the edge of the room's small storm and began to forget leaving.

Hal stalked in ahead of me.

'We found Iz,' she called, triumph in her voice.

The door closed behind me. It was easy then to forget anything beyond our yellow door, our red walls. The ice melting in the next room. Winter turning.

Acknowledgements

Thank you to the Social Sciences and Humanities Research Council, the Department of English and Faculty of Graduate Studies at the University of Calgary and the A. T. J. Cairns estate for financial support during the research and writing of this book.

I extend huge gratitude to two editors: Aritha van Herk, the original coach. And Alana Wilcox (Coxy), architect of the final draft. Both went above and beyond.

How do I begin to thank players and coaches on the University of Manitoba Bison Women's Hockey Team, seasons 1997 to 2000? Their voices and stories are in these pages; I owe them an ocean of beer. In particular, these former teammates and friends fielded 'research'-related questions in recent years and provided much inspiration: the Doerk, Houdie, Shmange, G, Rath, Warnick, Nano, Boris, Trash, Tetreault, Chukles, Bones, Romm (Amy Doerksen, Kim Houde, Andrea Keating, Jennifer Botterill, Trina Rathgeber, Alana Warnick, Nancy MacDonald, Lauren MacMillan, Trish Faurschou, Alison Tetreault, Karen Mamchuk, Jennifer Everard, Amber Rommelaere).

To my Calgary T.E.A.M.-mates, Jill Hartman and Brea Burton: thanks for letting me play hockey with their pirates and belly dancers. Thanks also to these 598 classmates at the University of Calgary (for their generous suggestions toward initial drafts) and other friends in Calgary and the writing community: Chris Ewart, Paul Kennett, Jeremy Leipert, Xay Saysana, Jessica Grant, Kathryn Sloan, Jane Grove, William Neil Scott, Phil Rivard, Heather Ellwood-Wright, James Dangerous, Jani Krulc, Lee Depner, Andre Rodrigues, Jason Christie, derek beaulieu, Travis Murphy, Brett Smith, Angela Rawlings, Jordan Scott (for collaboration) – and so many other poets, writers and friends who helped make the vibrant Calgary writing community home for me while I was there.

Finally, I'd like to acknowledge and thank my family and Winnipeg friends for their incredible support: Liz, Eric and Emily Levin; Mar and Carrlon Appleby; Billie, Steph, Katie and Melinda Appleby; Pat, Doug, Mike, John and James Finkbeiner; Kaiya and Tawnee Hedley; Glen Eliasson; Preston Mandamin; Raechelle Mudray; Tanis Brako; Erin Fitzpatrick; Renee Read (for cover inspiration); Barb and Ryan Brako (for a space to write in last winter). Grandparents Bill Appleby and Shirley Hedley have provided me with so much encouragement along the way. This book is enriched, as well, by the memory of Amma (Connie Appleby) and Uncle Sir (Doug Hedley), whose strength and stories live on. My sister, Anne Hedley (former Bison Captain), has supplied me with ongoing inspiration and stories for the Scarlets and a million laughs. Lastly, I offer deepest thanks to my parents, Jim Hedley and Cathie Eliasson, for their unwavering support and encouragement.

Cara Hedley grew up in Winnipeg and on Coney Island, Lake of the Woods. After playing three seasons with the University of Manitoba Bison women's hockey team, Cara moved to Calgary, where she completed an MA in English Literature and Creative Writing. She's been a member of the *dANDelion* magazine editorial collective, performed as part of a poetry ensemble in Calgary, Toronto and Scotland, and worked on a number of films in Vancouver and Ontario. She is currently a Ph.D. student at the University of Alberta.

Typeset in Dante and printed and bound at the Coach House
on bpNichol Lane, 2007.

Edited and designed by Alana Wilcox
Cover design by Rick/Simon
Author photo by Kim Houde

Coach House Books
401 Huron St. on bpNichol Lane
Toronto ON M5S 2G5

416 979 2217
800 367 6360

mail@chbooks.com
www.chbooks.com